SPECTRUM

STONE SOCIETY BOOK 14

BY FAITH GIBSON

I0614572

Copyright © 2021 by Faith Gibson

Published by: Bramblerose Press LLC

Editor: Candice Royer

First edition: April 2021

Cover design: Jay Aheer, © Simply Defined Art

Cover photography: Adobe Stock

ISBN: 978-1736890004

Dedication

For Candy

Acknowledgments

I thank these fabulous women every time. It's because they are the steadiness in the chaos. Candy, Jennifer, Kerstin, and Nikki – big, big hugs.

To my beta readers and ARC team, you all rock. I appreciate your input and your words of encouragement.

Jay Aheer of Simply Defined Art, thank you for all you do.

To my reader group, thank you for chatting with me and playing along. It's nice to know you're there when I need you.

To the man: Here's to a better year. I love you.

EZEKIEL

CHAPTER ONE

California

December 2047

ZEKE WAS SO ready to be off this gods-forsaken jet. He had felt off from the moment he boarded the craft and had taken his seat in the back after booking the flight last minute. The plane landed on time, not that it mattered to Zeke. Rarely was he on a schedule, and today was no different. He had no one waiting at the end of the walkway welcoming him home. Had no time clock he had to punch. No real responsibility other than his brother Cyrus. He was just ready to be away from all the bodies surrounding him.

After what felt like an eternity, he was following the other passengers who'd been seated in the back through the airport. The customs line was long, so Zeke mentally prepared to wait. "Ezekiel?" an older woman's voice asked. Standing several passengers ahead of him was a familiar face. The woman came backward through the line and stopped in front of him. She was short, so he had to look down. "Are you Ezekiel Seymour?" she asked.

"Yes ma'am." He racked his brain trying to remember who she was. She appeared to be in her fifties, was still pretty without a lot of age lines, and her eyes reminded him of someone.

"Good heavens, you haven't changed a bit. You look like you did when we dated."

"Dated?" He smiled all the while trying to remember her name.

She laughed. "You don't remember me, do you? I'm Sheila Varner. I was Sheila Bentley back then. You have to remember my daughter, Stella. Where'd she go?" Sheila looked around and grabbed a younger woman by the arm. "Here she is. This is my Stella, all grown up."

Zeke felt like he'd been punched in the gut. Stella was a younger, prettier version of her mother. His brain kicked in, and he remembered dating a woman a couple times who had a toddler. *Holy fucking shit.* Stella held out her hand, and against his better judgment, Zeke shook it. He thought he was going to lose his stomach.

Stella must have felt the pull because she jerked her hand away. "What the hell?" she murmured.

Zeke turned to Sheila and lied, "I'm not the man you dated; that must have been my father. I'm Ezekiel, Jr. Please, call me Zeke." There was no way Zeke was letting something as trivial as him dating Stella's mother thirty years ago drive her away.

Sheila laughed, cocking her head sideways as she studied him intently. "Well, that sure makes a lot more sense. You're the spitting image of Ezekiel. I swear you could pass for twins. You even have the same scar above your eye that he did." Sheila continued talking, asking questions about the senior Ezekiel Seymour, and Zeke answered her questions as vaguely as possible about someone who didn't exist. The line crept closer to the check-in point, and Zeke was trying to think of some way to get Stella alone later. "So, Ezekiel, where are you coming from? We just got back from Egypt. Those pyramids were something else."

"You were in Egypt?" he asked Sheila, only he was looking at Stella. She had silky, straight black hair with dark

3

eyes to match. She reminded him of an Egyptian queen. "You could pass for Nefertari," he whispered. She lowered her eyes, blushing.

"Sir, you're holding up the line," an airport worker chastised him. Zeke made it through customs and waited on the other side for Sheila and Stella to come through. Thankfully, Stella was first, and she walked to where he was waiting.

"Your dad must have really been something. My mother still talks about him after all this time."

Zeke hated lying to her. If she was his mate – and he was almost certain she was – he'd eventually have to be honest with her, but until he knew without a doubt, he was going to avoid the topic. "Where are you off to?" he asked.

"Like mother said, we just got home from Egypt. I love her, but I need to put a little distance between us, if you know what I mean."

He sure did. "Stella, I'd love to see you again. After you get settled and jet lag has worn off, if you are interested, give me a call." He prayed she didn't have a boyfriend, or worse, a husband waiting on her at home.

"I think I'd like that," she said. "What's your phone number?"

Zeke told her his number, and she programmed it into her phone. His phone buzzed in his pocket. As he pulled it out, she said, "There, now you have mine, too. Ezekiel Seymour, why do you seem so familiar to me?"

He couldn't tell her the truth. Not yet. He wanted to spend time together and be one hundred percent sure she was his mate. "Sometimes the fates have a funny way about them."

She started to say something, but Sheila joined them. "Ezekiel, it was good meeting you. Please tell your father I said hello. Come on, Stella, I'm ready to be home."

Stella held out her hand again. Was she a glutton for punishment, or was she trying to see if there really was a

4

strange connection between them? Zeke placed his hand in hers, and her eyes widened. Instead of letting go, he brought her knuckles to his lips and kissed them. "I'll be waiting," he said.

"Bye, Zeke." Stella squeezed his hand before taking off after her mother.

Since they would more than likely be going to the same baggage carousel he was, Zeke ducked into one of the restaurants and ordered a drink so he didn't seem like a stalker. He sipped his whiskey as he thought about the first time he met Stella. He'd gone to pick Sheila up for their date. When she wasn't ready, he waited for her in the living room. The babysitter was already there, and a little girl waddled into the room. He remembered dark eyes staring up at him as she held onto his leg to steady herself. The little girl was babbling incoherently, and he'd been mesmerized. Zeke and Sheila had barely pulled out of the driveway when he felt sick to his stomach. He still took her out to eat, but he didn't gain his appetite back. A few days after their date, Ezekiel transitioned for the first time.

Zeke enjoyed two more glasses of whiskey before paying his tab and retrieving his luggage. On the way home, he called Jonas. His father answered the phone, frantic. "Zeke? Where are you? Is Sam okay? Did you find them? How's Sophia?"

"Slow down, Father. Everyone's good. I'm back in the States, but I left everyone else in Egypt. They were having a family reunion of sorts. Xenia knows the truth."

"Huh. Listen, I'm glad you called. Your mother and I have something we'd like you to take care of."

"Huh? All you can say is huh?" It was just like Jonas to focus on his own needs.

"The truth is out, and Samuel will take care of it. It's out of my hands. Now, about that favor."

"I need to ask you something first. Is it possible to mate with a small child?"

"Are you crazy? Why would you even ask that?" Jonas hissed.

"Not that way! Gods, you really think I'd do that? What I meant was could being around a child cause the transition?"

"I suppose if the fates are willing to put someone through a test of sorts it could be possible. Why are you asking?"

"I ran into someone I haven't seen since they were really young. I met her when I dated her mother. Soon after, I went through my transition. Back then we didn't know the cause, but since we now do, I'm thinking she is the reason. I felt the mate pull strongly in her presence just now."

"Wait a second. How do you know the cause?" Jonas snapped.

"How we know isn't important. The fact that you hid it from us is. If you hadn't kept it a secret, I might be with my mate right now. All of your offspring have transitioned with the exception of Cyrus. I'm on my way to Montana to rectify the situation. Back to my original question, is it possible?"

Jonas was silent for a moment, and if Zeke hadn't heard breathing on the other end of the line, he would've thought his father had hung up. Finally, Jonas responded, "It isn't something I've ever heard of, Son, but I wouldn't say it is impossible. Now, about that favor..."

Zeke listened to his father drone on and on about some experiment he was currently working on. Since Tessa and Sam were out of the country, he wanted Zeke to help him. Zeke declined, reminding his father he was going to see Cyrus. He wouldn't put off the trip because Jonas had a wild hair up his ass. Maybe by the time he returned from Montana, Stella would be ready to see him.

He left the New San Diego airport and headed north toward his beach house. He had a feeling that one day very soon he would no longer need the soothing sound of the waves as a balm to his spirit. As much as Zeke loved the

6

beach, he'd had enough sand to last a while being in Egypt. He was looking forward to the open skies and mountain air of Montana. Cyrus lived on four hundred acres flush with trout-filled streams, cross-fenced pastures, and wildflowers blooming in the spring and summer. Since it was December, the land wouldn't be as beautiful unless it was covered in white. Zeke loved the brisk air and quiet of snow-laden fields. It was exhilarating and so completely different than the almost always sunny days of New Oceanside.

If things were different, Zeke would remain in California and spend time with Stella. His beast was demanding he do so. But he couldn't in good conscience put off going to his brother. Not when Cyrus had yet to transition. With that being the case, the male had the opportunity to know his mate from the beginning, unlike Zeke who had lived his life with no clue as to who she was or when they'd met.

Better late than never.

That was true. Zeke was positive Stella was his mate, and he would have her, but not until he visited with Cyrus and told him the truth of who and what he was. Once Cyrus knew he was a half-blood, he would need to make preparations to sell the few horses he owned. Animals didn't do well around shifters, sensing the beast within. The horses and dogs Cyrus owned were going to be riled when Zeke visited, but it couldn't be helped.

Zeke unpacked his bags and tossed his clothes in the washing machine, then grabbed a beer from the near empty fridge. He took the bottle to one of his spare bedrooms where he kept the clothes he didn't wear in his everyday life. Since he was headed to Montana, he grabbed the jeans and flannel shirts he'd bought specifically for visiting this particular brother. Now that Cyrus was the last of his siblings to need watching, Zeke could get rid of the various wardrobes he never wore, because who needed heavy canvas coats on the beach? Not that he needed them in

7

Montana, either, considering he was Gargoyle. But he had to look the part wherever he went. If Zeke had his way, he'd be in board shorts, T-shirts, and flip-flops every day.

After swapping the clothes over to the dryer, Zeke finished off the six-pack while staring at his phone. He contemplated calling Stella just to see if she'd made it home okay. He knew nothing about his mate other than who her mother was. Zeke remembered where Sheila lived back when he took her out, but that didn't mean she still lived in the same house or that Stella lived close by. Maybe just a text...

Zeke: *Just seeing if you made it home okay.*

Rubbing his temples as he cursed his father, Zeke mentally prepared for the talk with Cyrus. His siblings' reactions were always a crap shoot. Some sensed there was something different about them; they just couldn't figure out what. Others laughed their asses off until he phased and showed them pictures of the family. They always resembled either Jonas or Caroline closely enough to pass for siblings, but when he explained they were their parents, that got another laugh. Explaining how those who brought you into the world didn't look older than their thirties was always a treat. Not. None of what he had to explain was pleasant, especially why they had been given up for adoption.

Zeke wasn't ready to get on another plane, having spent the last twenty-three hours in the air, even if it was a short three hours compared to driving eighteen.

Stella: *Made it to Mom's. I live up in New Fallbrook, so I'll be driving back this afternoon.*

Zeke: *Good to know. Be careful on your drive home.*

He needed to get to Cyrus sooner rather than later, and driving would give him too much time to think. Or make a detour to New Fallbrook. Flying it was. Zeke pulled out his phone and checked the flights leaving that afternoon. Several seats were available on the four-thirty departure, so he booked it. He would wait until he arrived at the airport to upgrade if first class was available. Zeke hated sitting crammed between noisy and nosy humans. He had enough of both on the trip home from Egypt. He much preferred driving where he didn't have to talk or try to avoid odors humans didn't realize they gave off. He loved being a half-blood most of the time, but sitting next to a man who enjoyed garlic-laden pizza while waiting on his flight or a woman who doused herself in too much perfume was hell on shifter noses.

Stella: *I take it you made it home okay too?*

Zeke: *Yes. I live in New Oceanside, so not far from the airport at all.*

Stella: *Maybe we can get together soon?*

Zeke: *I'd love that, but I have to take a business trip up to Montana. I shouldn't be gone more than a week, so rain check?*

Stella's reply wasn't immediate, and Zeke prayed she didn't think he was giving her the brush off. He stared at his phone, willing it to buzz. When she finally responded, Zeke about dropped his phone.

Stella: *Sorry, one of my kids had a question about the assignment the substitute gave them. Rain check is fine.*

One of her kids, as in she had at least two. If there were children, then there was a father somewhere. Someone as stunning as Stella wouldn't have remained single, but the thought of his mate being intimate with another male set his beast on edge, even if it wasn't fair for either his beast or him to begrudge the female happiness. If she was accepting a rain check, she had to be single. Zeke hadn't spent much time in Stella's presence, but she didn't come across as the cheating type. Either she was divorced or widowed. Those were the only two options he would accept. As soon as he returned from Montana, he would find out.

Zeke: *I look forward to seeing you again. I'll call you when I get back. Until then, take care of yourself.*

Stella's reply was a smiley face emoji with hearts around it. Zeke wasn't an emoji kind of male, but seeing

9

that particular one made his heart beat a little faster.

STELLA WANTED TO recall the stupid emoji. Zeke didn't respond after she sent it, and he probably found it childish. Oh well. It was out there. At least he knew she was interested, but now she had to wait several days for him to get back to Cali. At least her week would fly by. Instead of taking vacation with her mother during the holiday break, they had gone two weeks prior, and Stella had one more week of school. Leaving her tenth graders with a substitute for one day wasn't an issue, but having been gone over a week meant chaos had probably ensued, as was evident by the latest email. Kids were master manipulators, especially teens. She had learned that in her first year teaching Sophomore English. In her ten years of being an educator, Stella had learned all their tricks.

Stella's inbox had more than one message from students regarding the assignment given by the substitute. Kerri Barnett was a capable teacher. The older woman had taught high school for almost thirty years before her first grandchild came along. At that point, she decided to retire. She didn't need Stella telling her how to lead the class, but as with all substitutes, Stella left a detailed outline of what she expected the students to learn in her absence. So the emails from the students had her rolling her eyes before responding with, "Yes, you have to do the report," and, "No, you can't do it over winter break if you want it to count."

Sheila asked Stella to stay for lunch, and reluctantly, she agreed. Stella wanted to get home where she could think about Ezekiel. Having spent the last ten days with her mother was more than enough bonding time, but Sheila was on divorce number two, thus the trip to Egypt. Stella didn't blame her mother for the number of husbands she had accumulated. Wanting to be loved was something everyone dreamed about, but Sheila's luck with men was shitty at best. Stella's father passed away before she was born, and Sheila had started dating again when Stella was two. Stella didn't remember Zeke's father, and the fact that her mom had gone out with the man was beyond strange.

Stella poured lemonade while Sheila made their sandwiches. Her mom had been unusually quiet since running into Zeke. Stella hadn't been kidding when she told the handsome blond her mother talked about his father all the time. Sheila felt like he was the one who got away, but she didn't know why after only two dates.

Sheila set their plates on the table, then took her seat. "You always asked me what Ezekiel looked like. Now you know. If you stood them side by side, you wouldn't be able to tell them apart. I always thought after he never called again, it was because I had a kid. He was fine on the first date, but after he met you... It was strange. As soon as we got in the car to go eat, he said he didn't feel good. The man did look green, so maybe he was telling the truth."

"If I am the reason, then I'm sorry, but since he had his own child, I don't see why you having one as well would have mattered." Stella wanted her mom to find a man worthy, but if she were being honest, she was glad Zeke's dad hadn't stuck around. If he had, she and Zeke would possibly have been stepsiblings. There was something about the man that called to her like none had before. Maybe it was from watching her mom go through several men without finding the one to go the distance, but Stella was particular. She had been on plenty of dates. And yes, she'd had a couple short-term relationships, but she never found the one who would fulfil all her dreams and desires. Never found the man she'd dreamed about ever since she was a little girl.

"He never mentioned a child, but it's possible Zeke Jr.

11

lived with the mother at the time. Whatever the reason, it wasn't meant to be."

Stella wanted to believe that reason was because she and Zeke were destined to be together. She believed in karma and fate. Believed the stars aligned at precisely the right time for certain occasions because what were the odds the two of them returned from the same place on the same flight?

Stella's phone rang, and her heart skipped a beat thinking it was Zeke. When she looked at the caller ID, she groaned, then hit *ignore*.

CHAPTER TWO

STELLA SLUMPED AGAINST the door as soon as she closed it, dropping her bags to the floor. Ten days with her mother was about five too many. She loved Sheila, but when her mom was depressed, fun wasn't in her vocabulary no matter if they were in an exotic location. Before she could get past the laundry room, her doorbell rang. Groaning, Stella went to see who it was. When she spotted her next-door neighbor through the peephole, Stella leaned her head back and stared at the ceiling. Mrs. Goss was nice enough, but why the hell was she bringing Stella flowers?

"Mrs. Goss," Stella greeted when she opened the door.

"Hello, dear. These came for you this morning, and I told the nice man I'd keep them until you got home. I told him you were supposed to be back earlier, and when you didn't get home this morning, I got worried something happened to you. I thought about calling, but, well, I didn't want to bother you if you were at the hospital. Here." The older woman shoved the roses at Stella. "I didn't peek at the card, but I assumed they were from the handsome man delivering them. Since they're roses, you probably know who he was. I didn't know you had a man friend in your life." Mrs. Goss looked over Stella's shoulder, probably searching for her nonexistent man friend.

Stella blocked the doorway lest the woman try to barge in. It wouldn't be the first time she had. "Nope. No man friend. Thank you for bringing these. I'll talk to you later once I've had the chance to unpack."

"Aren't you going to check the card?"

13

Not with you standing here. "I'll do that later. Again, thank you." She shut the door in the woman's face, because if she hadn't, Mrs. Goss would have stood there all day. Stella took the flowers to the kitchen and stared at them. If they were delivered that morning, they wouldn't be from Zeke. He didn't know her address. That left only one person. Stella sighed and pulled the card from the plastic stick.

Welcome home, Beautiful. I missed you and can't wait to see you Monday.
Yours, Bradley

Ugh! Stella ripped the card in two, then tossed it along with the flowers, vase and all, into the trash. She turned to go to the laundry room, but her conscience wouldn't allow her to leave the glass in the bin, so she pulled the flowers out of the garbage, pulled them from the vase, then tossed the roses back in, smushing them down for good measure. She poured the water out of the vase, then wiped it out with a paper towel before shoving the glass in the cabinet where she kept random items like a plastic tea pitcher, bottles of rum and vodka, an empty cookie tin, and packing tape.

Two weeks away from the man hadn't been nearly enough. If Stella could get through the next week, she would have another reprieve from his relentless pursuit. Maybe Zeke would come home sooner than expected, and Stella could tell Bradley she had a boyfriend, whether it was true or not. Although the last time she said she was seeing someone, Bradley hadn't taken the news well.

With both suitcases empty and the washing machine full, Stella turned up the thermostat, ran through the shower, then dressed in sweats, a hoodie, and thick socks while waiting for her house to heat up. Plopping down on the sofa, she turned on the TV and pulled up the shows she had recorded while she'd been in Egypt. When the first show ended, Stella couldn't remember a single thing about it. She'd spent the last hour thinking about Zeke. Pausing the recording, Stella went to the laundry room, tossed the wet clothes in the dryer, then started another load.

Returning to the sofa, she restarted the show. About ten minutes in, her phone rang. Stella contemplated not getting up, but if it were Zeke and she missed the call, she would kick her own ass. It wasn't Zeke, but it was her mother.

"Miss me already?" Stella joked, but her mother had been unusually quiet after they ate lunch. No, it was after she told her mom about Zeke texting.

"I always miss you." Sheila cleared her throat. "I got to thinking after you left. I know you believe in all that mystical stuff, so maybe the reason Ezekiel and I didn't work out is so you and his son could one day meet and have a shot. I saw the way he looked at you, and I have to tell you, no man has ever looked at me that way. Not even your father. When Zeke saw you, his whole demeanor changed, like you two were the only people in the airport. And when you got his texts? You lit up the same way. I might not believe in the stars aligning and all that hoodoo, but I do believe when you have instant chemistry, it means something."

Stella had those same thoughts, and she wanted to see if there was something there. "And you're okay with it? It won't be weird for you?"

"He's not my Ezekiel. If he were, then yes, that would be weird for me. But it's been thirty years, and it was only two dates. I want you to be happy, and I think Zeke could do that for you."

Stella thought he could too.

ZEKE THANKED THE agent and went outside to retrieve his

rental. After navigating out of the airport, he headed north. He planned to stay with his brother, but if things went sideways with Cyrus, Zeke would need a room for the duration. He wasn't leaving Montana until Cyrus had the truth and had all his questions answered. And there would be so many questions. Zeke could write a how-to manual at this point. He kept in touch with all his siblings he'd met over the years, even if through a quick email or text. Some had new lives and families and weren't interested in anything more than an informal relationship. Others, like Lilly and Dane, became part of his life. Maybe that had more to do with Tessa having been their watcher. His niece was a force of nature, and anyone who met her loved her. Maybe Zeke should have sent her to talk to Cyrus.

New Evaro was a quick four-mile drive from New Missoula. It took longer to get out of the airport than it did to travel to Cyrus's place. Zeke had made this particular trip several times but had never approached his brother. Now he wished he had. The sun had set while Zeke was in the air, and the two-lane road leading to Cyrus's property was desolate. Zeke pulled into the long driveway, thankful there wasn't a gate.

The house was dark when Zeke arrived. Cyrus's truck wasn't in the driveway, so he turned around and drove past Cyrus's parents' ranch. He stopped on the road and peered toward their home where he found Cyrus's truck. Zeke couldn't confront Cyrus there, and since he had no idea how long his brother would be, he made his way back to the hotel. He had really hoped to get the conversation started because the sooner Cyrus was aware he was Gargoyle, the sooner Zeke could return to California and get to know his mate. He had plenty of time to kill, so Zeke stopped off at a diner he had bypassed on his other trips to watch over Cyrus. It was late, so the place was empty except for a couple of older men sitting at the counter talking to the waitress across from them.

16

"Sit anywhere," the woman said.

Zeke took one of the empty booths next to the window and picked up the laminated menu wedged between the condiments.

Maggie, according to her name tag, strolled over holding a coffee pot. She appeared to be in her late forties with blonde hair that didn't come from a bottle. Her blue eyes were framed with a few lines, but other than that, her skin was smooth. She wore minimal makeup, and what lipstick she'd applied earlier had faded. Maggie picked up his empty mug and filled it without asking. "Haven't seen you in here before. You visiting someone?"

"Yes, my cousin. Can I get a large water?" Zeke wasn't about to tell Maggie he was Cyrus's brother.

"Sure. Who's your cousin? I know everyone in these parts." She didn't make a move to go after his water, and the two men were turned his way. Maybe stopping there had been a bad idea.

"Cyrus Gillespie."

Maggie's smile fell, and one of the men groaned. "Here we go," he muttered.

"Cyrus doesn't have any cousins." Maggie's friendly demeanor turned icy. Everything Zeke knew of his brother told him Cyrus was a good man. He took care of his parents who were both getting on in years.

"We're distant cousins on his father's side."

"Look at the man, Maggie. Even I can see the resemblance from over here," one of the men said.

"I'll just get that water." Maggie returned with his water, sans ice or a straw. "Are you going to order food or just take up space?"

"I'll have the steak, medium rare, scrambled eggs with cheese, and an order of hash browns please."

Maggie scribbled his order on her pad and took it to the window between the front of the diner and the kitchen. She returned to her spot across from the men, glaring at both of

17

them.

"Come on, Mags. Cyrus is good people. Just because he—"

"Stop right there, Earl. I won't listen to you tell me how good he is. I know him a lot better than you do." Maggie crossed her arms, daring Earl to argue.

Okay, maybe Zeke didn't know his brother as well as he thought. Then again, he wasn't going to let this woman's opinion skew his own. The two men went back to sipping their coffees, and Maggie glared at Zeke. He ignored her by looking out the window at the mountains in the distance.

When the waitress brought his order, the eggs were over easy. Zeke cut into his steak, which was well done, and there were no hash browns. "This isn't..." Zeke didn't bother complaining. He grabbed the ketchup and squeezed a puddle onto his plate. He recognized pettiness when he saw it. Whatever happened between Maggie and Cyrus bled into the woman's treatment of his relatives. He hoped she didn't treat Cyrus's parents this way. But they probably didn't visit the diner knowing the bad blood between their son and this woman.

Two more men came in and seated themselves on the opposite side of the room. While Maggie was talking to them, the men at the counter whispered between themselves.

"She really needs to let that go. It was twenty years ago."

"True, but she gave that man five years and expected a ring."

"It's not like he left her for someone else. He's not dated since he broke things off with her."

"If you ask me, the man's queer. Why else would he live alone with his dogs after having a good woman looking out for him?"

The friends halted their conversation when Maggie went behind the counter to place the newcomers' order and gather their drinks. Their water included ice, Zeke noticed. The steak, although well done, had a good flavor and the ketchup wasn't needed. The eggs he left sitting because

18

Zeke hated runny eggs. He thought about the men's conversation as he ate his food. Was his brother gay? If he was, that didn't bother Zeke, but it would make sense why he hadn't dated since he broke up with Maggie. Or maybe Cyrus had known on some level that Maggie wasn't his mate. Zeke would be sure to ask Cyrus about it whenever they had their talk.

Zeke didn't bother asking for drink refills. He tossed enough cash on the table to cover the tab along with a good tip, even though Maggie didn't deserve one. It wasn't Zeke's fault what happened all those years ago. When he rose, the two men nodded his way, but the waitress didn't acknowledge him.

"Good evening, gentlemen. Maggie." Zeke didn't wait for a response. He strolled out of the diner vowing to never return. If his conversation with his brother was successful, Zeke wouldn't need to find somewhere else to eat. He would dine with Cyrus in his home.

The hotel he frequented was older, yet it had been remodeled since the last time he stayed there. Zeke had expected bright oranges and yellows, but the room was painted a light gray, and the bedding was stark white, more in line with upscale hotels. The bathroom had been updated too. Zeke didn't bother unpacking. It wasn't like jeans and flannel got that wrinkled inside his duffel.

Zeke picked up the remote and turned on the TV for background noise. After sitting against the headboard, he scrolled through the few texts he had traded with Stella. Zeke wished he'd taken a picture of his mate. Not that her beauty wasn't seared into his brain. He wondered at her heritage. Did she and Sheila have Egyptian blood flowing through them? He hadn't been kidding when he told her she could pass for Nefertari. His mate was exotic, and he had been blessed when the fates chose her for him. He wondered what their children would look like. Would they take after their mother with her dark hair and eyes? Would

19

they be blond-headed with blue eyes like Zeke? Or would they be a mixture of the two? As long as they were healthy, Zeke didn't care who they took after. Then again, her looks weren't what was important. It was her inner goodness that called to him. No, he didn't know Stella, but the fates wouldn't give him someone who didn't have a good heart.

It was then Zeke remembered Stella already had kids. He hadn't actually forgotten, but he'd put it out of his mind. Where had they stayed while Stella had been on her trip? Probably with their father. Instead of texting Stella, Zeke opened the search engine on his phone and did some digging. He wished he'd brought his laptop, but he hadn't planned on having much downtime. Now that he'd met Julian Stone, Zeke knew he could reach out to the male for computer help, but Julian was still in Egypt with the others. Even Tessa was a whiz when it came to searching. Zeke had contacted his cousin more than once for assistance over the past few years. Since she, too, was still in Cairo, he had to search on his own.

After a couple hours, Zeke knew Stella was a high school teacher. He found a photo from the local news outlet when she won teacher of the year. What he didn't find was a marriage certificate or birth announcements. Knowing she was a teacher, Zeke concluded the kids she had mentioned were students. At least he hoped they were. Not that he wouldn't accept her children if she had them, but it would be easier without an ex-husband in the picture. Zeke wanted to call and hear Stella's voice, but it would only rile his beast. His Goyle was already pissed he hadn't stayed in California.

Zeke needed at least a small connection, so he texted her.

Zeke: *Did you make it home okay?*

Stella must have been holding her phone because she responded straight away.

Stella: *I did. My next-door neighbor assaulted me*

20

immediately, but I got away from her as soon as I could.

Zeke: *You were assaulted? Did you call the police? Are you okay?*

Zeke was on his feet, ready to head to the airport when his phone pinged.

Stella: *Sorry, not that kind of assault. Mrs. Goss is just nosy.*

He blew out a breath. He wanted to spank Stella's ass for nearly giving him a heart attack.

Zeke: *You scared me.*

Stella: *I'm sorry. I'll be more careful with how I phrase things. So, how was your flight? You said you had business?*

Zeke: *The flight was short, and my meeting was canceled until tomorrow. I stopped by a diner, and now I'm sitting in my hotel room. I usually go for a run, but I wanted to make sure you got home okay.* Zeke wanted to ask so many questions, but doing so by text was too impersonal.

Stella: *I used to jog every night with Bruce, but he passed away last year.*

Zeke: *Bruce?* Zeke held his breath, praying Bruce wasn't her husband.

Stella: *Sorry. Bruce was my pit bull. He was the best dog ever. I got him right after I started teaching, which was almost ten years ago. Now I jog by myself, but it's not as fun.*

Zeke: *Not that I can replace your best friend, but I'd love to jog with you.* Zeke hated the thought of Stella out alone even if was around her neighborhood. It wasn't safe for someone as pretty as her to be without protection.

Stella: *You mentioned New Oceanside. Do you live close to the beach? Is that where you usually run?*

Zeke: *I have a house on the beach. It's nothing fancy, but it's nice to hear the ocean every night when I lay down. And yes, I run on the sand. Do you like the beach?*

Stella: *I love it, although I don't get to see it as often as I'd like. I do visit the coast for at least a week every summer once school lets out.*

Zeke: *You're welcome at my house any time.* Zeke deleted the sentence. It was too forward even if it was the truth.

21

Instead, he typed: *Once we get to know one another better, maybe you can stay at my house instead of a hotel or wherever it is you usually go.*

Stella: *Thank you for the offer. Since that's months away, I have a feeling we'll know each other pretty well by then.*

Zeke's heart stuttered. His mate felt their connection. If things went the way Zeke knew they would, it was possible she would spend all summer with him on the beach. And maybe that's how things would work. She'd keep her job, and they would live in her home during the school year, visiting the beach house during breaks when they weren't off traveling. Because they would travel, of that he had no doubt.

Zeke: *You're welcome, and I have the same feeling.*

Instead of letting Stella get her rest, Zeke continued chatting with his mate, getting to know little things like her favorite foods and TV shows. She talked about teaching, and he told her about his travels, leaving out why he visited so many different places. There would be a time for explanations once they were mated.

When he noticed how late it had gotten, Zeke insisted she get some sleep, promising to resume their chat later that day. After Stella wished him a good night, Zeke stared at the ceiling. His beast was antsy, and Zeke needed to expend some energy, so he changed out of his jeans and pulled on a pair of sweats and running shoes. He started off jogging on the street, but when he was out of sight of any businesses or homes, he turned toward the mountains. With it being so late, he didn't think anyone would see him. Zeke had found this particular trail the last time he visited. It appeared to be a deer trail by the prints, but Zeke hadn't encountered any wildlife the last time. If any animals were in the vicinity, they probably sensed the beast within him and gave him a wide berth.

Zeke jogged until he came to an open area, and then he let his shifter loose a bit. Running full speed was risky, but

22

not as risky as flying. Zeke did some rock climbing, using his claws to pull himself up. He didn't ascend to the top of the mountain. Instead, he stopped about halfway up and admired the view. It was so different than California. Zeke wondered how attached Stella was to her job and home. When Jonas hired Zeke and Sam to watch over the family, he paid them well to do so. His father had more money than the gods, and he was generous in what he gave them. Since Cyrus was the last sibling to watch over, Zeke would no longer need to travel in secrecy.

Once he and Stella completed their bond, would she be willing to give up her teaching job and see the world with him? Zeke had no plans to abandon those siblings he'd met just because they now knew the truth. With Sam and Monica reconnecting with Xenia, Sam would more than likely want to spend time with his daughter getting to know her. Not that Zeke saw his brother all that often. Sam and Monica lived in New York. Zeke's family was scattered around the world, and he had enjoyed his job. A job that, after talking to Cyrus, would no longer be needed.

Zeke scaled down the rocks, then headed back to the hotel. While he ran, he imagined Stella jogging alongside him. He didn't let himself think about getting to know her intimately, because running with an erection was no fun. By the time he got back in the room and showered, it was going on five a.m. He planned to drive to Cyrus's house early, before his brother had time to head to his parents'. Instead of lying down for a short nap, Zeke got dressed and headed out.

CHAPTER THREE

CYRUS'S TRUCK WAS in the driveway when Zeke arrived. Just as he reached for the handle, a couple dogs bounded around the house barking, Zeke didn't need to worry about Cyrus knowing someone was there. His brother strode onto the porch, casually pointing a rifle Zeke's direction.

"Hera, Leto, quiet!" Cyrus commanded the dogs. They stopped barking, but neither dog moved away from the car.

Zeke cracked his window. "Hello, Cyrus. My name is Ezekiel Seymour, and I need to talk to you about your family." He was vague, allowing Cyrus to think he was referring to John and Gwen Gillespie, the couple who adopted Cyrus.

Cyrus raised the gun a little higher. "I just spoke to Mom not five minutes ago. They both were fine."

"No, not your parents. Your birth family." As with all others, the Gillespies signed an agreement stating they wouldn't reveal who Cyrus's birth parents were. In all his years as a watcher, that agreement had never been broken. "It's important, Cyrus. Life or death important."

"Get out of the car slowly." Cyrus didn't loosen his grip on the gun.

Zeke pushed open the car door, and the dogs alternated between growling and whimpering. At least the horses weren't close by. Zeke brought his shifter to the surface, emanating his dominance over the dogs. Getting bitten would hurt, but he would heal quickly. The animals whimpered, then took off running around the back of the house. With them out of the way, Zeke walked toward his

24

brother. When he got close enough for the porch light to illuminate his features, Cyrus gasped. Zeke had stopped aging when he met Stella, so he appeared as though he was in his early thirties, not fifty-seven. At fifty-three, Cyrus looked like an older version of Zeke, both taking after Jonas.

"You look just like I did when I was younger. Brother?" Cyrus lowered the rifle as he took in Zeke's countenance.

"Yes. One of many. May I come in?"

"I… yes. This is…" Cyrus shook his head, then opened the door, holding it for Zeke.

"Have a seat. Can I get you some coffee? Although I think I'm going to need to add some alcohol to mine." Cyrus placed the rifle on a rack by the front door.

"I would love some coffee." Zeke followed Cyrus farther into the living room and took a seat on the sofa. Cyrus's house was a two-story cabin. The lower level was an open concept with only a few doors, one which led out back. A wide staircase rose to a loft overlooking the downstairs. "Nice place you have."

"Thanks. Dad and I built it when I graduated high school. I always knew college wasn't for me. I grew up on the ranch helping raise cattle. I was more at home atop a horse than in a classroom, but I also wanted a little bit of freedom. Their ranch is about three miles down the road." Cyrus must have been up for a while since the coffee was already brewed. He handed Zeke a mug. "Do you take cream or sugar?"

"No, this is perfect. Thank you."

Cyrus took his own cup to a cabinet where he added a healthy dose of whiskey to his coffee. "You said something about many siblings and life or death?"

"I wasn't lying about the siblings. There are fifteen of us still living. An older brother was killed several months ago, and I recently found out one of our sisters is really a niece, but that's a story for another time. What I'm about to tell you is going to sound far-fetched and unbelievable, but I

25

need you to keep an open mind, and when I finish speaking, I will show you proof."

"Proof of what? And what about the life and death situation you mentioned. Was that a lie?"

"No, just not as dire as I made it sound. Cyrus, have you heard of Jonas Montague?"

"The scientist who cloned the first baby? Yeah, everyone's heard of him."

"Jonas is our father." Zeke always started with that. Sometimes it went over well. Others?

"Are you saying we're clones?" Cyrus downed the whiskey and coffee mixture, then poured a mugful of liquor from the bottle he'd placed on the mantle. A lot of drinking and pacing accompanied these talks.

"No, not at all. We are the biological children of Jonas and his mate, Caroline."

"Mate? You mean he didn't wed the mother of his kids?"

"Here's where the story gets strange. Jonas is a Gargoyle. Meaning he appears human, but he has a shifter inside that can come out. Unlike stories about werewolves who fully shift into their animal, Gargoyles retain most of their human features when they shift with the exception of wings, claws, and fangs. The females don't have wings, nor do they have the same impenetrable skin the males do. Our mother, Jonas's mate, is fully human, making us half-bloods. The difference in the two is that full-bloods transition for the first time around puberty. Half-bloods don't transition until they meet their mate, and since you have yet to transition, you haven't met yours yet."

Cyrus, who had been staring at Zeke, burst out laughing. Zeke had been met with that reaction more than once, so he let his fangs drop and extended the claws on his free hand. Cyrus's laughter abated, and his eyes widened. "What the fuck?" His eyes darted to the rifle by the door.

Before Cyrus could take a step, Zeke set his coffee down

26

and sped across the room to stand in front of the weapon. "Did I mention super speed? We have extraordinary strength too. If you'd feel better holding the rifle" — Zeke pulled it down and held it out to Cyrus — "I'd be okay with that, but please don't shoot me in the head. One, it'll hurt like a mother, and two, you'll be the one cleaning up the mess." When Cyrus just stood staring, Zeke replaced the rifle in the rack. "Cyrus, I'm your brother, and I would rather die than hurt you. And no, that wasn't all parlor tricks. I can show you my wings if you need further proof."

Cyrus picked up the whiskey. Instead of adding more to his mug, he drank from the bottle instead. After wiping his mouth on the back of his hand, he dropped into the recliner. "Say I believe you. What does that mean for me? I can't do all that." Cyrus waved his hand in Zeke's direction.

"It's because you haven't met your mate. We only recently discovered what causes the half-bloods' transition. Unfortunately, I ran into my mate about thirty years ago and didn't know it. I've been living without her all these years because I didn't know she was the reason." Zeke left out the part about Stella being a toddler at the time. "If you had come across your female, or male if you prefer, you would have given over to your Gargoyle."

"If I haven't met them in fifty-three years, what makes you think I will now?"

"Because it is our way. Our niece, Xenia, only found her mate a few weeks ago, and she's forty-seven. Keene showed up for a date while Xenia was going through her transition. She was freaking out, throwing shit at Keene, yelling for him to get out of the house. Luckily, another niece, Sophia, showed up at that moment and walked Xenia through what was going on. All these years I thought Xenia was our sister, but Jonas had convinced our brother, Sam, to put his first-born up for adoption the way he and Caroline had with most of us. Not only did Xenia find out she was a Gargoyle but that the man who raised her was actually an uncle on her mother's side. Sophia found out the female she thought was her aunt was really her sister. It's all a little convoluted."

"Why did Jonas put us up for adoption? And you said most of us."

"When Jonas met Caroline, Gargoyles had never mated with humans. He was ostracized from his Clan, and he took Caroline and fled Italy. When she got pregnant with their first child, they were on the run. Caroline wanted children, but Jonas convinced her letting others raise most of their offspring was for the best. Two years after they had me, Gabriel was born. For whatever reason, they kept him, but they probably wish they hadn't. His story is tragic, but we'll get into that later. Caroline had seven more children, but when she got pregnant with Isabelle, their last child, Caroline refused to part with her daughter. When Isabelle was old enough to notice her parents weren't aging, Caroline left Isabelle with Jonas. When he deemed her too much to handle on his own, he sent her to live with a husband and wife who were friends of the family, while Caroline watched over her from nearby. Isabelle thought her mother had died, and it wasn't until a few months ago she found out that wasn't true." Zeke scrubbed a hand down his face. "There are so many stories surrounding our family, but those can wait until later."

"I'm not sure I want a mate if having one comes with such turmoil."

"It's worth it when you meet the one the fates send you. As Gargoyles, there is only one perfect being for us. You haven't met yours for a reason, although only the fates know what that reason is. I met mine in passing thirty years ago, then yesterday I was standing in line at the airport, and there she was. Our King, Rafael, spent almost six hundred years thinking he'd never find his mate, then one day the chief of police came calling regarding an incident at one of Rafael's warehouses, and boom – there she was."

"What if I had found a partner already? What happens to them when my mate comes along?"

"That has happened, but more often than not, the spouse isn't a good one. The marriage doesn't last for whatever reason. Rafael's cousin's mate was married when he found her, but the husband was a horrible human. He was killed after kidnapping Abbi, and now she and Frey are happily mated."

"If I never find my mate, what happens?" Cyrus had stopped drinking and was focused on all Zeke was telling him. Zeke took that as a win.

"Life as you know it will continue. You'll remain human. Keep aging. Nothing will change. If you do meet your mate, you'll know it because you'll feel sick to your stomach for no apparent reason. If that should happen, you need to get away from her as quickly as possible because you'll transition soon after, and you don't want her around for that. It's rather painful the first time."

"Him."

"Excuse me?"

"My mate will be a man. At least that would be my preference." Cyrus wouldn't meet Zeke's eyes.

"Then that is who the fates will send to you. But you will need to stay away from him until you have your phasing under control. That is what we call shifting. If or when it happens, you'll need to have the same conversation you and I are having. If he agrees to be your mate, you'll bite him, and that will seal the bond. You both will stop aging and hopefully live a long life together." At least that's what Zeke hoped happened. The females' outer appearance didn't change, and he figured it was because of the bite. "There's something else I should warn you about. Once you transition, your animals are going to become agitated. That's what was wrong with your dogs when I arrived. They recognized the animal within me."

"Will I have to give them up? I love Hera and Leto."

29

"I honestly don't know. Maybe since they're already loyal, they'll be okay with you being different."

Cyrus stood and stared into the fireplace. "I feel like I'm dreaming."

"Believe me, I understand. But you're not alone. I live down in Southern California, and it's only a three-hour plane ride. If you need me, all you have to do is call. Our other siblings are scattered across the globe. Isabelle and Dane are in New Atlanta where Rafael lives. Lilly lives in New Orleans. Sophia is mated to Rafael's cousin Nikolas. They also live in New Atlanta. Our brother Sam, Sophia's dad, lives in New York with his mate, Monica. Cordelia, who recently transitioned, is in New Mexico. Everyone else is somewhere across the pond."

Cyrus continued asking questions, and Zeke answered every one of them honestly. When it came time for Cyrus to get ready to head to work, Zeke made himself at home and whipped up a quick breakfast while Cyrus was in the shower.

"You didn't have to do that," Cyrus said as he poured a cup of coffee. "But I do appreciate it."

"It's the least I could do for your hospitality." Zeke plated their food, and the two brothers ate in companionable silence.

"I want you to go with me. I've always known I was adopted, but my parents said they didn't know anything about my birth parents, and I want them to meet you."

"Just don't tell them I'm four years older. That'll be hard to explain without letting them know I'm a Gargoyle."

"Damn, you look good for fifty-seven. And you'll look that way forever?"

"Yep. Jonas is nine hundred seventy-three, and he and I can pass for brothers."

"Nine hundred... He's lived almost a thousand years?"

"Yes. Gargoyles, males especially, have long lifespans. There are only two ways to kill males: beheading and some

30

rare poisons."

"Huh." Cyrus clasped his hands in front of him. "If I am going to find my mate, I hope it happens sooner rather than later. I'd prefer to live hundreds of years looking like this instead of a wrinkled old man. Before we go, can I see your wings? Or is that inappropriate to ask?"

"Not at all. Seeing mine, you'll know what to expect." After putting their dishes away, Zeke removed his shirt and called forth his wings. Cyrus reached his hand out, but Zeke took a step back. "Touching a Goyle's wings is reserved for one's mate."

Cyrus ducked his eyes. "Sorry."

"No need to apologize. We hadn't covered that." Zeke wrapped his wings around his body, then flared them behind him again. "They're good for protection and flying. That's another thing that takes some getting used to. Just make sure if you ever decide to take to the skies you are in a secluded area. We can't have humans aware of our existence."

"Except for our mates?"

"Yes, but the fates wouldn't give us a human mate who wasn't loyal. Whomever you end up with will be trustworthy and will love you like no other." Zeke retracted his wings and put on his shirt. "Are you sure you want me to come with you? I'll need to stay away from the animals."

"I'm sure. Mom doesn't have any pets, and all the horses and cattle are well away from the house."

"Then let's go." Zeke had never met any of his siblings' adopted families, and he was looking forward to seeing where his brother grew up.

STELLA'S EYES WERE gritty when she woke. Groaning, she turned over on her side to see the clock. It didn't surprise

31

her it was almost noon. She had stayed up late texting with Zeke. She had wanted to call him, to hear his voice, but he seemed to prefer texting. He didn't come across as shy, but maybe it was easier to reveal parts of himself over text. She had learned a few tidbits about the handsome blond, but mostly, he asked about her. On one hand, it was a positive he didn't drone on and on about himself. It showed he wanted to know about her. On the other, she hadn't gleaned much about him other than he had quite a few siblings who were scattered around the globe. That was intriguing considering he was so young. Had his father found a woman after Sheila who he connected with and gave him lots of children? Or was the elder Ezekiel a player with different baby mommas?

If that were the case, Stella prayed Zeke didn't take after his father. He did travel for his job after all. When she asked what he had been doing in Egypt, he told her it was a family reunion of sorts. Since Stella was an only child, she couldn't imagine having siblings to travel with and visit around the globe. Maybe if she and Zeke hit it off the way she imagined, she would get to travel with him.

After they said goodnight, Stella lay awake dreaming of a life with Zeke. He owned a beach house, and she had to admit living with him by the ocean was enticing. Stella loved teaching, and she could always change schools. That was probably in the cards anyway. With the way things had been going with Bradley, she didn't see herself staying at New Fallbrook High School after the current year was up. It had been a mistake to go out with the man, especially since he was the principal. There was nothing in the employee handbook about dating other teachers. In fact, there was a married couple who taught at the school.

Stella unplugged her phone from the charger and checked to see if she had any messages from Zeke. She smiled to see he had sent her a good morning text, but when she noticed the time he sent it, she frowned. Did the man not sleep?

Stella: *Good afternoon, and yes, I just woke up. Hope your meeting is going well.*

She didn't expect a response if he was busy, so Stella rolled out of bed and padded to the kitchen for a cup of coffee. She had cleaned out her refrigerator before leaving on her trip, so her options for breakfast were slim. While she waited for the water to heat in the coffee maker, she popped a piece of bread in the toaster. After both were ready, Stella took her meager breakfast to the living room and sat cross-legged on the sofa. Her laptop taunted her from the coffee table. With next week being right before winter break, she didn't have much to do in the way of planning lessons. The students' attention span would be shorter than usual. In past years, she had given them a short book to read and had them write a report on Thursday to turn in Friday. Why deviate from what worked?

Stella popped the last bite of toast in her mouth and grabbed her computer, setting it on her lap. Kerri had forwarded all the grades from past lessons, and Stella spent an hour going over what she needed to catch up on for Monday. A new email came through, and when she saw it was from Bradley, Stella held her breath. It wasn't unusual for him to send messages to all the teachers, but this one was from his personal account. Since that was the case, she left it unread. Professionally, she couldn't ignore a missive from her boss, but personally, she could. Stella didn't want anything to do with the man outside of school.

After taking care of business, Stella decided to run to the store. She didn't like cafeteria food, so she took her lunch every day. She wasn't getting any younger, and it was harder to keep her weight at a sensible level, especially since she didn't jog as often as she used to when Bruce was alive. If she and Zeke got together, she would need to get back in the habit so they could run together. By the looks of his body, Zeke did a lot of running. She had only caught a short glimpse at the airport. Her focus had been on the way his light blue eyes darkened the longer he stared at her. His blond hair had just the right amount of wave to it, and Stella longed to run her fingers through it.

Pushing off the sofa, Stella closed her laptop, and set it on the coffee table. She padded to her bedroom to change out of her comfy clothes. She wasn't as vain as some women, but she also wasn't one to go out looking like she just crawled out of bed. She pulled her long, black hair into a low ponytail, brushed some foundation on, then dressed in jeans and a beige sweater. Since she was only going for groceries, she left off a necklace. Stella had a large collection taking up two standing jewelry boxes in her walk-in closet. She began collecting them in college, and it was rare to see her without one. She had picked up a couple stunning new pieces while on vacation.

After getting the reusable shopping bags out of the pantry, Stella drove the short distance to the closest grocer, not wanting to travel half an hour to the Farm Fresh Market. She would grab what she needed for lunch, then go to the specialty market one day after school since both were in the same area. Stella loved to cook, but doing so for one person got tedious. She often made large batches of food and froze the leftovers. But the market had small, prepackaged meals that were perfect. All the ingredients were included in the box, and she didn't have to measure or worry about if she had the right spices. As she drove, Stella thought about Zeke. They had briefly touched on favorite foods, but you could only eat so many steaks – Zeke's favorite – or enchiladas – Stella's favorite.

Stella chose a cart and stowed the shopping bags on the rack underneath, then pushed it to the produce section. She was scanning the spinach when she felt someone step close behind her.

"Hello, Beautiful."

34

CHAPTER FOUR

STELLA CLOSED HER eyes, begging whatever goddess was listening for strength. She schooled her expression before turning to face her boss. "Bradley."

His megawatt smile faltered at her frosty greeting. "Did you get my flowers? I had hoped to deliver them myself, but your neighbor said you were running late. Did something happen to delay your homecoming?"

Stella grabbed the cart and turned it so it was between them. "I didn't realize I was on a schedule. Not that it's any of your business, but I had lunch with someone upon my return."

"Excuse me, I need to get to the lettuce." An older woman pointed behind Stella.

"Sorry." Stella turned and chose a bag of spinach instead of shopping for the loose variety. She tossed it into her cart and moved out of the woman's way. "I'll see you tomorrow, Mr. Calhoun." Using Bradley's last name always pissed him off, but Stella was past the point of caring. Before she could get two steps, he gripped her arm.

"Stella—"

"Let go." Stella jerked her arm out of his hold. She lowered her voice, not wanting to air their dirty laundry in the produce section. "I have made it clear I have no intention of going out with you again. Stop emailing, stop sending flowers, and for the love of Bast, stop interrupting my class for no good reason." Stella grabbed her purse, then left her cart where it was, rushing out of the store. She checked to make sure he wasn't following, and when she made it to her car, Stella locked herself inside.

"Damnit!" In her rush to get away, she'd left her reusable bags underneath the shopping cart. Thankfully, they were inexpensive and could be replaced. She didn't make much on a teacher's salary, but having tenure, she made more than the younger ones just starting out. She was frugal with her money during the year to save up for her vacations. The only things she splurged on were get-aways and her vast array of beaded necklaces. The trip to Egypt had cost a pretty penny, but she and her mom had gotten a two-for-one deal, so splitting the cost had helped. Still, she hated spending money when she didn't need to.

Stella was pissed that Bradley had ruined her shopping. She could either wait for him to leave the store, or she could come back later. Stella opted for neither, praying he didn't follow her. She started the car and headed toward the market she should have gone to in the first place. When she arrived, Stella circled the parking lot several times looking for Bradley's fancy car. When she didn't see it, she parked and went inside. Stella made it through the store and back to the parking lot unscathed except for the expense of purchasing new bags.

Stella wanted to call Zeke. She wanted him to know what was going on with her boss, but it was too soon to lay all that on him. She had a feeling he would be the kind of man to confront her problem for her. It probably spoke to her love of action movies, but Stella could imagine Zeke popping Bradley in the nose. Maybe she would mention it – the confrontation, not the violence – when she texted with him later.

Instead of taking the main roads home where she would have to sit through several traffic lights, Stella opted to go the long way. The two-lane road was quiet for a Sunday afternoon, and Stella turned up the radio, singing along with her favorite rock band, Cyanide Sweetness. Stella loved most types of music, but sometimes a girl needed to blast something a little heavy. Her mind went back to Zeke and the fact that he liked jazz. Stella imagined the bluesy tunes playing in the background while they cooked supper together. They would eat on his back deck overlooking the Pacific. If she hadn't been lost in a daydream, she might have noticed the truck racing up behind her.

There was a double yellow line, so she was surprised when the truck veered into the other lane to pass. Only they didn't pass her. The truck rammed into the side of her car, and Stella screamed. She jerked the wheel to the left, but the truck struck again, pushing her off the shoulder. Stella braked hard, but the tires caught gravel and fishtailed a few times before there was another hit. This time, the truck tapped her back quarter panel, sending her spinning. "Oh, goddess!" A million thoughts flitted through Stella's mind, but the one that stuck out the most was that she would never have the chance to find out if Zeke was the one.

No sooner than her car stopped, the door was jerked open. A large man reached in, unbuckling her seatbelt before hauling Stella out onto her feet. He never said a word. Holding her sweater with one hand, he swung with the other. She raised her arms to shield her face, but it did no good. The first hit to her head hurt like nothing she'd ever encountered before, but the punch to her stomach took her breath. At five-four and one hundred forty pounds, Stella was no match for the stranger, although she refused to stand there and not do something. Stella scratched at his face and arms. She tried to kick him. When she managed to draw blood with her nails, the man cursed her, then punched her in her temple. Stella went down, and soon, there was nothing but darkness.

MEETING CYRUS'S PARENTS was a different experience for

Zeke. When he'd spoken with his other siblings, it was usually after they had transitioned, and those meetings came with much arguing, some fighting, and lots of anger. Zeke didn't blame any of them. He only blamed Jonas. But being the bearer of the truth came with the need for tough skin and patience. He could commiserate with each and every one of them, having transitioned without his own mate at his side all those years ago. Luckily, for most of his brothers and sisters, they could narrow down who might have caused their phasing.

Cyrus introduced Zeke as his biological brother, and Zeke told the Gillespies half-truths and a lot of lies. He explained to Cyrus on the drive that his parents couldn't know the truth of Gargoyles. Cyrus had agreed, but the male didn't want to lie to his parents, so he let Zeke do all the talking. While Cyrus went about his daily chores, Zeke sat with Gwen, allowing the older woman to dote on him while peppering him with questions. While she was fixing their lunch, Zeke excused himself and walked outside. The kitchen door led to the backyard, which contained a picnic table, several Adirondack chairs surrounding a stone fire pit, and a large square plot of dirt that had been a garden in the summer. Cyrus's parents' house was worn and lived-in, but it wasn't in need of repair. Cyrus made sure of it. They had four hundred acres that would all go to Cyrus whenever they passed. The couple never had children of their own, so Cyrus had received all their love. Zeke wasn't jealous, but he did wonder what that would feel like. Not wanting to be rude, Zeke got on with the reason he had gone outside.

Zeke: *My meeting is going well. I might be home sooner than expected.*

Zeke sent the message and watched his phone, waiting for it to show Stella had read the text. It showed to be delivered, but after ten minutes, she still hadn't read it. It was possible she was driving. Maybe she was busy getting ready for class the next day. She could be in the shower. *Nope*. Zeke couldn't let his mind go there, because facing Gwen with an erection was the last thing he wanted. Having shifter hearing, he left the phone on silent. When she responded, it would vibrate. He tucked the device back in his front pocket and returned to the kitchen.

By the time Cyrus was finished for the day and ready to head home, Zeke still hadn't heard from Stella. His Goyle was sure something was wrong, and it was all Zeke could do to keep the beast from taking over. Zeke bit the bullet and tried calling, but it went straight to voicemail. He didn't leave a message, but when several more hours came and went with no response, he called back.

"Hello? Zeke?" Sheila's voice was scratchy. And why was Stella's mom answering her phone?

"Sheila, what's wrong? Where is Stella?"

"She was..." Sheila's voice broke. It was twenty-seven long seconds later before she answered. Yes, Zeke counted. "She was attacked coming home from the grocery store. She's... It's not good. I need to go."

Attacked? Godsdamnit, his beast had been right. Something was wrong, and instead of being there to protect her, he was almost thirteen hundred miles away. "Sheila, wait! Tell me where you are." There was no way Zeke wasn't going to be there for his mate.

"We're at the Tri-County Medical Center. I-I have to go." Sheila disconnected, and Zeke wanted to throw his phone against the wall.

"Everything okay?" Cyrus asked. Zeke had told his brother about meeting Stella in the airport and how they had texted back and forth.

"No. No, it's not. I have to go. Stella was attacked, and she's in the hospital. That's all I know."

Cyrus clasped Zeke's shoulder. "I'm going with you."

Zeke was taken aback at his brother's offer. He kept in touch with the siblings he watched over, but with the exception of Sam, he wasn't close to any of them. For Cyrus to offer to be there for him after just meeting meant the world to him.

"I appreciate the offer, but stay here and help your parents."

"Dad can call his buddy to help out for a few days. Let me do this."

"Okay. But we need to go. While you pack, I'll get us a flight." Zeke prayed there was one leaving soon, because he couldn't stand the thought of Stella lying in a hospital bed without him there longer than she'd already been. Cyrus was packed and ready before Zeke found their flights. It took several tries, but he got them leaving New Missoula in less than an hour and landing in New Santa Ana. "We'll have to drive part of the way once we land, but that's only an hour and a half. Let's go."

Cyrus called his dad on the way to the airport, and John told him not to rush home. To be there for his brother. Zeke's heart warmed at the sentiment. He already felt closer to Cyrus than any of his siblings with the exception of Sam, but Zeke could see that changing. Sam and Monica had reunited with Xenia, and with the lot of them still in Egypt close to finding where Cleopatra was buried, they finally had the opportunity to bond as a family. Zeke hoped they succeeded on both fronts.

During the flight, Zeke explained more about what he had encountered on his trip to rescue their brother and his mate. He recounted quietly how Sophia disguised herself as an old woman, kissing Nikolas right there on the street, then he explained how Jonas was a genius who created the disguises. Zeke didn't usually talk about their father much in the first few days. Now that they had figured out the trigger, bitterness grew inside Zeke. Jonas had given him life, but he had taken so much from Zeke too.

Once they landed and were in their rental, Zeke got quiet. The closer to his mate, the more he worried he would be too late. He had called Stella's phone, but it went straight to voicemail. Sheila had more than likely turned it off, and it irritated Zeke. Being close to midnight, the drive went quicker than the GPS originally indicated. It also had to do with Zeke speeding while praying he didn't get pulled over. The gods were on his side, and Zeke made it in record time. Cyrus had programmed his number in Zeke's phone during the ride, so he told Zeke to pull up to the door, then text him the room number. It was after visiting hours, but Cyrus told him he would be in the waiting room.

When Zeke called information earlier, he had been surprised to be given a regular room number. With Sheila's tone, he expected his mate to be in intensive care. That was the good news. The bad arrived when Zeke got to the fourth floor and a nurse tried to stop him from seeing Stella.

"You can't go in there."

"Ma'am, I understand there are rules, but I just got off a red-eye out of Montana. I couldn't get here any sooner, and I have to see her."

"And who is she to you? It's family only, and as far as we were notified, she has no family other than her mother."

Fucking Sheila. "I'm her fiancé. Stella and I decided to wait and tell Sheila when we took her out to dinner next week. I was supposed to be on a business trip until then."

The nurse placed a hand on her hip. "I don't remember seeing a ring."

"Right. Because of the surprise. I'll bring it and show you tomorrow, but right now, I need to see my girl. Please, just five minutes?"

"Are you aware of her injuries?"

"No. Sheila was distraught when I talked to her, and I jumped on a plane straight away. How bad is she?"

"She looks like she went three rounds with a heavy-weight boxer and lost." The nurse shook her head. "You need to prepare yourself. It isn't pretty."

Zeke took a deep breath, willing his beast to behave.

41

There would be time later for finding out who attacked his mate, then Zeke would make him pay. "I'm ready."

The nurse pushed open Stella's door and entered the room. It didn't look like she was going to give them privacy, and Zeke was fine with it. He had lied to get his way into the room. What if someone else tried the same thing, like whoever did this? Zeke would probably have to leave and come back, and it looked like he needed to stop and purchase a ring. As he walked through the door, Zeke gave his Goyle a stern warning.

Do not lose your shit, or the nurse will kick us out.

His Goyle didn't respond, but it was calm as Zeke entered the room. Stella's face was swollen, and bruises lined the left side of her face. He took her hand and cradled it gently while studying her injuries. "Who did this to you, Baby?" Zeke whispered. He reached behind him and dragged the chair closer to the bed. Once seated, he brushed Stella's hair back from the uninjured side and let the tears fall. Zeke leaned his forehead against the bed and sobbed. If he hadn't gone to see Cyrus... No. He wouldn't blame this on his brother. Or Jonas, even though it was his father's fault all the siblings had been kept in the dark. This was all on whomever had attacked Stella.

When he got himself under control, he wiped his eyes and turned to the nurse. "Do the police know anything?"

"I'm not sure. They had already come and gone by the time I came on shift. I do know Stella's mom talked to them."

"Where is Sheila? She should be here with her daughter."

"Stella's boss convinced her to go to a hotel and get some rest."

"Her boss? Why was he here?"

"From what I heard, he's the one who found Stella. I don't know all the details. I'm going back to the desk. Ring me if you need anything. I'm Connie, by the way." Connie didn't mention Zeke leaving, so he settled in.

Now that they were alone, his beast pushed at him to claim Stella.

Are you crazy? She's hurt. And I won't claim her without her consent.

It'll help heal her sooner.

You don't know that. But Zeke remembered how Frey bit Abbi when he thought she was dying. Only Stella wasn't dying. She would recover, and then he would never leave her side again. At least not until he proved they belonged together and she agreed to be his mate.

Stella stirred but didn't wake. Zeke texted Cyrus and let him know Zeke wasn't planning on going anywhere. Cyrus left to find a hotel and said he'd be back in the morning. Zeke spent the night talking to her when he wasn't dozing. Telling her how he claimed to be her fiancé just to get in the room, then everything he planned to say when she woke. He vowed to find who did this to her and make them pay. His beast was onboard with that. Connie came in a couple times during the night. The first time she seemed surprised Zeke was awake. The second, she brought him a cup of coffee, and they chatted for a few minutes. Later, she returned with a new nurse and introduced them.

"Zeke, this is Sunny. She'll be watching over Stella on day shift."

Zeke inclined his head to Sunny. "Thank you, Connie."

Connie left, and Sunny checked the machines at Stella's bedside. Zeke could tell her they hadn't changed all night. Well, her heart monitor had sped up a few times when he was speaking to her, but he didn't know if it was because he was talking about his Goyle or if she recognized his voice.

"So, fiancé, huh? That's an exciting time. I remember when my Raymond proposed to me. It was two weeks after we met. Everyone said it was too soon, but we've been married twenty-three years. Sometimes you just know." Sunny stood on the opposite side of the bed, and her

43

demeanor went from caring to concerned. "I have to say I'm surprised, though. When Bradley was here yesterday, he acted like Stella was his. He sat where you are, holding her hand the same tentative way."

Zeke had no idea who this Bradley was. Stella hadn't mentioned another male, and she had told Zeke she looked forward to getting to know him. Maybe he was an ex, and if that were the case, he could stay away. "I assure you Stella is mine. If I hadn't been out of town on business, I would have been here with her. If I hadn't been out of town, this wouldn't have happened in the first place." His tone must have convinced the nurse he was telling the truth. "Were you here when the police came by?"

"Yes. Stella wasn't coherent enough to answer their questions. They're coming back this morning. Then again, so is Bradley. This is my floor, Zeke, and I won't have you upsetting the patients. If you and Mr. Calhoun have issues, take them outside."

"Understood." Now Zeke had a last name. As soon as Sunny left to check on other patients, Zeke pulled out his phone and searched the man's name. It didn't take long to figure out Bradley Calhoun was the principal at the high school where Stella taught. Maybe Sunny misread the situation, and Calhoun was concerned about one of his teachers. That thought was nixed a few minutes later.

"Good morning, Beautiful. I brought you— Who the fuck are you?" Bradley Calhoun was a good-looking man in his early forties. He was as tall as Zeke but not as broad. His dark hair was plastered to his head with some type of product, and his green eyes blazed with fury. Bradley set the vase of red roses on the rolling cart beside Stella's bed, then crossed his arms over his chest.

Zeke didn't bother to get up. He continued caressing Stella's knuckles. "Ezekiel Seymour."

"And? That doesn't tell me shit. You need to leave."

"And you need to keep your voice down, Mr.

Calhoun," Sheila chastised as she entered the room. "I could hear you halfway down the hall. Good morning, Zeke." If Sheila was surprised to see him, she didn't let on. "I'm sorry I didn't return your call, but I figured you were on your way." Sheila wouldn't meet his eyes.

"Of course I was. I have to ask – how'd you get Stella's phone?"

Bradley puffed out his chest. "I brought it to Sheila along with Stella's purse."

Zeke wanted to punch the smarmy dick, but instead, he smiled. "Thank you for that. If you hadn't been so kind, I wouldn't have known so quickly Stella needed me." Zeke kissed the back of Stella's hand, and she muttered something. It was the first time she'd made a sound since Zeke arrived. "Stella? Open those pretty brown eyes for me, Baby."

Sunny entered the room and pointed between the three adults. "Only two allowed at a time. Mr. Calhoun, maybe you can come by later?"

"I'm not going anywhere. Stella is — "

"No," Stella groaned.

Chapter Five

ZEKE HELD HIS breath, waiting for Stella to make her wishes known.

"See? She wants me here. He needs to go." Bradley stabbed a finger in Zeke's direction.

"No. Bradley..." Stella opened her eyes, staring at Zeke. "Zeke. My Zeke."

"I'm here, Love. I'm sorry I wasn't here yesterday when this happened." Zeke prayed Stella could read his sincerity in his eyes.

"That's right, you weren't," Bradley said. "But I was. I'm the one who found her and got her to the hospital. I'm the one who saved her." Bradley puffed his chest out, and Zeke narrowed his eyes at the human.

"Saved her? Then you saw who did this to her. Who was it? Is he in custody? Did you beat his ass for doing this to Stella?"

"What? No, I... They were already gone when I found her on the side of the road." Bradley licked his lips. His heart was beating double time, and he was starting to sweat. If Zeke weren't a Goyle, he wouldn't be aware of these things. Bradley Calhoun was nervous.

"Right." Zeke would find out the truth, but it could wait. His mate was awake, and he needed to talk to her.

"Zeke? What did I tell you?" Sunny asked, her hands fisting her hips.

"You're right. This can wait." Zeke pulled Stella's hand to his mouth and kissed her knuckles. "Hey," he whispered to his mate.

"Hi," she returned, smiling.

"Mr. Calhoun, you need to leave. At least go sit in the waiting room." Sunny pointed to the door.

"Stella, Beautiful—"

"No, Bradley. Leave. Now," Stella managed to say, her voice strained.

"You heard the lady. Out, now." Sunny pushed against Bradley's arm until he left the room. Stella's boss turned at the door, his eyes narrowed on Zeke. Zeke ignored the man and turned his focus to his female.

Sunny asked Sheila to step aside so she could check Stella over. "How's your pain on a scale of one to ten?"

"Fifteen," Stella whimpered.

"I'm going to administer extra pain relief," Sunny said as she turned a small dial on the IV line. "It'll make you sleepy, but that's what you need right now. The doctor is on the floor, and he'll be in to speak with you soon."

Sheila, who had silently watched the two males, stepped back up to the other side of the bed. "How are you feeling?"

"My head hurts." Stella hadn't taken her eyes off Zeke. "You're really here. I thought I was dreaming."

"I got here as soon as I could. I sat with you all night, so you may have heard me talking to you." Stella's eyelids fluttered like she was fighting sleep. "Rest, Baby. I'll be here when you wake up."

"Promise?"

"Yeah, I promise." Zeke ran his fingertip down her right cheek, and Stella smiled as she closed her eyes. He waited until her breathing evened out, then turned his attention to Sheila. "Tell me about Calhoun."

Sheila sighed, fussing with the sheet covering Stella. "He's her boss. The principal at the high school."

"I know that much. What I don't know is why he thinks he has a right to her."

"Like you do? I may have dated your father, but I don't

47

know you," Sheila snapped.

"No, you don't, but Stella does.

"How? You met her Saturday. Bradley has known her for years."

"So what? They dated? Lived together? Planned a future together?"

"No, it was one date, but—"

"But what? One date does not a relationship make." Zeke wanted to add she should know that, but being petty wouldn't win his mate's mother over to his side.

"And texting does?" Sheila huffed out a breath. "Can we talk about this after we make sure my girl's going to be okay? It's up to her who she wants in her life."

"And you think she wants him?" Zeke pointed to the door Bradley had exited.

"No, I don't." Sheila picked up Stella's hand and cradled it between both of hers. "We talked about you. I have never seen my daughter light up the way she did when you were texting her. Then, after she got home, I called her to say…" Sheila looked at Zeke. Really looked at him. "I can't get over how much you look like your father. I understand sometimes genes are strong, but *my god*, it's like looking at him all over again."

"You aren't wrong, but it has been thirty years, so I'm sure you are forgetting subtle differences." Zeke hated himself a little, but there was no way Sheila would understand. Hell, Stella might not once he admitted the truth, but he was counting on the mate bond to help.

"Anyway, I called her to say I'm okay with the two of you dating. It was weird at first. Remembering the date I went on with Ezekiel and how he ghosted me afterward. I thought it was because of Stella. That your father didn't want me because of her, then Stella and I talked about it. Why wouldn't he be okay with her since he had a child of his own?" Sheila wiped a tear from under her eye, and Zeke's heart went out to the woman. She had truly cared for him, and as she said, he ghosted her after that second date. But he had transitioned shortly after. He kept to himself those first few weeks.

"Sheila, I'm sorry for what you went through back then. I am one of those who believes everything happens for a reason, no matter whether we understand it at the time or not. I believe fate brought Stella and me together at the airport because she and I are meant to be. Yes, we just met, but I know in here" — Zeke thumped his chest above his heart — "she is my forever. I have spent my whole life looking for my other half, and Stella is that for me. There won't be 'one date' and then everything falls apart. There will be a lifetime of me doing everything in my power to take care of her, provide for her, love her. Make her happy. What happened yesterday..." Zeke brushed a strand of hair off Stella's mottled cheek. "That will never happen again. The fact that it did happen tears me up inside, but I want to make sure whoever did this to her pays for it. I need to know everything."

Sheila sighed. "I only know what Bradley told the cops. That he was driving home from the store and saw Stella on the side of the road. He called for an ambulance. I'm her emergency contact, so when the hospital called me, it took a couple hours to get here, and he was in the waiting room since she was still in the ER. Bradley is fixated on Stella. He came to the high school as principal about two years ago and immediately asked her out. Stella put him off for quite a while, then finally gave in. It only took one date to know there wouldn't be a second. She has been in a couple of relationships over the years, but for whatever reason, they didn't work out. I think seeing me accept men into my life who are less than what I deserve made her leery of letting herself remain with those men when it was less than perfect. She didn't want to end up like me."

"Or maybe what you went through taught her how to wait for the perfect male to come along. Waiting isn't a bad

49

thing. Whatever the reason her past relationships didn't work out, I'm thankful for it. But I am concerned about this fixation Calhoun has with Stella. If the date was a year ago, he hasn't moved on. Has he harassed her at work? Does he interfere with her classes?" There was so much Zeke didn't know about his mate.

"If he has, Stella hasn't mentioned it. She doesn't want me to worry about her."

"I can understand that, but until she can tell us more about what he has or hasn't been doing, I don't want him anywhere near her. Since I'm new in her life, I don't know her routines. I'm not familiar with the area she was driving, but I do find it suspect he just happened to be in the right place at the right time to find her."

Sheila gasped, clutching at her throat. "You think he did this to her?"

"Anything is possible." Zeke picked up Stella's hand and examined it. "Her nails are jagged, which means she fought her attacker. No doubt a forensic specialist swabbed under her nails for skin cells. If the attacker is in the system, they'll find him."

The doctor entered the room, interrupting their conversation, and Zeke rose to greet him. "Zeke Seymour. I'm Stella's fiancé. Please tell us you have good news." Zeke waited for Sheila to dispute him, but her focus was on the handsome doctor.

"Dr. Crabtree." The man shook Zeke's proffered hand, accepting Zeke's title as the truth. "And you must be Miss Bentley's sister," Dr. Crabtree said to Sheila.

Sheila pushed her hair behind her ear as a blush rose on her cheeks. "I'm her mother, Sheila."

"Sunny informed me Stella woke up for a few minutes and was coherent. This is good news. There are no fractures to either her orbital socket or her jaw. She does have a concussion, but it should heal in a week's time. I'm going to keep her another night for observation, but if she's alert during the day today and has no issues tonight, she can go home tomorrow."

"Should we be waking her every couple hours because of the concussion? Did you do that last night?" Sheila asked first the doctor, then Zeke.

Dr. Crabtree's face softened when he spoke to Sheila. "That isn't necessary. There is no internal bleeding, therefore the best thing for Stella is rest."

"We'll make sure she gets it." Zeke had no doubt Sheila would want to watch over Stella, and he would allow it for a day or two. Then he was going to insist Sheila return home so he could tend to his mate. Stella had mentioned how exhausting her mother could be, and he wouldn't allow her to hinder Stella's recovery.

"The police mentioned they'll be here this morning to get Stella's statement. Concentrating will be unpleasant for Stella, but it's in her best interest to talk to them sooner rather than later so they can do their job in finding who did this to her." Dr. Crabtree was speaking to them both, but he couldn't keep his eyes off Sheila.

Sheila clutched her hands to her chest. "Thank you, Dr. Crabtree."

"Please, call me Anson. I'll be back later to check in. Will you still be here, Sheila?"

"Yes. I'll be here."

"Then I'll see you soon." The older man smiled at her.

Zeke thanked the doctor and walked him out, and when they opened the door, Bradley was waiting in the hallway.

"How is Stella?"

"Who are you?" Dr. Crabtree asked.

"I'm Bradley Calhoun, Stella's boss. She's a teacher at my high school. I'm the one who found her." Bradley had been so focused on Dr. Crabtree that he hadn't noticed Zeke. When he did, he scowled.

"Since you aren't family, I'm not at liberty to discuss

my patient. If the family wishes to talk to you, that is up to them."

"He's not family," Bradley said, pointing to Zeke.

"He is Stella's fiancé," Dr. Crabtree responded. Bradley opened his mouth to argue, but two police officers stepped up beside him.

The female of the duo, Officer Dowd according to her nameplate, frowned at Bradley. "Mr. Calhoun? What are you doing here?"

"I came to check on Stella. Did you find who did this to her?" Bradley's mood shifted, and a fine sheen of sweat appeared above his lip. Zeke would bet his beach house Bradley knew more than he had told.

"That's why we're here. Now if you'll excuse us, we need to speak to Stella," Officer Dowd said, dismissing Bradley by shouldering past him. "Did I hear correctly that you're Miss Bentley's fiancé?" she asked Zeke.

"Yes. Zeke Seymour. I was out of town when Stella was attacked. I got here as soon as possible."

"Do you have anyone who can corroborate your whereabouts?"

"Absolutely. I went to visit my brother up in Montana. I can give you his contact information. I also have flight and rental car receipts if you'd like to see them."

Officer Dowd produced a business card. "Please forward them to my email. Is Miss Bentley awake?"

"She wasn't a few minutes ago." Zeke gestured for the female to walk ahead of him into the room. When her partner was inside, Zeke shut the door in Bradley's face before walking around Stella's bed. He brushed a kiss against her forehead. "Stella? Baby, the officers need you to wake up and talk to them."

"Zeke," she murmured.

"I'm here, Love. Can you open your eyes for me?" Zeke couldn't help but speak to Stella as though they had been together a while instead of having just met. He already

52

knew she was his forever.

Stella blinked a few times, then focused on his face. Her smile was weak but instantaneous. "Hi."

"I'm going to raise the bed a little so you can talk to Officer Dowd, okay?"

Once Stella was in a seated position, she turned to the cop. "I'm ready."

"Miss Bentley, do you know who did this to you?"

"No. He was large, about Zeke's size, but his hair was dark, and he had a scar running down his left cheek."

"Can you walk us through what happened?" The officer held a tablet in front of her, ready to take notes.

"I was driving home from the grocery store. I went the back way because..." Stella glanced over at Zeke.

"What is it? Did you remember something?" Zeke sat next to her and took her hand.

"I usually shop at the Farm Fresh Market, but I didn't want to drive that far, so I stopped at a store closer to my house. Bradley was there, and I didn't want to talk to him, so I left and went to Farm Fresh anyway. I was still a little shaken from seeing my boss, so I drove the long way home because it's all back roads, and the scenery is nicer. A truck drove up behind me and crossed the double yellow line. I thought he was going to pass, but instead, he rammed into my car. He hit me a couple times, and I spun out. The man pulled me out of my car and hit me until I blacked out."

As Stella spoke, Zeke had to calm his beast. Hearing Bradley had been in the same store didn't sit well with Zeke, and he figured there was more to the story.

"Did the man say anything to you while he was hitting you?"

"No. I have no idea why he attacked me."

"Miss Bentley, why didn't you want to speak to your boss? Do you not have a good relationship with him?" Officer Dowd's partner asked.

"I went out with him about a year ago, and ever since,

53

he's tried to get me to go out with him again. He sends flowers and calls on the weekend. He disrupts my class. I've told him I'm not interested over and over, but he won't take no for an answer."

"If you have a fiancé, shouldn't that give him the hint you aren't interested?" Office Dowd asked.

Zeke didn't want Stella to have to lie, so he answered for her. "Our engagement is new."

Stella grinned at Zeke, squeezing his hand.

"Is this true, Miss Bentley?" Officer Dowd was watching them closely.

"It is. We haven't even told my mother. We were going to announce our engagement when we took her to supper next week. It's why I'm not wearing my ring." It was all Zeke could do to keep a straight face. Either Stella had grasped what he said to her during the night, or she had some amazing psychic abilities. As for Sheila, she crossed her arms over her chest but didn't dispute her daughter.

"The forensic specialist was able to get skin from under your fingernails. It's being run through the various databases. Hopefully, your assailant has priors and is in the system. This isn't like television where results are instantaneous. This could take up to a week if not longer."

"And if he isn't in the system?" Zeke asked.

"We'll find him. I'm going to go back to Farm Fresh and ask to see their security feed. Hopefully, he followed Stella from the store and his truck was caught on camera. Miss Bentley, what kind of car does your boss drive?"

"A black Mercedes. Why?"

"Just covering all my bases. Your fiancé has my card. If you can think of anything else, please give me a call."

Stella nodded, her eyes drooping. But still, she smiled at Zeke and mouthed, "Fiancé?"

Zeke grinned back and shrugged. He leaned over and whispered, "It was the only way the nurse would let me in last night. Did you hear me talking to you last night?"

"I thought I was dreaming."

"Stella," Sheila started, so Zeke sat up. When Stella turned toward her mother, Sheila's eyes were filled with tears. "Why didn't you tell me how bad things were with Bradley?"

"I didn't want you to worry."

"It looks like I have good reason to."

"Not anymore, you don't." Zeke's phone pinged. "Excuse me." When he checked the message, it was from Cyrus. Zeke had forgotten about his brother, and he felt like shit for it. "I need to call my brother. I'm going to step out in the hall for a second." Zeke stood, then leaned over and softly kissed Stella on the lips. "I'll be right back."

"Okay," she responded dreamily. Whether her expression was from the pain meds or the mate bond, he didn't know.

"Hey, Cyrus. I'm sorry I left you hanging. I know you didn't come with me to sit in a hotel."

"Nah, don't worry about me. How's Stella?"

Zeke stepped into the stairwell and relayed everything.

"Damn, Brother. I'm sorry."

"It's not your fault."

"It kind of is. If you hadn't come to visit, you'd have been here with your female," Cyrus stated, almost as though he had read Zeke's mind.

"No, that is all on her attacker. But what's done is done. Stella will be okay in a few days. I'm taking her to my beach house. You're welcome to come with us. There's plenty of room, and I'd like to spend more time getting to know you."

"Yeah? I've never been to the beach. If you're sure, I'd love to take you up on your offer."

Zeke realized he wanted that a lot. He wanted to be alone with Stella, but he wouldn't be able to claim her until after she was feeling better. Plus, he still had to tell her the truth.

"Absolutely. We won't be going home until tomorrow

at the earliest, so if you'd like to go ahead and take the rental, I can give you the keys as well as the security code. You'll be more comfortable there than in a hotel."

"Sure, I'd love that. Is there anything you need me to bring you?"

"Actually, there is." Zeke told Cyrus the one thing he wanted his brother to pick up for him, thanked him, then headed back to Stella's room.

CHAPTER SIX

"PLEASE TELL ME you were both joking about being engaged," Sheila said as soon as the door closed.

Stella wished they hadn't been kidding, and wasn't that crazy? And what was even crazier was the dream she had where Zeke told her about being some kind of shapeshifter. How the two of them were fated mates, destined to be together for a long time. Stella wasn't one to remember her dreams, but she remembered that one. She blamed it on the drugs.

"It was the only way Zeke could get in last night."

Shelia brushed a strand of hair behind her own ear. "I need to call the office and ask off for next week. Anson said you need to rest for the next few days."

"Anson?"

"Dr. Crabtree." Her mom blushed and walked over to stare out the window.

"Is he hot?" Stella asked. She was fading, but she didn't want to fall asleep again until Zeke returned.

"What? Who?" Sheila grabbed Stella's cup and took it to the bathroom. When she returned, she refilled it with fresh water.

Stella grinned. "Anson. Who else?"

"He's, well yes, but... Anyway, he said you can go home tomorrow barring any setbacks today."

"She'll be coming home with me," Zeke announced as he entered the room. "I'm taking Stella to my beach house. I think she needs to put some distance between her and Calhoun while she heals."

Stella knew Sheila would protest, but there was nothing more Stella wanted than to go with Zeke. "Thank you, Zeke. I appreciate the offer. I need to call Kerri Barnett and see if she's the one covering my classes this week."

"Stella—"

"No, Mom. This is what I want. Besides, you used all your vacation time for our trip." Stella yawned, and her head throbbed. "Please hand me my phone so I can call Kerri, then I need a nap."

Sheila did as asked, but she wasn't happy with Stella's decision. Things with Zeke were moving at Mach speed, but she didn't care. She trusted him. The way she knew Bradley wasn't right for her, Stella knew Zeke was. She had already planned on visiting him in New Oceanside during winter break, but now she got to do that a week earlier. Kerri admitted Bradley had called her in to sub, then Stella briefly explained what happened.

"Everything okay with your brother?" Stella was trying hard to stay awake. She wanted nothing more than to talk to Zeke.

"Yes. When I found out what happened, he offered to come with me. He'll be here in a little while to get the key to the beach house, and then he's going to drive there this afternoon instead of staying in a hotel."

"Stella, I don't like this." Shelia had no trouble speaking her mind, and it often embarrassed Stella. "You're going home with not one but two strangers."

"Mom, Zeke isn't a stranger. I've never given you reason not to trust me. I'm a good judge of character, and I was planning on visiting him over winter break anyway. Now I get to see the ocean sooner."

"Sheila, you're more than welcome to come visit. To see for yourself I'm taking good care of our girl."

Stella held back a groan. *She* didn't want her mother intruding. Even though Zeke's brother would also be there, she had a feeling he wouldn't have a problem giving them their space, unlike her mom who would try to take over.

"You say beach house like it's not your only home. Do you have more than one house? And what do you do for a living?"

"Mom!" Stella was curious as well, but she had more tact.

"It's okay," Zeke said as he sat down in the chair and ran his fingertip across the back of Stella's hand. It was comforting as well as arousing. Stella was a young woman who had enjoyed sex whenever she was in a relationship, but there had always been something missing. The sex hadn't been bad with her past partners, but it was nothing like what she read in romance novels. The softest touch from Zeke had her ready to kick her mom out of the room.

"I do have two houses, the other being in Tennessee, but I prefer the one here in California. As for my job, I am a consultant, meaning I work for myself. I am good at investing, and I have enough money saved that if I didn't want to work anymore, I wouldn't have to. If Stella wanted to stop teaching and travel the world, I can offer that to her. But more than money, I can offer Stella a life filled with love."

"But you just met."

"This is true, and I will take things as slow as Stella needs, but I will do that by her side."

If Stella had any doubts Zeke was the one for her, he just obliterated them. She felt the sincerity in his words. His honesty, his strength, everything about the gorgeous blond washed over her, and she closed her eyes, knowing he would be there when she woke.

ZEKE WAS THANKFUL when Dr. Crabtree interrupted to check on Stella. Sheila's whole demeanor changed in the presence of the man. Zeke understood the woman's disbelief that Zeke and Stella were a done deal. She had no idea of the bond between the two, and it wasn't something Zeke ever planned on sharing with her. Maybe if he hadn't dated the woman, if he hadn't transitioned when Stella was a toddler… No, not even if that weren't the case. The only ones who needed to know the truth were the Gargoyle and their mate.

"Sheila, could I interest you in a cup of coffee?" Dr. Crabtree had barely stepped foot in the room before he turned his attention to Stella's mom.

"You could, thank you." Sheila stood, but before she left with the doctor, she pulled the sheet up higher over Stella's chest and brushed her hair back. Zeke had no doubt the woman loved her daughter, but it was now Zeke's responsibility to care for her. Maybe Sheila and the doctor would hit it off, and she would turn her focus on someone other than Stella.

Zeke breathed a sigh of relief as soon as they were out of the room and spent the quiet time studying his mate. The bruises hurt his heart as well as pissed him off. If the police didn't find the man responsible, Zeke would call on his new friends from the Stone Society. His new Clan. For so many years, Zeke had longed for the closeness he found when spending time with both his family and their mates in Egypt. The males had accepted him, no questions asked. Both Sophia and Tessa were in good hands with their mates.

Cyrus texted when he arrived at the hospital, and Zeke stood to meet him at the door. Cyrus handed him the item, and Zeke admired the purchase, then thanked his brother for retrieving it.

"I'm sorry," Cyrus whispered, getting a look at Stella's bruises.

"Hey, none of that." Zeke squeezed Cyrus's shoulder. "She's going to be fine. Here." Zeke handed his brother the key to the house as well as a piece of paper with the address and alarm code. "Is there anything special you want from the grocery store? I'm going to place an order for delivery to arrive later so you have time to get settled before it arrives."

"I'm not picky, as long as there's coffee and sandwich stuff. I am a pretty good cook, and I'll gladly take over that duty while I'm visiting so you can focus on your mate."

"And I'll gladly take you up on that, but don't feel obligated. I want you to enjoy your stay."

"Oh, I plan on it. Like I said, I've never even seen the ocean, so this is going to be like a vacation. Now, I'm going to hit the road. I can't wait to stick my toes in the sand."

"Don't expect to get a tan. The weather is chilly this time of year. Then again, you're used to Montana."

"True. Still, I'm excited. Thank you, Zeke. I'll see you both tomorrow." Cyrus pulled Zeke in for a hug, and Zeke welcomed it. He was excited too, but it was for his future. He had not only found his mate, but Zeke felt as though he and Cyrus would become close. He looked forward to getting to know his brother, and when the time came, helping him through his transition.

Sheila returned from her coffee break with the doctor, and her mood was different. She didn't argue with Zeke. In fact, she offered to go to Stella's house and pack a bag for the upcoming week. While she was gone, Zeke made some calls. After finding Stella's car, he made arrangements to have it towed to a body shop. He planned on buying her a new vehicle, but in the meantime, he would have her old one fixed.

When she woke from her nap, Stella felt well enough to eat. She had missed lunch, and Zeke was glad to see his mate polish off her supper. Other than the bruises, her color was returning, and her eyes held more life than earlier. Her smile... gods, her smile was everything. Zeke never wanted it to diminish, so he hoped the gift he had would help keep it there.

"I have a gift for you." He picked up her left hand and

slid the ring on her finger. After telling Connie he had a ring, Zeke got online and found the perfect one, then had Cyrus pick it up. He wasn't sure of the size, but it was close if maybe a little loose. "This isn't a proper proposal. Yet. It is a promise. A vow to get to know one another. A vow to take care of you until you are sure I'm the male for you. I will give you as long as you need, but until then, I'll be by your side, doing everything in my power to make you happy."

"Zeke," Stella whispered. "It's perfect." Her eyes filled with tears, and Zeke brushed them off her cheeks before leaning in and pressing a soft kiss to her lips. Being this close to her had his beast itching to claim her, but Zeke pushed back, shutting that shit down. They had waited thirty years for their mate, and another few days wouldn't hurt. He promised to give her all the time she needed, but having been around others who found their mates, Zeke knew she was feeling the bond, and after he told her the truth, it wouldn't take long until she agreed to the bite.

Stella was released the next morning, and Zeke was ready to get her home. Sheila surprised them both when she said she was going to work instead of seeing Stella off. The woman was upset even if she pretended she wasn't. She had gushed over the stunning ring on her daughter's finger, but the words had been nothing more than lip service. If Stella recognized her mother's lies, she didn't let on. Zeke would prove by his actions he was the male for her daughter. Not that her opinion made that much of a difference. He had his own parent - Jonas - who he no longer felt the need to appease. Caroline was a different story. Zeke loved his mother beyond measure.

Zeke had a rental car delivered to the hospital. Once he got Stella home and settled, he would see about retrieving his own car from the airport. Zeke called Officer Dowd to inform her he was taking Stella to New Oceanside, and she promised to keep them apprised of the case. Bradley hadn't returned, but Zeke didn't see the male forgetting about

62

Stella just because Zeke was in the picture.

It was after noon when they arrived at the beach house, and Cyrus greeted them with a smile. He held the door open as Zeke carried Stella inside. "Stella, this is my brother Cyrus. Cyrus, this is my Stella."

"It's a pleasure to meet you, although I wish it were under different circumstances." Cyrus was dressed in jeans and a flannel shirt. His feet were bare, but that didn't surprise Zeke. His brother was used to the colder climate of his home state.

"Bed or sofa?" Zeke wanted Stella to be comfortable.

"Sofa please."

"I'll give you a tour of the house when you feel up to it. For now, let's get you settled." Zeke placed his mate on the couch, knowing it was comfortable. He was of the mindset that furniture was for function more than looks. Cyrus held out a soft blanket Zeke didn't remember having.

"Since I only brought a couple changes of clothes, I went shopping last night. I saw this and thought it would keep Stella warm." Cyrus blushed as he explained where the blanket came from.

"Thank you, Cyrus. That was very thoughtful." Stella brushed her hands over the covering, smiling at Zeke's brother. His beast bristled inside.

Stop it. Stella is ours, and Cyrus is gay. He was doing something nice for our mate.

But we take care of our mate.

And we will, but I want them to get along. They are both important to me, and I want Cyrus in my life too.

By the wonderful aroma wafting from the kitchen, Cyrus had been cooking. "What smells so good?" Zeke asked.

"I fixed a pot of soup and some cornbread."

"I can't wait to try it. Stella, do you feel up to eating?"

"Yes. I'm surprised you both can't hear my stomach protesting. Plus, I need to eat something so I can take my medicine." Stella looked around the living room. Zeke hadn't decorated much in the ten years since he bought the place. The walls were painted light blue with gray accents. The living room opened to the dining area just off the kitchen. French doors opened to a large deck on the back of the house overlooking the ocean. Steps off the deck led to a small stretch of sand. Most of the houses were stacked on top of each other, but Zeke had managed to find the one on the strip with the most property. He had neighbors on either side, but they weren't so close they could easily see in his windows.

"I love it here," Cyrus said between bites of soup. "I took a walk on the beach and met some of the neighbors. Everyone is friendly without being nosy."

"I know what you mean. When I stopped off at the diner the night before you and I met, everyone knew who you were." Zeke hadn't told Cyrus about meeting Maggie.

"Please tell me you didn't run into Maggie."

Zeke grinned after wiping his mouth on a paper towel. "Sure did. I have to say, you broke the woman's heart."

Cyrus shook his head. "She needs to let that go. It's been years. Don't get me wrong. I feel bad for how things ended, but it was during that time I realized I was gay. I broke it off because it wouldn't lead to marriage the way she wanted. I could only make so many excuses about why..." Cyrus glanced at Stella and blushed. "Anyway, I can't say all of our problems were my fault. The woman has dated several men since me, and yet she's still single."

"Wait, you said the night before you met." Stella arched her eyebrows at Zeke.

Fuck. "Yeah, I have several siblings who were given up for adoption. Cyrus was one of them, and before this week, we had never met. It's a long story, one I promise to tell you soon. There's some things we need to talk about."

"Is Cyrus like you?" Stella asked, absently stirring her soup.

64

"Like me?"

"Different. I heard you talking to me, or maybe I was dreaming. Never mind. Cyrus, this soup is delicious. Where did you learn to cook?"

Zeke had thought Stella was asleep when he rambled on about being a shifter. But if she heard him, why wasn't she freaking out?

"My mom taught me. I grew up an only child, and I learned about ranching from my father, but my mom was of the opinion I needed to know how to take care of myself too, so she taught me how to cook, wash clothes, sew on buttons, things like that. Dad taught me to drive, change the oil in my truck, build things. I'm pretty well-rounded."

Stella smiled at him. "They sound like wonderful parents. I never knew my dad, and the men my mother married afterward were less than stellar. Don't get me wrong, I love my mom, but she was more concerned with finding a husband than a good father figure." Stella shrugged and took a bite of cornbread.

Zeke decide now was as good a time as any to test the waters. "Yes, Cyrus is like me, and no, you weren't dreaming. Everything I told you was the truth. I didn't know you could hear me, so I thought I would practice what I wanted to tell you."

Stella held out the tray her food was on, and Zeke took it, placing it on the coffee table. "So both of you are these shapeshifters? What exactly do you turn into?"

Zeke had been sitting in the recliner next to the sofa in case Stella needed help. He knelt in front of her. "Do you remember what I said about meeting our mates? How that was the catalyst for shifting the first time?" Stella nodded. "Cyrus hasn't met his mate yet. It's why I went to visit him. When I told your mom I was a consultant, it wasn't the truth. I am what is called a watcher. Me, my brother Sam, his daughter Sophia, and my niece Tessa, the four of us were tasked with watching over my siblings who had yet to transition. Our father knew what prompted the initial shift, and that was coming in contact with our mate. Cyrus is the last sibling who has yet to transition, and I went to meet him so he didn't go through what some of the others have.

"Not aware there is a shifter inside you, then all of a sudden you become this thing you don't understand... It's alarming to say the least. I knew what our family was, so it didn't surprise me when I shifted. But our father sent us out to help after the fact, not before. I didn't want that for Cyrus."

"If he's the last one, then you've already met your mate?" Stella paled, and Zeke prayed she wouldn't pull away from him. He took her hands in his and kissed her knuckles.

"You are my mate. I just didn't know it until I met you in the airport."

"So you hadn't shifted until we met last week?"

Zeke didn't want to lie to her. He couldn't lie. "Not exactly. Once our Gargoyle surfaces, we stop aging. I'm actually older than Cyrus by four years." Stella looked between the two brothers, her forehead wrinkling.

"But we just met... No. No, no, no. Please don't tell me you're my mother's Ezekiel."

"No, I am *your* Ezekiel. But yes, I met you when you were a toddler."

"Oh, Bast. You didn't... you and her, did you...?" Stella placed a hand over her mouth.

"No! No, we were never together like that. Stella, I didn't date a lot, but once I transitioned, I never, I mean, it didn't feel..." Zeke blew out a breath. "I haven't been with anyone since before I transitioned."

"Really?" Stella searched his eyes, and Zeke tried to smile. It was a long time to go without sex. Even though he didn't know what caused his beast to come forth, Zeke never felt the urge to find a female. Not until Stella.

"Really. I don't know why the fates made me wait all

these years for you, why they put you in my path when you were so young. There are others who have dealt with the same thing – meeting their mate only not knowing who they are. I'm praying the gods will intervene with them the way they did for me. Knowing you have a mate yet not knowing who they are is a pain I don't wish on anyone. Once we find our mate, there is no other for us. You were designed especially for me. If you decide you want to be my mate, you will never want another if you accept the mate bond."

"What happens if I don't accept the bond?"

"You will be free to date whomever you want." It pained Zeke to admit those words.

"And will you be free as well?"

"No. My heart and soul belonged to you the moment we met, and that will never change."

CHAPTER SEVEN

STELLA HAD NO intention of dating anyone else, but she had to ask. Knowing Zeke would never have anyone other than her, even if she refused the bond, hurt her heart for him and all the others of his kind. It shouldn't have been so easy to believe what he was telling her, but Stella had always considered there were other beings walking among the humans. Sheila hadn't raised Stella in church, but Christianity was alive and well in America. If Christians believed in angels and demons, why couldn't there be Gargoyles? The Unholy weren't human, and they were real.

"Will you show me your shifter?" Stella believed Zeke was telling the truth, but seeing it for herself would go a long way to letting her know she wasn't riding the crazy train.

Zeke stood and took a step back. He held out his hands, and claws elongated from his fingertips. Stella couldn't help but gasp. When she looked up at his face, sharp canines protruded over his lower lip. He withdrew his claws and removed his T-shirt. Stella's eyes traveled from Zeke's face down his torso. Her man was ripped. "One, two, three…" Stella counted his abdominal muscles under her breath. Holy cat, he had an eight pack. And those sexy dips at his hips that led to —

"Stella."

"Huh?"

Zeke's eyes were hooded, and she curled her fingers into a fist. If he had been close enough, she would have probably licked the man, he was so sexy.

"Stella, Baby."

"I'll just get out of your way," Cyrus said chuckling as he moved to the other side of the room.

Zeke stepped into the middle of the room, and within seconds, a pair of wings were spread behind him.

"Holy Bast! Turn around." Zeke did as she asked. No wonder the room was so large. The glorious wings spread out behind him. Stella wanted to run her fingers over the rigid edges, but before she could scoot off the sofa, the wings disappeared like magic. There was no sign of an opening on his back, just smooth, tanned skin. "That's... Holy Bast," she muttered again. Zeke pulled his shirt back on, and Stella wanted to protest. Since they weren't alone, she thought it was probably for the best.

"Do all Gargoyles look like you? With the" — Stella twirled her finger in the direction of Zeke's abs — "muscles and, uh." She lost her train of thought.

"Yes. Well, the males are muscular, but the females, while fit, don't necessarily look like they spend hours in the gym. They do have claws and fangs, but they do not get wings or the impenetrable skin. We all are much faster and stronger than humans. Once we transition, we stop aging. I will never look older than I do now. As soon as Cyrus meets his mate, he, too, will stop aging."

"Gotta say, it sucks that you're older and look twenty years younger." Cyrus winked at his brother as he walked back to take a seat.

Stella had so many questions, but she asked the one she couldn't get out of her head. "You said there is only one mate for you, but what happens when I continue getting older? I'm human, and relatively speaking, will die way before you."

"Once a mate has accepted the bond, they also stop aging. While it is nearly impossible to kill a male, females are still susceptible to diseases and regular tragedies. Barring those, you will live as long as I do. Our mother, who

69

doesn't appear older than you, is two hundred forty-six."

"How will I explain that to my own mother?"

"You won't. It is imperative you keep our secret. If you wish to remain in California to be around Sheila, my father can provide you with a prosthetic that you wear when around her. It is how he has blended in with the same people in New Atlanta as long as he has. Jonas is the chief of staff at the hospital there and has worn prosthetics to not only hide his age but also his true identity. The world around him knows him as Joseph Mooneyham, when he is, in fact, Jonas Montague."

Stella knew that name. Hell, everyone knew who Jonas Montague was. "The scientist who cloned the baby?"

"Yes. The baby was my cousin Tessa, who you will no doubt meet in the near future. Jonas is a genius, but he has different ideas of how we interact with full bloods." Stella listened to Zeke speak of his parents meeting and subsequent escape. He explained how they put most of their children up for adoption, and how that led him to Cyrus. "If he had shared with us how we transition upon meeting our mates, I wouldn't have spent these last thirty years feeling so adrift. I would have watched over you from afar, then as soon as you were old enough, I would have claimed you."

Stella couldn't allow herself to think about Zeke dating Sheila. That was just too weird. At least they hadn't slept together. Stella would never, ever tell her mother who Zeke really was. It would not only be strange, but hurtful. She held out her hand, and Zeke sat on the sofa next to her. Stella threaded their fingers together, smiling at her handsome blond. "It does suck that we missed out on all those years, but we have each other now."

Cyrus gathered their dirty dishes. "I'm going to put these in the kitchen, then I'm going for a walk on the beach."

"Thank you, Brother."

As soon as Cyrus was out the back door, Stella asked,

"How do you complete the bond? You said something about a bite?"

Zeke touched Stella's unmarred cheek. "Yes, if you decide to accept our mate bond, I bite you."

"I've read romance books with shifters, and anytime a claiming happens, it's during sex. Is that the case here? With us?" Now that Cyrus was out of the room, Stella wanted to strip her clothes off and get horizontal, even with the pulsing headache. She had never found any of the men she dated irresistible. Never thought of herself as wanton, a term she laughed at in her romance novels. But here she was, ready to climb Zeke, her headache be damned.

"From what I've heard, that is usually when it takes place, yes. But it doesn't have to be during sex. One of the King's cousins bit his mate when he thought she had died to connect himself to her forever."

"Wow, that's romantic. And sad. Please tell me she lived."

"She did, and now they are mated and married. Abbi's is a sad story, one she will tell you when you meet her, but *theirs* is a story for the ages, much like ours."

"You keep saying when I meet these women. Is there like some initiation for me to become one of the Clan?"

Zeke smiled and kissed Stella's knuckles. "No, nothing like that. Tessa and Sophia are important to me. They both live in New Atlanta, along with two other siblings whom I wish to get to know better. I had hoped to visit them whenever we go to our house in Tennessee. That is, if you want to."

"I'd like that very much. It has always been Mom and me and my two stepfathers. Neither one had kids of their own, and their parents lived out of town. My mom's parents died when I was young. We never visited my father's family after he passed, so I've never known what it was like to have a big family."

"As odd as this sounds, neither have I. Even having

71

fifteen siblings, I haven't met all of them. With Sam and Tessa splitting watcher duty with me, then Sophia being added lately, I only met five of them. I would like to rectify that in the next few years. If you wish to continue teaching, we'll travel during your summer breaks."

Stella had yet to see the rest of the house, but if it was anything like the living room, she would love it. Plus, he had another house in Tennessee, so he had to have quite a bit of money. Not that money mattered to her. She only wanted to be loved well.

"What will you do now that all your siblings know the truth?" she asked.

"I like flipping houses. Buying something in disrepair and bringing it back to life has always been fulfilling. My home in Tennessee was one of the first ones I fixed up. I loved it so much I kept it."

"Is that something we could do together?" Stella loved teaching, but she loved the thought of spending her days with Zeke more. "I mean only if that's what you would want. I don't want you to get tired of me."

"Oh, My Love, there is no chance I'll get tired of being around you. The fates choose our perfect partner. It will be harder to *not* be around you than to work side by side with you. Take Sophia for instance. Before she met her mate, Nikolas, she researched the full-bloods, detailing everything about their lives. Nik is the archivist for the Clan, so their interests fully align. Does flipping houses interest you? Because if not, we can find something we both enjoy."

"I do love to watch home improvement shows, so yes, I think it is something I can see myself doing. And quite honestly, I don't want to go back to my job. Not with Bradley being there every day."

"Then you won't. Once we are mated, everything I own becomes yours. We will have a lifetime of figuring out how we want to spend our days. Whether it's traveling, flipping houses, or something completely different, we will do it together. Can you see that in your future?"

"I can." Stella figured it was the mate bond drawing her to Zeke, but she couldn't find it in herself to care. He already explained how the fates chose the perfect partner for the Gargoyle, so that meant he was also perfect for her. "But I also see a nap, because the pain meds are starting to wear off. Will you show me to a bedroom?"

"I will take you to *our* bedroom." Zeke stood, then gently scooped Stella into his arms. She wrapped her arms around his shoulders and nestled her face against his neck, inhaling his masculine scent. The master suite was just as light and airy as the living room. The king-sized bed was like being placed on a cloud. If she felt better, she would invite him to sleep beside her. But she really was fading fast. Zeke went back downstairs to get her medicine. After taking two of the pills, he told her to get some rest. "I'll be out on the back deck, but if you need me, all you have to do is say my name. I'll hear you." Zeke pressed a kiss to her forehead, and Stella closed her eyes.

LEAVING STELLA TO nap alone was one of the hardest things Zeke had ever done. If it weren't for Cyrus, Zeke would have lain down beside his mate. They hadn't completed the bond, but her acceptance was there in her eyes. In the way she smiled at him. The way her heart beat a little faster when their hands joined. Then again, if he stayed in bed with her, his Goyle would insist on taking things further than Stella felt up for. They had waited thirty years. Another day or two wouldn't kill them.

Zeke stopped off in the kitchen and grabbed a bucket, filling it with ice and longnecks. He took them to the back deck and sat in one of the Adirondack chairs while waiting for his brother to return from his walk. Zeke wanted to be alone with Stella, but he would never make Cyrus feel unwelcome in his home. He had a lifetime with Stella ahead of him, but he had a lot of years of catching up with Cyrus to make up for. *Damn you, Jonas.* Where Sophia and Tessa adored Jonas, Zeke resented the male. Resented the fact that he and Caroline continued having offspring only to pawn them off on unsuspecting humans. Why have kids if you weren't going to keep them?

His thoughts trailed off to his mate, wondering if she wanted children. Zeke could imagine how being around so many kids over the years might lessen the shine of having her own. There was so much they needed to talk about, but as he told her, they had a lifetime of getting to know one another. Zeke twisted the top off his beer and took a sip. The cold liquid felt good going down, and Zeke leaned his head back as he searched the shoreline for his brother.

The beach outside Zeke's home was mostly deserted this time of year. The other houses in the area were family-owned, and those who lived there rarely took to the sand during the colder months. With the breeze coming off the ocean meeting with the cool temperatures, most humans, at least those he had met, preferred to enjoy the view from inside their heated homes. With Zeke being Gargoyle, the cold didn't bother him. Seeing his brother walking barefoot next to the surf, Zeke smiled. It didn't seem to bother Cyrus either.

A dog barking followed by a male yelling had Cyrus turning his attention toward the only other two beings Zeke could see. His protective nature had Zeke sitting up a little straighter. The stretch of beach between his deck and the water wasn't large, and if Cyrus needed him, Zeke could be there within seconds. The golden lab bounded up to Cyrus, who bent down to give the dog some love. The pup's owner jogged up, apologizing profusely. The smile on Cyrus's face was brighter than the sunshine. Cyrus rose, and the two males shook hands, only they didn't immediately turn loose.

74

Zeke leaned forward, studying the man who had his brother's attention, and he listened in on their conversation.

"*Sorry about Nonna. She never meets a stranger.*"

"*Oh, that's no problem. I have two at home who are the same.*" Cyrus stood and stretched out his hand. "*Cyrus Gillespie.*"

"*Thomas Kinsey.*"

"*It's a pleasure, Thomas.*"

"*I think the pleasure is mine.*"

Nonna stepped between the two men, begging for attention. When they released their hands, Thomas ran a hand through his dark, windblown hair. "*So, Cyrus. Do you live around here?*"

"*No. I'm visiting my brother. I live in Montana.*"

Thomas smiled. "*That explains the bare feet. You must be used to the cold.*"

Cyrus grinned and shrugged. "*I am, but this is my first time on a beach, and I couldn't let the opportunity to feel the sand between my toes go to waste. What about you? Is one of these houses yours?*"

"*No. I'm visiting my sister. She lives in the fifth house down. Nonna is her dog, and I volunteered to take her for a walk. Would you like to join us?*"

Cyrus glanced toward the house, and Zeke raised his bottle in agreement. "*Yes. I'd like that.*"

Zeke leaned his head back, smiling. Had Cyrus traveled all the way to California to find his mate? Time would tell. By the time Zeke finished off all the beer, Cyrus hadn't returned, but Zeke wasn't worried. He took the empties into the house and disposed of them in the recycling bin, then went to check on Stella.

STELLA'S HEAD WAS no longer pounding. Her eyes took in the bedroom, and she could see herself waking there every morning with Zeke by her side. Speaking of her sexy Gargoyle, she wondered where he had gotten off to, so she pushed back the covers and slung her legs over the side of the bed. When she caught sight of herself in the mirror above the dresser, she paused. Why was she wearing her clothes from the day she was attacked instead of her sweats? Stella didn't remember changing back into them. *Why would she have put them back on before washing them?* She pulled the hem of the sweater out, studying the stain across the bottom. Was that blood?

Stella looked around the room, searching for her sweats. When she didn't find them, she decided to change into something of Zeke's. Opening the top drawer, she found it empty. They all were. Stella rushed to the closet and slung open the door. Empty hangers hooked over the bars on both sides of the large walk-in. *What the hell?* Was this not Zeke's home? Even if it were a vacation house, there would have been evidence of him being there somewhere.

After closing the door, she padded into the attached bathroom. There were no toiletries. No toothbrushes or accessories lying about. No towels hanging on the bar. The shower curtain was pushed back revealing a spotless enclosure. "No, no, no." Nothing about this scenario was right.

Stella made her way through the upstairs. Zeke hadn't shown her any of the house before her nap. Every door opened into empty rooms. There was nothing but bare walls and spotless floors. Stella's heart pounded harder with each second she spent searching for something. Some indication this house was lived in. She needed to calm down, so she took a few cleansing breaths, drawing on her yoga instruction. Stella walked over to the far wall where a curtainless window looked out over the back of the house. The waves rolled onto the sand as though they were furious. Stella had been on the beach during storms, but the sky wasn't dark and ominous. She didn't understand the science behind the tides or the way the water moved at the moon's insistence. She had always enjoyed the beach without questioning its magical nature. It simply was.

Making her way downstairs, Stella didn't hear any noise. No television. No voices. Zeke and Cyrus must be outside. When she reached the living room, Stella froze. "Bradley?"

"Hello, Beautiful."

"Wh-what are you doing here?" Better yet, how had he found her?

"I've come to take you home where you belong." Bradley was sitting in an armchair with an ankle crossed over the opposite knee. He was dressed in his usual khakis with a button-up shirt tucked in. His dark hair was gelled into place. What wasn't normal we're the splotches of blood dotting his otherwise pristine beige shirt and the long knife clutched in one hand.

"What did you do?" Stella looked around, searching for any sign of Zeke or Cyrus.

"What was necessary. Did you really think I'd let you run off with that monster?" Bradley rose from the chair and stretched his neck, the popping eerily loud in the otherwise quiet room.

"Y-you killed him?" Stella's throat threatened to close. No, he couldn't have. Zeke couldn't be killed except by... "No!" She wouldn't believe it.

"You're mine, Stella." Bradley took a step toward her, but she wouldn't go with him. She couldn't. She had to find Zeke. Her mate. They were supposed to be together forever, except they hadn't completed the bond. Stella would continue to age, and Zeke would... "No! Zeke! Zeke!" She rushed through the house toward the back door. She had to find him. Throwing open the French doors, Stella ran across the deck and down the stairs to the sand. The wind whipped her long hair around her face, blinding her.

"Stella." Strong hands gripped her arms, but she jerked away.

"No! You can't have me!" Stella ran toward the sound

of the waves. She had to get away from Bradley. She wouldn't let him take her.

CHAPTER EIGHT

"STELLA, I'M HERE." Zeke's strong voice called out to her. He wasn't dead.

"Zeke?" Stella still couldn't see her Gargoyle. "Where are you?"

"I'm right here. Open your eyes." Gentle fingers brushed her hair off her face. Stella blinked her eyes open, and Zeke was sitting on the side of the bed, his brow furrowed. Stella sat up and threw her arms around his neck.

"You're here. You're not dead."

"No, Love. I'm fine. You were having a bad dream." Zeke held her tightly, rubbing circles over her back and pressing kisses to her temple.

Stella leaned back, searching his face. "Hi," she whispered.

"Are you okay?" Zeke stroked her right cheek, always avoiding the bruises.

"I am now." Stella pushed herself back, and Zeke fixed the pillows so they were between her and the headboard. When she was settled, Stella reached for Zeke, encouraging him to move closer. "I want to complete the bond."

Zeke picked up her hand and kissed her fingertips. "We will, when you're feeling better."

Stella shook her head. After the dream, she wanted it to be sooner rather than later. "Being your mate will make me feel better."

"Baby, the bite bonds us for centuries. Are you sure you don't want to get to know me better?"

"I've never been more certain of anything in my life.

79

But before we complete the bond, I think you should kiss me." Stella cupped the back of Zeke's neck, ready to make the move if he didn't.

"Is that right?" Zeke's blue eyes sparkled. Stella could tell he was trying not to grin.

"Mmmhmm. I mean, you wouldn't buy a car without test driving it, would you?" Stella threaded her fingers through Zeke's hair as he leaned closer.

"No, I don't guess you would." Zeke closed the distance between them and pressed his lips to hers. He had kissed her in the hospital, but that had been sweet. This one started off the same way, but a fire flamed from deep inside. Stella nipped at his lower lip, begging for more. Zeke teased her mouth with his tongue, and Stella answered the challenge. Kissing this man was like coming home, only instead of four walls, home was his warrior soul. Their breaths mingled as their tongues danced a slow, seductive number. Stella's fingers tangled with his hair, keeping his head where she wanted it. A low growl emanated from within Zeke's chest, and Stella pulled away, curious as to what she'd done wrong.

"Did you just growl at me?"

"No, I growled at my Goyle. He's being a pushy bastard."

Stella smirked as she ran her pointer finger over Zeke's lips. "Yeah? What's he saying?"

"He's demanding I mark you."

Stella leaned back against the pillows, missing the heat from her blond, but she had to know how he felt. "And you don't want that?"

"More than I want my next breath, but you're hurt, and I won't do anything to add to your injuries."

"Bast, you're sweet. But I need you, Zeke. I know it's crazy how fast this is happening, but who am I to tell the fates to eff off?"

"Stella—"

80

"Shh." Stella placed her fingers against Zeke's lips. "I trust you, and I trust the fates. I've always believed in the mystical. In the stars and planets aligning." Stella pushed the covers down her legs, then lowered the top of her sweatpants only far enough to show off a tattoo.

Zeke brushed his fingers over the ink. "I'm not familiar with the symbol, but the moon and stars are sexy on your hip." Zeke slid off the bed to his knees and pressed his lips to the ink. Stella shivered and grabbed a handful of his hair, the meaning of her ink forgotten.

"Don't start something you don't intend to finish. I'm already tempted to throw myself at you to get what I need."

Zeke pulled the sweats back up, then set his chin on her hip. "What do you need? I will give you anything."

"I need you. I need your weight on top of me, and I need you filling me up. I need you to bite me and make me yours."

"You are mine. You have been mine since the day you toddled over to me and grinned with those big brown eyes shining." Zeke stood and began removing his clothes. "I will have to be careful of your injuries, but I won't deny you anything." Stella's eyes were transfixed on his body as he exposed his skin. When he stood before her in all his glory, she licked her lips.

"Oh, my."

Stella had never been aggressive in bed, but she'd also never had a man like Zeke standing before her unabashedly naked with his erection leaking, tempting her to lean over and taste. In the past, she had given blow jobs because it was expected. She'd never been thrilled about it. But now? It was as though tasting Zeke was as essential as breathing. Pleasing him was important. Not because he expected it, but because he deserved it. Deserved her attention. Her mouth. Her body. Stella moved to sit on the edge of the bed and leaned over, licking the moisture from his tip.

"Stella, My Queen." Zeke gripped her shoulders,

neither pulling her forward nor pushing her away. She took that as permission and leaned in again, this time taking the flared head into her mouth. While she had never enjoyed giving head before, she used the previous practice to please her mate. Maybe one day she would be able to add husband to his titles, but for now, Zeke was all hers, no matter what she called him.

Using her tongue, she teased the slit again before taking him as far as she could into her mouth. She wrapped her fingers around the base, sliding her grip up and down his length along with her mouth.

"Stella, that feels too good. I want to be inside you when I come. Do you want that?"

"Yes." They didn't talk about protection, but Stella was on birth control. Even if she hadn't been, she wouldn't have stopped this moment for anything, even the prospect of getting pregnant. Zeke pulled her to her feet, then gripped the edge of her sweatshirt and carefully pulled it off, being mindful of her bruises. He divested her of the sweatpants, leaving her in her underwear. Stella was exotic looking, but her body was nothing special. Her breasts were a small C-cup, her stomach wasn't flat, and she had cellulite on her thighs. But the way Zeke devoured her with his eyes, he didn't care. *Thank you, fates.*

ZEKE WAS FIGHTING his Goyle big time. They had waited thirty years for this moment, and Zeke wasn't going to allow the beast to screw it up. As he slowly divested Stella of her lacy underwear, Stella stood before him bare. He could feel her reticence. He wasn't sure if it was because this was their first time or if she was self-conscious about her body. She had no need to be either. "Look at you." He allowed his desire to shine through his eyes and words. "You are stunningly perfect. I have waited my whole life for

82

you." Zeke cupped her cheek. "As a Gargoyle, I don't carry diseases, but I can get you pregnant without protection."

Stella leaned into his touch as she reached out and ran her nails down his chest. "I'm on birth control," she said softly.

That didn't answer the question of whether or not she wanted children, but now wasn't the time for talk. Zeke lifted Stella in his arms and lay her in the middle of the bed before crawling between her legs. She parted her thighs, and Zeke stared at the juncture. A dark thatch of hair topped her pubic bone, and he bent his head and inhaled deeply before licking her entrance. He teased her clit with the tip of his tongue while spearing her channel with two fingers. Gods, his mate was ready for him. As much as he wanted to make her come with his mouth, he couldn't hold off taking her, making her his mate.

Zeke nipped at the tender skin of her inner thighs. "Are you sure about this? Once I bite you, there's no going back. We will be connected for the rest of our lives, and that could be hundreds of years."

"I'm sure." Stella slid her bare foot down his side, then hooked it under his armpit, urging him forward.

Zeke gave her nub one last lick, then he placed his large body over hers, his dick hard and ready. Stella wrapped her legs around his waist, and Zeke entered her body in one slow, slick slide. *Fucking heaven.* Using her heels for leverage, Stella met him eagerly. He wanted to make love. Wanted their first time to last, but this was a claiming, and he lost control after less than a minute. As Zeke increased their rhythm, Stella scratched her nails down his biceps before gripping his arms tightly.

"Zeke, ungh. Please..." His mate kept her eyes on his, but her words became sounds of pleasure, ramping his own need.

Zeke allowed his fangs to drop, and Stella's eyes widened, and her breathing hitched. His hips stuttered, thinking she'd changed her mind, but then she moved her hair out of the way, baring her neck to him. Zeke lowered his head and latched onto the creamy skin. Her body convulsed around his cock. His own orgasm tore through him as her tangy copper flavor flooded his mouth. Zeke retracted his fangs and roared as his wings spread out behind him.

Breathing hard, Stella stretched out her fingertips, and the second she touched the edge of his wing, he came again, pulsing his seed into her already filled core. For just a second, he wished she weren't on birth control. But that second passed. Zeke wanted it all with this exquisite creature laid out before him, including children, but they now had all the time in the world. Their mating had been quick, but such was the way of Gargoyles. Well, some of them. Tessa had put Gregor off for three years. How she did it, Zeke couldn't fathom. There was no way Zeke could have held off that long.

Back when he was younger and dating, Zeke had not been a monk. He'd had sex, but it had never been as earth-shattering as with his mate.

Duh.

Oh, shut it.

Zeke bent his head and dotted Stella's face with sweet kisses before finding her lips. When he moved to pull out, Stella gripped his ass, holding him in place.

"Not yet." Her eyes were wet, and Zeke was afraid he hurt her until she smiled. "I have no words." Stella slid her hands up his back, then around to his chest.

I have the words for both of us, My Queen. You are my mate, and one day soon, my wife. You are my everything.

Stella gasped. "I can feel you. I can feel your heart beat inside my chest. And..." Stella licked her lips. "I can hear you in my head."

Zeke grinned and kissed her nose. "That's the bond. We're connected now."

"Does the bond have anything to do with healing? Because the ache in my head is gone. Or maybe it was the powerful orgasm?"

Zeke pushed up on his forearms. The bruises on her face were already fading. Gargoyle saliva held powerful properties, as he'd already explained, but even he was surprised at the quickness with which it had coursed through her veins.

"I'm going to chalk it up to the orgasm," Zeke joked as the sound of the French doors opening signaled Cyrus's return. "My brother is back. As much as I'd love to stay in bed the rest of the night, I need to feed you. Let's get cleaned up and see how Cyrus's walk went."

Zeke wet a washcloth with warm water, then wiped away the evidence of their mating. As they dressed, they couldn't stop grinning and kissing. By the time they walked into the living room, twenty minutes had passed. Cyrus was sitting on the sofa staring at the wall.

"Brother? You okay?"

When he turned Zeke's way, Cyrus had a funny look on his face. "I think I'm in love."

Zeke smiled, but he couldn't let his brother fall for the human if he wasn't his mate. "I'm not sure if that's good or not." He hated to bring Cyrus's mood down. "Don't forget, you have a mate somewhere."

Cyrus scrubbed his hands down his face. "Yeah, I remember, but what if it's Thomas? He's absolutely perfect."

"For your sake, I hope he is. And if that's the case, you'll know soon enough. Are you hungry? I need to feed my mate, and I was going to cook."

"Oh, no thank you. Thomas and I walked to a place called Dockers after dropping Nonna off with his sister."

"If things were going so well, why aren't you still with him?"

"I don't feel so good. I think something I ate didn't

85

agree with me."

Zeke winced. "Brother? Do you remember what I said about meeting your mate for the first time?"

"Oh. *Oh!*" Cyrus jumped up from the sofa and paced in front of the fireplace.

Zeke stepped into his path and placed his hands on Cyrus's arms. "I'm not saying you've for certain met your mate, but if you have, you need to get ready. The transition is painful, but I'm here to help you through it."

"Oh, god. Yeah. Okay. I can do this." Cyrus froze like a statue and closed his eyes. Zeke grinned at his brother.

"Cyrus, you can relax. As a matter of fact, why don't you have a drink?"

Cyrus opened one eye. "Sorry, I'm just a little nervous."

"No, I get it. And not to put a damper on the situation, but it may just be something you ate. If that's the case, you probably won't want a drink."

"No, I definitely can handle a little alcohol." Cyrus walked over to the cabinet where bottles of liquor were stored and poured himself a drink. "Would either of you... Stella? Your face."

Zeke turned toward his mate, worried about whatever it was that had Cyrus freaking out. His mate's bruises were gone. Completely. Zeke walked over to her and cupped her cheek. "Any pain at all?"

Stella shook her head. "Nope." She smiled at Cyrus. "I was injected with Gargoyle miracle serum."

Cyrus choked on the sip of whiskey he'd just taken. "Uh, TMI," he muttered when he got the coughing under control.

Stella's mouth dropped, and her face flushed crimson. "Not that! Oh my god. Zeke bit me."

Cyrus shook his head. "Yeah, that's not much better."

Zeke pulled Stella's back to his chest. "Just wait, Brother. When you get to bond with your own mate, you'll want to shout it from the rooftops. It's the best feeling in the world."

Cyrus rubbed the back of his neck. "Yeah, you're right. And I'm really happy for you. Both of you. I hope —"

Zeke's phone rang. "Hold that thought." Zeke walked over to where he'd left his phone earlier. "It's Officer Dowd," he said before answering. "Hello?"

"Mr. Seymour, this is Officer Dowd. I tried to call Miss Bentley's phone, but it's gone straight to voicemail several times, so I was wondering if she's with you?"

"She is. Hang on a second." Zeke held out the phone to Stella, and she put it on speaker.

"Hello? This is Stella."

"Stella, this is Officer Dowd. I wanted to call you with an update. We were able to apprehend the man who attacked you."

Stella's eyes widened. "Oh, that's uh... That's good. Did he say why he attacked me?"

"He claims he was paid to do it. He says he was only supposed to rough you up a bit, but he hit you harder than intended."

"Who paid him?" Stella asked, her eyes filling with tears.

"That's what we're still trying to figure out. He was paid in cash, so we can't track the money, but he does have a description. I don't want to say anything further until I have proof, but I wanted to let you know what we've learned so you can remain vigilant. Whoever paid the man is still out there, but I promise, we're doing everything we can to catch him. I'll call you when we have more."

"Okay, thank you." Stella swiped the tears from her cheeks. Zeke disconnected the phone, then pulled Stella into his arms.

Stella leaned her cheek against Zeke's chest. "Who would pay someone to hurt me? I don't have enemies."

Zeke didn't want to upset his mate further, but he wouldn't lie to her. "I have a theory." Stella looked up at

87

him, and Zeke kissed her forehead before continuing. "I have a feeling it's Calhoun."

"Bradley? I know he's unhappy that I won't go out with him, but paying to have me assaulted? That's going a little far."

"It is, but he is the one who found you. It's too coincidental he happened along at just the right time."

"Crap. If they don't catch him, I can never go back home." Stella thudded her forehead against Zeke's chest.

"You can if that's what you want. I'll be watching over you from now on. He won't get anywhere near you. That's a promise. In the meantime, you can stay here. This is your home now. Or we can visit Tennessee. The mountains are splendid no matter the time of year."

"I need to call someone about my job. Normally, he would be the one I'd contact, but under the circumstances…"

"You could call the school board. Explain how he's been harassing you. Even if he isn't responsible for the attack, they need to know what kind of man they have as their principal."

"That's a good idea. I'll do that first thing in the morning."

"Good. Now, I'm going to fix something to eat."

Stella stood on her toes and kissed his cheek. "I'm going to find my phone and call Mom. She's probably going nuts by now."

Zeke kept his eyes and ears open for both his mate and brother as well as his senses on the area surrounding the house. If Bradley was responsible for the attack, it wouldn't surprise Zeke if the human had followed them to New Oceanside. He threw together a quick stir fry, and he and Stella ate at the dining room table while Cyrus retreated to his room to lie down. As they were eating, Zeke told Stella about Cyrus meeting Thomas. Then he told her what would happen if Cyrus did transition. She had lots of questions, and her concern for his brother was touching.

After they polished off the stir fry, Zeke showed Stella around the house. It wasn't as large as some of his family's homes, but it was theirs, and there was room enough to start a family.

When they were back in the living room, Zeke pulled Stella down onto his lap. He lifted her left hand and played with the promise ring, which was as unique as his mate with the onyx stones surrounding the princess-cut diamond. "Do you want children?"

"Do *you*?" Stella asked.

"I wouldn't mind a little girl with dark hair and eyes." Zeke wanted a houseful, but he wasn't going to scare her with the truth. "But only if it's what you want, and not anytime soon. I want to spend a few years getting to know each other. Our mating happened rather quickly, as is the case with some fated mates."

"And I'd love a son with your blond hair and blue eyes. I've never given much thought to having kids because I honestly never thought I'd find a man I wanted to spend the rest of my life with. But I agree we should wait. I just found you, and I selfishly want you all to myself." Stella moved out of Zeke's hold to straddle his lap. She twisted her fingers through his hair. "I want to learn all about you." Stella nuzzled Zeke's neck before nipping below his ear. His mate leaned back, then gripped the hem of his shirt. Zeke reached behind his head and pulled the garment off, tossing it on the floor.

Stella pushed off his lap and got on her knees between Zeke's thighs. She ran her fingers down his chest and through each dip in his abs. "Your stomach is crazy sexy." Stella's hair fell around her face as she pressed open kisses to his muscles. Zeke gathered the long strands in a fist so he could watch. His dick was hard as stone, but he let his female set the pace. When she reached out to unfasten his jeans, Zeke opened his senses to his brother to make sure

Cyrus wasn't going to interrupt them. He wanted Stella's mouth on him, but he didn't want her to be embarrassed if they were caught.

His mate on her knees was a sight to behold. Stella lowered the zipper and released his dick from its confines. She captured the drop of moisture from the tip and brought it to her mouth while watching him. Zeke's chest rumbled, and her eyes widened. Zeke winked, letting her know she was good to continue. Stella grinned, then lowered her head, licking a stripe from base to tip. When she closed her lips around him and sucked, Zeke hissed. Her mouth around his erection was the second-best feeling in the world.

"Gods, that feels good," he muttered. It was better than good. If he died in that moment, he would go out a happy male. Stella used her mouth, tongue, and fist, setting up a steady tempo that had Zeke ready to blow within minutes. "I'm close," he warned. Instead of pulling off, Stella stroked faster and sucked harder. Having his mate get him off was so much better than his own hand. "I'm coming, Baby." Stella didn't hesitate to swallow his load. She worked him over with her hand until the last aftershock subsided. He grabbed her wrist and pulled her back onto his lap. Stella licked the corner of her mouth, then smacked her lips.

Zeke grinned, then pulled her to him so he could taste himself on her tongue.

"Zeke!" Cyrus called out. His brother was in pain.

"Fuck. I'm sorry, Baby. It looks like Cyrus is getting ready to transition."

Stella scrambled off his lap. "What can I do to help?"

"Gather the stock pot from the cabinet. Fill it with ice, then add water. Grab a washcloth out of the bathroom. I'll need to lower the thermostat, so you might want to bundle up." Zeke took off up the stairs, trusting Stella to do what he asked. He turned the heat off and the air down. He then rushed to Cyrus's door and knocked before entering the

90

room. Cyrus was writhing on the bed.

"Oh, god. It hurts."

"Let's get you stripped. You're going to feel like you're burning up from the inside. Stella's bringing some icy water, and that'll help cool you down, but it won't take the heat away completely." Zeke helped Cyrus out of his clothes but insisted he keep his underwear on. He didn't want Stella around another male, even if it was his brother, but he also knew she wouldn't look on Cyrus's body with lust. They were mated, and she would never stray, even in her thoughts.

Stella came in a few minutes later and set the pot on the nightstand. She rung out a washcloth and handed it to Zeke before taking another and pressing it to Cyrus's forehead. Stella sat on the bed facing away from Cyrus's lower body.

"Stella, when I tell you it's time, I need you to head back downstairs and stay there until I say otherwise. Cyrus won't have control of his shifter immediately."

"I can do that."

The two of them continued to dip the cloths in the cold water and wipe Cyrus down until he let out a guttural scream.

"It's time. Please close the door behind you."

Stella did as asked, and as soon as the door was closed, Zeke told his brother, "This is going to be excruciating, but don't fight it. I'll be right here the whole time." And Zeke would be.

91

CHAPTER NINE

STELLA LEANED AGAINST the wall just outside Cyrus's door as the man's cries became louder and more frantic. Zeke asked her to wait downstairs, so she pushed off her perch, went to his bedroom – she guessed it was their bedroom now – and grabbed more clothes. The house was cooling down quickly with the air conditioning turned low. Once downstairs, she added the layers and reclined on the sofa. After a few minutes of staring at the unlit fireplace, she padded into the kitchen and dug around the cabinets. Finding what she needed, Stella started a pot of coffee.

Leaning against the counter while waiting for it to brew, Stella's brain was overloaded with all that had happened in the last few days. She touched her fingertips to her cheek. There was no pain. No bruises. Her concussion no longer made her head throb. Gargoyle saliva, or whatever it was in the bite, was a miracle serum, but she wondered if it only worked on mates? What if it helped others? They could sell it on the black market for a mint. Stella imagined Zeke dropping his fangs and spitting into a jar. Then she laughed at the ludicrous thought.

When the coffee was ready, Stella fixed herself a cup, adding just a splash of milk, then started for the living room. Before she got there, someone knocked on the back door. Stella froze. What if it was Bradley? Slipping behind the wall which separated the two rooms, Stella peeked around the corner. It wasn't her former boss, but a handsome, older man. Stella didn't know him, but he didn't appear to be someone who went around accosting women.

Then again, what did she know about what irrational men looked like? Bradley was charming and handsome. The irrational part of the man was on the inside where one couldn't access his thoughts and intentions.

"Cyrus? Are you there?" the man called out.

Ah, this must be Thomas. But Cyrus was currently indisposed, and Stella couldn't let him inside. Still, she wouldn't leave him standing there. Deciding to take a chance he wasn't evil, she walked to the French doors and cracked one open.

"Hi. Cyrus isn't feeling well, but I'll tell him you stopped by."

Movement from behind Thomas caught Stella's eye, but it was too late. Bradley hit Thomas over the head with the butt of a handgun, dropping the man to the deck. Stella tried to shut the door, but she was too slow. Coffee sloshed over the side of the cup, burning her hand. Thank goddess for the milk, or she might have been hurt. Bradley grabbed Stella's wrist, pulling her outside, causing Stella to drop the mug on the kitchen floor.

"Let me go!" Stella tried to jerk away, but his grip was too strong.

"You're a whole lot of trouble. Sometimes I wonder if your worth it, then all I have to do is look at your beautiful face." Bradley grabbed her small frame and tossed her over his shoulder.

"Zeke!" Stella yelled as she beat her fists against Bradley's back. His hold on her was too tight for her to wiggle loose. "Zeke, help!"

"Shut up. He can't help you now, and if he tries, I'll kill him."

"You have no idea who you're messing with." Stella wasn't worried about Zeke. Unless Bradley had a sword or certain poisons, he couldn't harm Zeke.

Bradley didn't respond. He trudged as quickly as he could through the dense sand with her on his shoulder. That particular stretch of beach was dark this late at night. The moon was shrouded behind clouds, and the only light was from a lamp outside one of the houses. Stella's fists did no good, so she raised his shirt and dug her nails into his back hard enough to draw blood.

"Gah! You bitch!" Bradley dropped Stella onto the sand and drew back to hit her.

"Don't you fucking dare!" Zeke's low tone sent shivers up Stella's spine. Bradley spun around and pulled Stella in front of him, using her as a shield. He pointed the gun at Zeke and fired. Stella cried out, waiting for blood to appear, but it didn't. Bradley fired the gun in rapid succession as Zeke closed in on them.

"What the fuck?" When Zeke was within striking distance, Bradley swung the pistol at Zeke's head, but Zeke grabbed Bradley's wrist, bones popping as he crushed it, sending the man to his knees.

"Stella, go call 911." Zeke twisted Bradley's arm behind his back, keeping him on the sand. "You fucked up, you fucking psycho," Stella heard Zeke curse as she tried to run back to the house.

"But I shot you! Six times!"

Trudging through sand wasn't easy nor quick, but she pushed her short legs as hard as they'd go. When she reached the back door, Thomas was no longer on the deck. Stella glanced around the house as she hurried for her phone. He was nowhere in sight, but she figured he'd gone back to his sister's home. Stella placed the call, and when they asked for the address, she stuttered, "Uh, I have no idea. Can you trace my phone?" How embarrassing. She didn't even know the street name.

"You'll need to stay on the line," the operator explained at the same time Cyrus yelled, "Get out of here!"

"Oh, shit," Stella whispered.

"What was that?" the operator asked.

"Nothing, just feeling kind of dizzy." Stella had no idea

how long she had until the cops showed up, but she had more pressing matters. Praying they were able to access her location in the few minutes they'd been on the phone, she disconnected, then ran up the stairs. Cyrus was standing in the middle of the room, fangs bared, claws out, and wings spread behind him. The bedroom wasn't small, but his imposing figure took up most of it. Thomas was on his ass with his hands out in front of him.

"Please don't hurt me," the older man begged.

"He won't hurt you," Stella said, stepping in front of Cyrus. "You *won't* hurt him, Cyrus. Thomas is your mate."

"I know that, but fuck! I don't want him to see me like this."

"Tell your Goyle to stand down. You can do it. Tell him he's scaring your mate." Stella hoped she was saying the right thing. Zeke spoke to his shifter like they were buddies. "Cyrus, you can do this."

Cyrus closed his eyes and took a deep breath. Stella stepped back toward the door, holding her hand out to Thomas. "Come on, we need to go downstairs."

Thomas scrambled to his feet, not looking back as he rushed from the room. Stella closed the door behind her, then followed the older man.

"Wh-what was *that*?"

"Long story really short, that was Cyrus transitioning into his Gargoyle for the first time. He is a shifter, and you are his mate. Being around you caused the shift. You are his destined life partner, chosen by the fates to be his one and only. I know it sounds strange, and it looks frightening. It's really not, once you get used to it. Cyrus is still the same man you met earlier, only now he's more. I need to get back down to the beach. My boss hit you over the head, then tried to kidnap me. My own mate is down there waiting on the cops. Maybe you need to come with me and let the EMTs check your head."

"I've had concussions before. I'll deal with it because I

am not leaving until I know Cyrus is okay."

"Spoken like a true mate. Okay, but if you need them, there are pain relievers on the end table. I had my own concussion just yesterday." Stella took off toward the back door but turned at the last second. "You're probably torn between disbelief and wonder, but please let Cyrus get through these first few hours. He's getting a handle on controlling his inner Gargoyle, and he would never hurt you on purpose, but if he did harm you accidentally, it would kill him."

"I'll just…" Thomas sat down on the sofa. "Why's it so cold in here?"

Stella didn't hang around to explain. She rushed back down to the beach. In all the excitement, she'd forgotten to grab shoes. In her double-socked feet, she ran straight for the edge of the water, then turned right and jogged on the packed sand. Sirens rent the night, and by the time she reached Zeke, several police officers were headed between two of the houses in their direction.

Zeke released Bradley's arm and stepped back with his hands up. Bradley pointed his good hand at Zeke. "Arrest him. He broke my wrist!"

"After you tried to kill him!" Stella yelled. She didn't know how to explain the fact that Zeke had been shot but not injured, much less killed.

"This man tried to kidnap my fiancée. He shot at me several times, but he missed as I zigzagged out of the way. His gun is over there," Zeke said, pointing to the weapon. "He followed Stella here after paying someone to attack her. You can call Officer Dowd with the New Fallbrook police department."

"She's not your fiancée! He's lying. Stella, you have to believe me," Bradley begged. Stella almost told the cops about Bradley hitting Thomas, but then she remembered the man had bigger headaches than talking with the cops, and Stella didn't want them anywhere near the house when

Cyrus was dealing with his transition.

Stella held up her left hand, waggling her ring finger. "He most certainly is my fiancé." A couple of officers slapped handcuffs on Bradley and hauled him off. Stella had only heard the term kicking and screaming until that moment. After giving their statements, they were allowed to go home.

"We need to hurry. Thomas must have heard Cyrus screaming because he went upstairs and saw Cyrus in all his Gargoyle glory."

"What? Come on." Zeke picked Stella up, and faster than was humanly possible, ran with her across the beach to their house. Thomas was where Stella left him, only he now had the blanket she'd used earlier wrapped around his shoulders. He jerked his head in their direction when they entered the room.

"I've got Thomas. You go check on your brother," Stella urged. Zeke held Stella's arms, staring at her. "I promise I'm fine. You saved me."

"How did he get to you anyway?"

"I opened the door to tell Thomas Cyrus wasn't feeling well, and Bradley hit him over the head with his gun. Then he grabbed me and took off. I knew you'd come after me."

"Always, but fuck, Baby. I've never been more frightened in my life than when I heard you yell my name."

"And I was only scared until I remembered his bullets wouldn't hurt you."

Zeke cradled Stella's face, his forehead still wrinkled. She reached up and smoothed the skin with her fingertips before arching up and kissing her male. "Go." Zeke pressed his lips to her temple, then rushed upstairs.

"Would you like some coffee?" Stella offered Thomas who was staring at her.

"Do you have anything stronger? Because that" — he gestured upstairs — "requires it."

"I understand. And yes, we have... I actually don't

know what all is here. Let me look." Stella perused the cabinet where Zeke's liquor was stored. She rattled off the various kinds of alcohol available, and Thomas opted for Scotch. After pouring a generous amount into a glass and handing it over, Stella found her discarded coffee cup she'd dropped earlier and put it in the sink before fixing another cup. When she returned to the living room, she sat on the other end of the sofa.

"Now, how about I tell you the long version?"

ZEKE HATED LEAVING Stella for even a second, but his brother needed him. He knocked on the door. "Cyrus, it's Zeke. I'm coming in." He wasn't sure what he expected to find when he entered the room, but it wasn't Cyrus calmly sitting on the end of the bed.

"I'm sorry I had to run out on you, but Calhoun tried to take Stella."

"Is she okay?" Cyrus asked as he extended his claws and retracted them yet as quickly.

"Yes, she is. And Calhoun's on his way to jail. Looks like you're getting the hang of things." Zeke leaned against the doorframe, keeping an eye on his brother while he listened in on his mate telling Thomas all about Gargoyles and half-bloods. The fates chose well when they gave Stella to him.

Cyrus opened his mouth and extended his fangs. "I'm trying. The claws aren't bad, but these damn teeth..." Cyrus winced when the sharp ends cut his bottom lip. He retracted them, then wiped his mouth with the back of his hand. Zeke pushed off the door and went into the bathroom for a washcloth. After wetting it with warm water, he returned and handed it to his brother. "You'll need this for a while. What about your wings?"

Cyrus narrowed his eyes, and a few seconds later, his wings spread out behind him. Cyrus stared at his reflection in the mirror on the wall across from where he was sitting. "I can't believe this is all real."

"It'll take a while to get used to it, more so having another voice in your head than the actual shifting."

"Yeah, uh, Stella actually helped with that. She told me to talk to it... Him."

Zeke chuckled. "It's okay to call your beast an it. You'll be calling it several things for a while, none of which are nice. You just can't let it control you when it tries to take over. That's the hardest part of being Gargoyle. Your shifter will be headstrong and combative, especially where your mate is concerned."

Cyrus turned sad eyes to Zeke. "I probably won't have to worry about that. I phased in front of him and yelled at him to leave. I doubt I get the chance to explain things to him."

"I wouldn't be so sure about that. He's currently sitting on the sofa with Stella, and she's explaining things from her perspective. He didn't leave when you told him to, so that's a good sign."

"Really?" Cyrus turned his face toward the door, cocking his head to the side. Zeke figured his brother was listening in on the conversation taking place downstairs. "I can hear them." Cyrus stood. "I need to go — "

Zeke held his hand out. "Hang on, Brother. I know you want to talk to him. Hold him, and claim him. Your beast is going to demand it. That's going to be the hardest thing you'll ever face – not claiming him immediately. But you need to be in control before you're alone with Thomas, and that's not going to happen quickly. I know you would never hurt your mate intentionally, but until you have some time to get used to the shifter inside, you need to keep your distance." When Cyrus's fangs dropped, Zeke pointed. "Case in point. You're pissed, and you need to tamp that shit down now."

"Sorry." Cyrus took a step back and got his beast under control.

"I'm proud of you, Brother. You're doing much better than I was at this point. Better than most of our siblings I helped through their transition."

"Like I said, Stella helped. She told me to talk to my Goyle. How did she know? It's not like she's a shifter."

Zeke smiled, thinking about his mate. "I may have spoken aloud to my beast in front of her. Plus, she can hear it in her head now that we're mated."

"Holy shit. Are you serious?"

"Yep. Not all couples have that level of bond, at least not right away. But I think me dressing down my Goyle gave her the idea."

"I'm glad she did." Cyrus stretched his neck, popping it from side to side. "Do you have any pain killers? My body feels like I got run over by a bull."

"I do, but right now, they won't help. Your body is adjusting to the changes and will be for a few more days. The aches will abate."

"If you say so. Say, will you go talk to Thomas for me? Explain things from our perspective and ask him to give me a few days?"

"I'd be happy to. For now, you have a little chat with your beast and let it know who's boss." Zeke clapped his brother on the shoulder, squeezing gently.

Now that Cyrus had gone through the burning up portion of the transition, Zeke flipped the heat back on, then headed downstairs. Stella and Thomas were facing each other from opposite ends of the sofa with Stella talking about the mate bond.

"Everything okay down here?" Zeke asked after telling his virtual assistant to start the fireplace. His house in Tennessee was wood burning. It fit the log-and-stone structure, but he appreciated being able to have insta-fire thanks to his electric unit. When he turned around, Zeke gave Thomas his attention.

"I honestly don't know. This morning, I met the man of my dreams, then tonight I find out he's not a man at all."

Zeke crossed the room and picked Stella up. He sat in her spot, settling her on his lap. "Cyrus is the same man you met this morning, but now he is more. His core values haven't changed. Gargoyles were put on Earth to watch over humans. Before I explained about our family, Cyrus's life revolved around his parents and their ranch. Now that he's transitioned, I don't see that changing, except for where you come in."

"But we just met," Thomas said, unwrapping the blanket from around his shoulders.

"Stella and I met less than a week ago. Now, we're mated. She's wearing my ring, and we're planning our future. As she explained to you earlier, mates are different than human couples. The fates choose that perfect being for you. The one who will love you above all others. Unconditionally. They will be your lover, your spouse, and your best friend for the rest of your lives. Our parents – our birth parents – have been together over two hundred years, and they're as much in love now as when they met, if not more. The bond only gets stronger as each day passes. I understand it's a lot to take in, but I promise Cyrus is the other half of your soul, the same way Stella is mine."

"Is that why I was drawn to him immediately? Usually, I'm too shy to even talk to another man." Thomas's skin blossomed red as he turned his head.

"Thomas, are you not out?" Stella asked.

"No, I am, at least to my family. Well, my sister. She and I are close. Our parents have both passed away, and she's the only one I have left. But she knows. She's tried to fix me up several times with friends of hers, but it was always a train wreck. I..." Thomas blew out a breath. "I've never been in a relationship. I'm fifty-one, and I don't know what it's like to have a boyfriend or partner. The few dates I went on once my parents passed were lackluster at best."

"Same here," Stella admitted. "I was in two short-lived relationships that went nowhere. I think it was because I was waiting on Zeke. I think the stars weren't aligned for you either because you were waiting on Cyrus."

"But look at him, then look at me. He's... well, he's an older version of you." Thomas pointed at Zeke.

"Actually, I'm four years older than my brother. I happened to go through my transition in my late twenties, and the aging process slowed, keeping me looking the way I do now. The same thing will happen to Cyrus. He will forevermore appear to be in his fifties. The same as you will if you agree to the bond. You'll be the handsome man with the flawless skin and a head full of dark hair."

"How will I explain that to my sister? Won't she wonder why I stopped aging?"

"After a few years, yes. But our biological father has developed prosthetics that can either show you with a few wrinkles, or he can give you a completely new look. My niece who is in her twenties used one of the masks to portray an old woman, and her own mate didn't recognize her. It's the same way our father has been able to stay in New Atlanta with no one realizing his true age or identity. We've been dealing with hiding in plain sight for centuries, and we have it down to an art. The easiest way to get around it is to move every ten or so years."

"What if someone were to find out the truth, and say, go to the press?"

"Would you believe someone if they told you Gargoyles exist without proof? What would you have said if Cyrus told you what he was going to become this morning?"

"I'd have thought he was mental. Oh, okay. I see what you're saying. This is a lot to take in." Thomas looked over his shoulder toward the stairs. "I don't hear any screaming, so does that mean he's okay now?"

"The worst of the pain is over, but now he has to learn how to gain and keep control over the shifter. He asked that you give him a few days, because being around you riles his beast."

"Oh. I... Does the beast not like me?"

"It likes you too much. It knows you are their mate, and it's trying to convince Cyrus to come down here and drag you upstairs, then keep you locked up for days. Cyrus doesn't have enough control though. Not yet."

Thomas clapped his hands on his legs, then stood. "I guess I'll go then. It's been an exciting night for all of us. Stella, I'm glad your stalker didn't hurt you, and I appreciate you talking with me. Zeke is a lucky man. Uh, male."

"I'm the lucky one, but you're welcome. I'm here if you want to talk further. Just maybe give me until about noon tomorrow. It has been a long day, and I plan on sleeping in."

Well, maybe not sleep. I hope I get to snuggle my hot fiancé and get naked at some point.

Zeke chuckled, then nuzzled Stella's neck. "I heard that," he whispered.

"I should let you two..." Thomas pointed his thumb toward the stairs. "I'll show myself out, but please tell Cyrus to call me if he wants to talk. I want to know how he is."

"I'll call you tomorrow," Cyrus called from upstairs.

Thomas snapped his head around, and Zeke explained, "Shifter hearing."

"Uh, I look forward to it," Thomas responded to Cyrus. He shook his head, but the man was smiling. "Until tomorrow."

Zeke stood with Stella cradled in his arms and walked Thomas to the door, both bidding him a goodnight. He then carried her up the stairs to their bedroom. After placing her on the bed, he sat down beside her and cradled her hand between his. "I'm so proud of you. You did well talking

Thomas off the ledge."

"I understood what he was going through. Yes, he might have been tossed into the deep end of the Gargoyles-are-real pool without a life preserver, whereas you explained it to me first, but I told him everything you told me. He's a very nice man, and from what little I know of Cyrus, I think they'll be perfect together. Thomas owns his own business and can work from anywhere, so if they do complete the bond, I can see him moving to Montana."

"I sure hope so. But enough about Thomas. You've had a long day, and I'd be a terrible mate if I kept you up any later."

Stella cupped Zeke's face, rubbing her thumb over his jaw. *You'd be terrible if you didn't.*

Zeke's beast rumbled in agreement. "If you insist."

EPILOGUE

STELLA WAS IN heaven. She had never been to Tennessee, but she never wanted to leave. The house Zeke brought her to was nestled at the base of the Smoky Mountains. Where their home in California was light and airy with the ocean outside the doors, this one was wood and stone and surrounded by trees. The fireplace roared with real cut wood. The scent of oak permeated the room, and the warmth enveloped Stella like one of Zeke's hugs. Her mate gave the best hugs.

It had been a crazy few months since she and Zeke met in the airport. After Bradley was arrested, it came out that he had planned the attack while she was in Egypt with Sheila. The man who ran her off the road admitted Bradley paid him up front to follow Stella as soon as she returned from her trip. With Bradley showing up at the beach house, attempting to kidnap her, then shooting at Zeke, he was arrested on multiple counts and currently sat in jail where he would stay, hopefully for a long time. Stella put it out of her mind and focused on getting to know Zeke as well as Cyrus and Thomas.

Cyrus got control of his beast while Thomas remained at his sister's house, visiting daily with Stella. The two became fast friends as they took walks along the water with Nonna. After a couple weeks, Cyrus and Thomas were finally together with Zeke acting as chaperone. When Cyrus had his shifter under control, he and Stella left the two men alone and went back to Stella's house for a few days where they packed all her belongings. Stella put her house up for sale since they didn't need it. They planned to use the money to purchase their first project. Before they got busy flipping a property, they were going to enjoy each other while nestled in what Zeke called their cabin.

The cabin was larger than the beach house, but to her, it felt more like home. The small town nearby was filled with friendly people, stunning scenery, and the best down-home cooking Stella ever tasted. Stella bought several cookbooks so she could replicate the meals they had while eating out. Zeke proved to be an excellent cook, and between them, they created some stellar dishes. Fried chicken with biscuits and gravy was Stella's favorite. They worked off all the calories later in bed. In her previous relationships, Stella could take or leave sex. With Zeke? She was insatiable.

Speaking of her husband, Zeke was on the phone with his brother. Cyrus and Thomas had returned to Montana, and according to Cyrus, Thomas had taken to ranch life like he had been born to it. Even though he could work from anywhere, Thomas sold his business so he could focus on helping Cyrus and the elder Gillespies. As an apology of sorts from Jonas, he sent Tamian to Cyrus's place and his parents' ranch to "speak" to all the animals. When Stella asked Zeke about Tamian, he admitted he hadn't been aware of his cousin's ability to talk to animals. He also didn't know how Jonas was aware of Cyrus's trip back home, but he chalked it up to Julian being involved somehow.

"That's wonderful news, Brother. Congratulations. Of course Stella and I will be there." Stella already knew Cyrus had proposed. Thomas texted her almost every day, filling her in on life on the ranch. She was excited about visiting Montana and seeing the couple again.

She and Zeke had gotten married in a little chapel in New Gatlinburg the first Saturday after they arrived in Tennessee. They had been walking around the tourist town, stopping in all the shops, sampling everything from fudge to flavored moonshine, of which Stella was a fan. They had passed by more than one chapel when Zeke mentioned there was no waiting period. A few hours later, they came home with matching wedding bands and several mason jars filled with different varieties of moonshine, and every night after one of their home-cooked meals, Stella sipped the tasty alcohol.

Stella glanced down at the stunning band which matched her promise ring. Zeke admitted to purchasing the rings at the same jeweler before they left California. When he asked if she wanted to wait until her mom could be there with them, Stella told him no. Sheila had her own life now with Dr. Crabtree, and Stella prayed he would be the man who finally stuck around.

After Zeke hung up with Cyrus, Stella went to him where he sat on the sofa and straddled his lap. Curling her arms around his neck, she leaned in for a kiss. "I take it we're going to Montana?"

"Yes, but you already knew that." Zeke nuzzled Stella's neck, kissing the spot just below her ear that drove her crazy.

"Thomas told me Cyrus proposed." Stella gripped Zeke's hair, tugging his head back so she could see his eyes.

"What? I can't kiss my wife?"

"Not like that. You know what that spot does to me."

Zeke grinned. "But you're the one who straddled my lap knowing what that spot does to *me*."

Oh yes, Stella knew, but she couldn't help herself. "How long do we have?" she asked, wiggling her butt over his erection.

In one of his faster-than-should-be-possible moves, Zeke had Stella flat of her back on the sofa with his weight on top of her. Her legs spread automatically, and his erection pressed against her. Zeke rubbed his denim-covered hard-on against her, and Stella wanted more. She always wanted more.

107

"Not long enough for all the things I want to do to you, but long enough for me to do this." Zeke unbuttoned Stella's jeans and slid them and her panties down her legs before latching onto her clit with his mouth.

"Holy Bast," she muttered. Zeke had perfected the art of oral on her. Whenever they didn't have time to get completely lost in each other, he made sure she was sated. As soon as she came, Stella was reaching for his zipper. She had also learned what her mate liked, and Zeke loved Stella's mouth.

Half an hour later, with clothes righted and teeth brushed, Stella stood by Zeke as he welcomed some of his family into their home. Stella felt as though she already knew Sophia, Nick, Tessa, and Gregor, but meeting them in person was so much better.

"Oh my gods! You could pass for an Egyptian queen," Sophia declared as soon as she walked in the door, her nose scrunching like a bunny. It was the cutest thing Stella had ever seen.

Tessa, the feisty redhead, made herself at home, going straight to the refrigerator while Gregor asked Zeke where to put their bags. The two couples were visiting for the weekend, and Stella was beyond excited. Growing up an only child, she had missed out on so much. Having Zeke's family there was a dream come true for Stella, even when Tessa found the strawberries-and-cream moonshine and proceeded to chug the whole jar. It was a good thing Stella had a case of it in the garage.

Sitting on Zeke's lap, sipping moonshine, and listening to her new family tell stories of their travels was the most fun Stella ever had in her life. And this was only the beginning. One day, they would all add kids to the mix. Stella could imagine the cabin decorated for Christmas and filled with their family as they celebrated together. She could also see everyone at the beach house, having barbecues and fires on the sand. Her first thirty years had been dull and a little lonely, but the next thirty? They would be filled with family and her Ezekiel. The future had never looked brighter.

REMY

PROLOGUE

Toulouse, France

2007

DRESSED IN HIS finest, Remy strolled through his family's hotel. After four hundred years of being without a mate, he caught the most glorious fragrance on the air. Somewhere between the stone walls of *Chateaux de Durand* was his female. He first caught her scent in the restaurant, then in the entrance to the maze garden. He was determined to find her, so now he was going floor to floor. When he reached the door to room four thirteen, he found what he was looking for. Instead of standing there like a stalker, he returned to the lobby and waited at the end of the check-in desk.

"Is there something I can help you with, *Monsieur* Durand?"

"Yes. I need to know who is in room four thirteen."

James frowned. "Is there a problem with the room?"

"No. I just need the name, please."

James tapped a few keys. "*Monsieur* Felix Hogan."

"Thank you, James." Remy wasn't one to jump to conclusions. This could be a father or brother. The male could have reserved the room in his name for an employee.

Or it could be her husband.

It could be, but I'm her mate, so I'll just have to be patient.

What was another few years after waiting four

111

hundred?

Remy turned from the desk when he heard a woman's laughter coming from where the elevator was located. That intoxicating scent met his nose right before the most mesmerizing female in the world stepped into view. All Remy could do was stare. Dirty blonde hair was piled on top of her head in soft curls. Blue eyes so pale they seemed translucent met his, and the woman stopped walking, her hand falling away from an older man's elbow. The man paused when he noticed the woman was no longer walking with him.

"Isla, what's wrong?" The man turned to see who she was staring at.

"Nothing's wrong, Dad," Isla said, her eyes never leaving Remy's.

Remy broke out of his trance and stepped forward with his hand outstretched. "*Bonjour.* I am Remy Durand. I hope your stay at *Chateaux de Durand* is meeting your expectations."

Felix Hogan grasped his hand tightly. Being Gargoyle, it took a lot of pressure to get Remy's attention, but he knew in that instant that the male before him wasn't human. When Mr. Hogan released Remy's grip, he took a step closer to his daughter. Remy was relieved to know the man who had secured the suite Isla was staying in wasn't a significant other.

"The Chateau is everything we expected when I booked it. Now, if you'll excuse us..."

"Of course, *Monsieur.* If there's anything you need, do not hesitate to let me know," Remy said, but his eyes were on the gorgeous female who was his mate.

"Come along, Isla." Her father's tone was gruff, and it rankled Remy. No one, not even his mate's father, should speak to her in such a way.

Isla winked at him, mischief glowing in her pale eyes, and she mouthed, "Later."

Remy's heart tapped double-time behind his ribs. He could do nothing but stand there and stare as she walked away. As soon as they were out the door, Remy went into the office and did something he shouldn't have. He grabbed a blank key card and ran it through the machine to code it to her suite. He calmed himself before heading out to the lobby. He would be humiliated if James figured out what Remy was going to do. Instead of going directly to the elevator, he made his way to the restaurant and spoke with the chef about the day's menu. Remy didn't micromanage. His family hired only the best, so the chef was taken aback when Remy showed up.

"I only asked because the cassoulet is a favorite of mine, and I've been craving it."

"*Oui, Monsieur.* You only have to ask. I can rearrange today's menu."

"*Non.* That won't be necessary, but if you could manage to work it in sometime this week, I would be forever grateful."

"Consider it done."

"*Merci.*" Remy inclined his head and exited the kitchen. He made his way to the bank of lifts at the back of the hotel and rode one to the fourth floor. He reached out with his shifter senses to assure there was no one around. When he was certain the coast was clear, Remy let himself into Isla's suite. *Isla.* A lovely name for a lovely female. *His* female. His beast was rumbling inside as their mate's essence assaulted them strongly. Remy felt like a creep, but he wanted to know a little more about his mate before he spoke to her alone. And he would get her away from her father. His quick perusal of her room didn't offer much about her personality. The only thing he garnered from snooping was she wore lacy underwear. When he opened the drawer and saw the frilly bras and panties, Remy had to grip his cock harshly. He also had to get out of her room.

"Hey, what are you doing in there?" a rough voice

asked when Remy stepped through the door.

Remy turned to find a younger version of Isla's father glaring at him. The male's nostrils were flaring, and his fists were clenched at his side. "I was checking the thermostat to ensure it had been fixed."

"And you often go into occupied rooms while the guests are unaware?"

"*Non*. Only when I want to assure there are no issues which would cause less than a memorable stay at my hotel."

"Your hotel?"

"*Oui*. I am Remy Durand."

The male's eyebrows rose as though he didn't believe Remy. "Well, Mister Durand, stay out of my sister's room."

"I was under the impression this was your father's suite. Now, if you'll excuse me, I have a hotel to oversee." Remy didn't give the male time to say anything further. He turned on his heel and strode toward the stairway, needing to put much space between himself and Isla Hogan's suspicious brother. Instead of returning to the lobby, Remy went upstairs to his own suite and closed himself in. He laughed at himself for getting caught, but his laughter turned into a groan when he thought about Isla wearing the lacy undergarments. Instead of taking care of his throbbing hard-on, Remy called the florist who supplied the arrangements scattered around the hotel. With her brother hanging around, Remy would have to be sneaky getting the flowers into his mate's room, but he would make it happen.

Remy paced his suite hours later. The flowers had been delivered, and Remy had handwritten a note, praying Isla's father and brother didn't see the roses and sabotage his plans. It was close to midnight when a soft knock broke him out of his pacing. One sniff and Remy knew she was there. He strode to the door and opened it. Isla stood before him, a dream in cream-colored pants and a soft lilac sweater.

"I got your note," she whispered. Remy held open the door for her. Isla stepped across the threshold, but instead of venturing farther into the room, she stopped in front of him. Remy held his breath as she slid her arms around his neck, grinning. "Hello, Mate."

CHAPTER ONE

REMY TOUSLED HIS son's hair after kissing him on the temple. Rain had missed two years of school, but he was thriving with Marigold as his teacher. As soon as Amelia found out Rain was going to be homeschooled, she begged Frey and Abbi to let her do the same. Her parents had agreed, saying it might help Rain feel more comfortable having an ally. Amelia was a whirlwind, making everyone who met her smile, including Rain. She reminded Remy of a mini version of his mate. Isla had the same effect on anyone who was in her presence. Amelia and Connor had taken Rain into their duo, and the three were thick as thieves. Connor was younger, but his little mind was brilliant. He had his own tutor since he was a few levels above the other two.

Lorenzo was assigned to watch over the kids while their parents were at work. Remy was learning about running the Pen. Abbi had started teaching dance classes at the gym, and Frey was there to watch over his mate while running the Clan in Rafael's absence. If Isla were still alive, Remy would have been by her side too. His lovely mate had been a force of nature. At four hundred twenty-three, Remy had almost given up finding his mate. Then one day, there she was in his hotel. Isla was on a business trip with her father when Remy caught her scent. Remy waited in the lobby every day until he finally found the female whose very essence called to his beast.

Things weren't easy for the two of them. Her father had taken one look at Remy and refused to allow Isla to mate below her station. Not only were the Hogans from an Original bloodline, they were also one of the richest families in Australia. It didn't matter that Remy's family owned several vineyards in South France. Their wealth was nothing compared to that of the Hogans. Isla, being her own female, had given her father an ultimatum: respect her wishes or lose her forever. Her father relented, but her brother, Nash, had been happy to see her go. With Isla out of the picture, he stepped into her spot as second in control of the family's company.

Remy and Isla remained in France. Instead of staying at *Chateaux de Durand*, they moved to one of his family's vineyards. They had a charmed life, one which became even more enriched when their son was born many years later. The two had tried for years to have a child, but their love never wavered when it didn't happen. Everything had been perfect until Isla took Rain to visit her parents. Nash called Remy with the news that both Isla and Rain had been killed in a car crash. Being the asshole he was, Nash also informed Remy the family had Isla and Rain cremated. Instead of getting on a plane and heading to Australia, Remy fell into a depression. Staying at the winery was no longer an option. He couldn't remain where the memories of his family were greatest, so he moved to the States. He fell in with the Stone Society in California. When they offered Remy a job running the penitentiary they were building, he took it. Remy had no experience with such things, but he had a brilliant mind for business, and he came to New Atlanta to learn everything he could from Gregor Stone.

Finding his son alive had nearly broken Remy, but it also brought him back to life. No longer going through the motions of making it through each day, he had something – someone – to live for. Knowing it was Nash who sold Rain to Dr. Craven had lit a fire in Remy. He was a male on a mission, and when he found his mate's brother, he was going to tear him apart. It had been months since Rain had been returned to Remy, and that was where Remy's focus was – taking care of his son. Henry Palamo, the Clan's new computer expert, was currently searching for Dr. Craven while also figuring out who had targeted the Clan by hacking into the system. Once they found Craven, Remy planned to force a confession out of the man with regards to Nash and Rain. When he had that, Remy was going to take it to Isla's parents and demand retribution.

When Rain was found, Remy had a moment's hope his mate was still alive. He had called her mother, not to inform her Rain was with him, but to ask about Isla. Before he could ask what he wanted to know, Felix had grabbed the phone and demanded Remy never contact them again. They blamed Remy for Isla's death, which made no sense. He had been thousands of miles away at the time. Maybe that was the reason. He hadn't been there to protect her.

Remy made his way to the office as soon as he arrived at work. Since Deacon had retired to spend time with Sabrina, Gregor had promoted Aldredge to assistant warden and had left training Remy to the male. Aldredge had worked at the Pen for over ten years, so he was knowledgeable with the ins and outs, whereas Remy was learning from the ground up. With the New Atlanta Penitentiary being privately owned by the Stone Society instead of funded by the government, they had more leeway with how they ran things. That included housing the Unholy in what Gregor called The Basement. The lower level contained the monsters the Clan managed to get off the street.

Isabelle, along with her father, had recently perfected the formula for changing the Unholy back to their former human selves, so not only was Remy learning the administrative portion of running the prison, he was also helping administer the serum. Changing the creatures back was time consuming. They had to be monitored closely, but they also had to be moved to the upper levels away from those who had yet to be changed. Frey and Gregor were in the process of converting one of the Clan's many warehouses into a holding facility. It was going to be a different type of prison. One where the males could get counseling while being evaluated as to their state of mind. Most of the ones who became Unholy in the first place had been former soldiers coming back from overseas without the means to return to civilian life. Men like Sabrina's baby brother. They had been promised a place in Gordon Flanagan's army not knowing the serum they were being given would turn them into nothing more than killing machines. Although it was Flanagan who created the Unholy, it was the Stone Society who were taking it upon themselves to undo the damage. They had the money, and now they had the antiserum.

Remy was checking the monitors for each floor when Aldredge came in carrying a paper sack. "Good morning, Brother." Aldredge set the white carry-out bag on the desk, and Remy smiled.

"Morning, and thank you." Remy pulled out one of the pastries and took a bite, moaning at the sugary goodness. Aldredge's mate owned a bakery, so every morning after dropping his mate off, Aldredge brought Remy a different treat. The bakery had been in Jessica's family for several generations, and the female had taken over when her parents decided it was time to relocate.

Aldredge didn't check the security feeds in the office. He trusted Remy to tell him if something was amiss. Although they had access to the cameras, Caleb manned the control room during the days. He had come on shift an hour earlier, and the male was more than capable of doing his job. There were few humans who worked in the Pen. Those who did were unaware of The Basement. The last human – a doctor – who had access to the lowest level had been killed

119

when he went below without backup. Even Isabelle, knowing about the Unholy, wasn't given access. Not because Gregor didn't trust her. He did. But there was no way the male would allow his brother's mate to be harmed accidentally. Dante also didn't allow Isabelle to administer any type of medical assistance to the Reborn nor the human inmates without a Gargoyle present. Her safety was of utmost importance.

The computer beeped, and Remy tapped a few keys. It was an incoming video conference. Aldredge rounded the desk and stood behind Remy. Frey, along with several others, was already logged on. Frey didn't waste time getting to the point. "Henry has located Craven. He's in south Mississippi. Remy, I know you want answers, so I'll leave it up to you whether you go after him or not. Rain is welcome to stay with Abbi and me."

"I'm in. I need to do this, Frey." Aldredge squeezed Remy's shoulder, offering encouragement.

"Tamian will be going with you. Gregor and Dominic are in New Orleans. They're going to leave right after the call and head that way. After we're finished here, Tamian will get with Gregor and decide where to meet. Santiago is getting Tamian's jet fueled, so you can leave as soon as you're ready. I assume you want to spend a little time with Rain before you leave?"

"Yes. I need to know he's okay with me being away from him for a few days."

"I figured as much. If something happens and you decide to stay in town, Lorenzo will go in your place. If you do go, Deacon has offered to cover your shift at the Pen while you're gone."

"Thank you, Deacon."

Deacon inclined his head. "If I didn't have my mate to watch over, I'd take the trip with you. I want this piece of shit taken down for what he did to Sabrina's brother."

"No. Helping cover at the Pen is more than enough."

Remy was grateful for such a good Clan. It was like being with his own family back in France.

"Okay. Henry has coordinated with Tamian, so he will take lead. Remy, I know you want to kill the bastard, but we need answers first." Frey's tone was stern. He was a fine leader, and Remy respected the hell out of the large male.

"Understood."

"After you see Rain, meet Tamian at his place. He'll drive you to the airport."

"I'll text you my address," Tamian said. He was a half-blood and a clone, but he had Original blood flowing through his veins. He had extraordinary powers, and Remy was more than happy to let the male lead their mission.

"I'll see you soon." Remy disconnected and dropped his head into his hands.

Aldredge squeezed his shoulders again. The two had become good friends in the short time they'd worked together. "Go, Brother. Go see Rain, then get this bastard. We'll hold down the fort until you return."

Remy raised his head and blew out a breath. "Thanks. I know Rain will be fine with Frey and Abbi, but I worry about leaving him so soon after I got him back."

"Your boy's tough. I can check in after my shift if you'd like."

"Thank you. I doubt that'll be necessary, but I'm glad to know the offer's there." Remy didn't hang around. There was no need considering he was a trainee. He drove the few miles to get to his boy, keeping just above the speed limit. The front door of Frey's home opened before Remy was on the porch.

"Daddy!" Rain rushed him, and Remy picked his son up. Remy internally frowned at the moniker, but his boy had been through a traumatic experience. Rain could call Remy whatever he wished. He had a feeling Rain was mimicking Amelia. Speaking of the whirlwind, she was dancing in circles right inside the door while she waited on

121

Rain to return. Remy placed Rain on his feet but kept hold of his little hand.

"Did you come to eat lunch with me?" Rain asked.

"It's a little early for lunch, but I came to hang out a while. Plus, I want to talk to you about something."

Marigold was standing in the doorway. "Do you want me to take Amelia in the other room?"

"Thank you, but that's not necessary."

"I'll go get a snack together." The young female smiled adoringly at both kids before leaving them alone. Abbi had done well when choosing a tutor.

Remy sat on the sofa and pulled Rain down on his lap. "How would you feel about having a sleepover with Amelia for a few nights? Papa needs to go out of town. It shouldn't take more than a couple days if that, but it might be longer. If you don't want me to leave you, I won't."

"Where are you going?"

Remy had already decided to be honest. "To find Dr. Craven and put him in jail where he belongs."

"He's scary." Rain's whispered words wobbled as did his bottom lip.

"Not as scary as me." Remy vowed to himself the doctor would never hurt another child, or anyone else, again.

Amelia had stopped twirling as she listened intently. Frey didn't hide much from his daughter. She was aware of the Gargoyles but had never once uttered their secret. It was why Remy felt comfortable talking in front of her. She plopped down beside them and took Rain's hand in hers.

"Your daddy is strong like mine."

Rain stared at his friend, chewing his bottom lip. When he turned his watery eyes back to Remy, he gave a small smile. "You can go."

"Are you sure?"

"Yes. I want you to capture the bad man."

Remy hugged his son tightly to his chest, resting his

cheek against Rain's hair. The three of them sat quietly until Marigold brought in some sliced veggies and fruit. Remy stayed at Frey's for a couple hours. When he was certain Rain was truly okay with him leaving, he left his son with his little friend, their tutor, and Lorenzo watching over them all. He drove home and packed the necessities, then met Tamian at his home. They drove in companionable silence to the small airfield where Santiago was waiting.

GREGOR PRESSED A kiss to Tessa's hair while they waited for Dominic to unlock the door. He enjoyed hanging out with the pirate immensely. Dominic was like Tessa – his own person. The male dressed and spoke however he wanted with no qualms whether anyone liked him or not. And Lilly, Dom's mate and Tessa's cousin, was a breath of fresh air. The pretty witch was a stark contrast to his own mate, but she complimented Dominic perfectly. Gregor never hesitated when Tessa wanted to spend time at her place in New Orleans. He considered it their second home as much as she did.

Just as they passed the threshold, Gregor's phone rang. When he saw it was Frey, he answered immediately. Things were still shaky back in New Atlanta with the unknown hacker on the loose. "Frey? Everything okay?"

"Henry located Craven. He tracked him to the DeSoto Forest just north of New Biloxi. He's not alone. Craven's traveling with four others, and you can assume they're Gargoyles, Unholy, or Reborn. I thought since you were close, you might want in on the hunt."

"Fuck yeah, I do."

Dominic, who had been headed toward the parlor, stopped and gave Gregor his full attention. Gregor put the phone on speaker, even though the other male didn't need

123

him to do so. Having Dom as backup would be nice. Frey relayed everything Henry had found, and Dominic nodded, pulling out his own phone and stepping out of the room.

"I'm going to give Remy the option of joining you considering what Craven did to Rain. Tamian has already agreed to fly him down there. If Remy stays here, I'll send Lor."

"Dominic and I will head out soon. Tell Tamian to call me with a location, and we'll pick them up when they land."

"Thanks, Brother. I want this bastard alive. Once we have some information, I'll turn Remy loose on him."

"Understood. How's everything else going?" Gregor had felt guilty for leaving his cousin behind to watch over the Clan, but Frey was the strongest of them all. He was the perfect male to take over while Rafael tended to Kaya.

"Things are quiet. Dante and Isabelle have been administering the antiserum to the Unholy, and so far, it's been successful. Construction on the warehouse is going as planned, so it shouldn't be too much longer before we have somewhere to put the Reborn."

"That's great news. As soon as we catch Craven, Tessa and I will be back to help."

"I'm looking forward to it. Stay safe, Cousin."

"Always." Gregor disconnected and held his arm out for his mate.

Tessa clapped her hands together. "Let's get this bastard."

Gregor rolled his eyes but didn't argue.

Lilly frowned at Tessa. "Wait. You're going with them? I know you're a half-blood, but..."

"She thinks she's Lara Croft," Gregor muttered.

Tessa gave him a middle finger. "I've been doing this cloak-and-dagger stuff for years. Besides, I figure while the males are going against the baddies, I can concentrate on the good doctor. He won't get away this time. No offense to Paxton."

Gregor pulled Tessa to him so her back was to his front. "Yeah, well, don't let him hear you say that. He's still beating himself up over it."

"I'll be taking some of my crew with me," Dominic said. "Tessa, you can stay here, Lass."

"And you can stuff your parrot," she replied.

Dominic winked at her, but Lilly said, "He's right. You don't need to go."

"Yes, I really do. Lilly, this bastard used a small boy as a fucking pin cushion. Took his blood. Kept him in a dark tunnel."

Lilly's demeanor went from worried to pissed. "I want in on this."

Dominic stepped behind his mate and wrapped his arms around her, settling his hands on her round belly. "Oh, no. You, my little witch, will stay here and protect my girls."

Lilly looked up at Dom over her shoulder and melted against him. "Okay," she whispered before he pressed their lips together. Gregor caught Tessa staring at the couple. He knew she felt guilty for not being pregnant already, but he had assured her more than once it would happen if it were meant to.

CHAPTER TWO

THE FLIGHT TO New Mobile, Alabama, was quick. When they touched down, Gregor, Tessa, and several males were waiting. Tamian had explained Dominic Dubois was the leader of their Clan in the southern portion of the States. If Tamian hadn't already told Remy about the male's penchant for dressing as a pirate, he would probably have laughed. But the look truly fit the roguish male instead of making him look like a character out of an old black-and-white film. Remy wasn't surprised to see Tessa standing alongside Gregor. He had met the female several times and had heard her story. Not only did she have Gregor as a mate, but Tamian was her clone, and there was no female on the planet more guarded in that moment. It didn't hurt that she was a badass in her own right.

Dominic stepped forward and introduced himself and the two males with him. Sully and Fallon were dressed in black military pants and boots. Unlike their leader, they appeared ready for battle. Remy didn't let Dom's clothing fool him. The male was a Gargoyle, so his appearance had no bearing on his ability to fight. They piled into two vehicles. One was a large SUV, and the other was a transport van.

Tamian had loaded several of the Clan's specially coated swords, including a smaller one for his sister. Remy grinned to himself, thinking Dominic probably had more experience with a sword than any of them. He had been a real pirate many years ago, so a sword was necessary for his swashbuckling days. Then again, Remy had been a soldier in The Napoleonic Wars, so maybe not.

Henry wasn't certain who was with Craven, but they all decided he would be surrounded by both Gargoyles and Unholy. Surprisingly, Tamian handed Tessa a holster and two powerful-looking black handguns. When she caught him looking, Tessa explained they weren't taking any chances. Yep, badass.

Henry didn't say how exactly he found Craven, and Remy didn't want to know, especially if it was somehow illegal. All that mattered was getting the human off the streets. Upon reaching the forest, they parked well away from where Craven was supposed to be. Tamian handed out communication devices to everyone. Julian had perfected the small earpieces, and they transmitted from a few miles away. Tamian was leading one team, which included Dominic and his males. Gregor led the other. He, Tessa, and Remy were coming in from the south, while Tamian's team came in from the north. After they went over the plan once more, Tamian and his team took off their shirts so they could shift. The De Soto Forest had been abandoned for the most part, as had most of the smaller parks around the country. If there were humans in the area, they wouldn't be in the dense portion where Craven was hiding out.

Since Tessa couldn't fly, their team remained on the ground. The female surprised Remy with her stealth. Her normal chatty self was replaced by a determined warrior. Remy had been surprised to see her with the others. If that had been Isla, he would never have allowed his mate on such a mission, but seeing Tessa in action proved this wasn't her first time doing something dangerous.

"We have visual," Tamian said half an hour later through the comms. "There are two Gargoyles and four Unholy we can see. Craven must be inside the cabin. We're going to take the guards out."

"Craven is mine," Remy reminded them.

"Copy that."

No longer worried about being quiet, Remy picked up the pace. Gregor and Tessa easily kept up with him. By the time they reached the cabin, both Gargoyles had been taken down. The Unholy were bound and secured against four trees with Dominic's males and Tamian standing guard. They had agreed to leave them alive if at all possible. Tamian pointed to the door, and Remy turned to see Dominic pushing a shaking Craven outside.

Remy shook with anger, but he reined it in. He needed answers. "How did you come by the boy?"

"I can't tell you. Drago will kill me." Craven didn't appear afraid, but Remy could smell the fear pouring from the human.

"Drago is dead, and if you don't tell me everything I want to know, you'll end up like your comrades over there." Remy pointed with his sword.

The doctor swallowed audibly and closed his eyes. When he opened them, his shoulders slumped. "Drago found the boy. Him and his mother." Remy called on his shifter to keep himself from showing any type of emotion. "When he first approached me about the antiserum, he had vials of blood. For whatever reason, he couldn't get more blood shipped, and soon after, the boy showed up."

"And you thought it was okay to use a child in such a way?" Remy growled. He sensed the presence of the others at his back. They no doubt sensed he was struggling to control his shifter.

"I didn't hurt the kid."

"You took him away from his mother! You stole his fucking blood! Kept him locked alone in a dark tunnel beneath a church! He's only seven for the gods' sake." Remy's voice was barely a whisper when he finished railing.

"I didn't kidnap him; his uncle did. So take that up with him," Craven had the nerve to say.

"Do you know where the uncle is?" Tessa asked.

Craven snarled, "Hello, Andrea. Might have known

128

you'd have your nose stuck in my business. It's a shame your father couldn't find you."

Tessa pulled both pistols faster than Remy could blink. The sound of her cocking the weapons was loud in the woods. Craven's eyes widened, his snarl turning into a grimace.

"The name's Tessa, and Flanagan wasn't my father. Anyone who threatens or harms my Clan *is* my business. Now answer the godsdamned question."

"No, I don't know where he is. I never met the male. That was all Drago's doing."

It was hard to get a read on the scientist considering he had two pistols pointed at him and six Gargoyles holding swords. Tamian stepped up next to his sister and whispered the man was telling the truth. Remy wasn't aware of all Tamian's abilities, but if he said the human was being truthful, Remy had no reason to doubt him.

"Where is the rest of the serum?" Tamian asked, but Craven kept his eyes on Tessa.

"There isn't any. I was waiting on Drago to send me the money he owed before I made more."

Tessa stepped up to the doctor and placed the end of one gun against his forehead. "Where is the rest of the serum?"

Craven flinched. "Th-there isn't any. I sw-swear."

Tessa took a step back and shot the man in his right kneecap. He howled out in pain, dropping to the ground. "You bitch!" When she pointed at the other leg, Craven held his bound hands up. "Stop! I'm sorry. Don't kill me."

"Oh, I'm not going to kill you. We're going to take you to the Pen and put you in the Basement with the Unholy you created. We'll let them take care of you." Tessa tucked her pistols in the holster and moved away from the man.

"No! I can help you. I have money. Please!" Snot and tears ran down the man's face as he begged for his life, no longer the self-assured doctor he first presented.

129

"We don't need your money nor your help. Since you have no useful information, there is nothing you have left to bargain with." Tessa joined Gregor who grinned at his mate. Obviously, he had no issue with her shooting the human.

Tamian pulled the keys out of his pocket and tossed them to Sully. "Please go get the vehicles and bring them here." Sully and Fallon phased to fly back to where both SUVs were parked.

Dominic sheathed his sword. "What are you going to do about those two?" he asked, pointing at the decapitated Gargoyles.

"Santiago's brothers are on standby. They will retrieve the bodies and dispose of them in the swamp."

"Aye, that's effective." Dominic not only looked like a pirate but sounded like one as well. Remy liked the Goyle. If things were different, Remy could see himself hanging out with the male.

While they were waiting on their transport, Gregor approached the Unholy. He pulled several vials out of his cargos pocket and administered the antiserum. Dominic offered for Sully and Fallon to drive back with Tamian to watch over the Unholy. Remy, Gregor, and Tessa would fly Dr. Craven back on Tamian's jet. Remy wasn't sure he could be around the human without taking his head, but he wanted to get back home to Rain.

When the vehicles arrived, Gregor dug around in the back for a black case. He returned with it, and after placing a tourniquet around Craven's leg where the doctor was still lying on the ground moaning, Gregor gave him a shot of some type. Remy would have preferred to let the human suffer. He had to concede they didn't need to explain a pool of blood to the car rental company. Once everyone was loaded, they took off for the airport. About ten minutes into the drive, Craven passed out. Remy sat in the passenger seat far enough away from the human he wasn't tempted to let his beast loose. Tamian had already called Santiago to tell him they were on their way as well as to give the pilot's brothers the coordinates to where the dead Gargoyles were.

After getting Craven loaded and secured on the jet, Dominic shook their hands. Everyone except Tessa. "It was a pleasure as always, Lass. Lilly and I will pack your belongings and bring them to New Atlanta."

"But she's about ready to pop," Tessa countered.

"She has a couple months yet, but my Lillian wants to be with family when the girls arrive."

"That's great. You can stay with us," the redhead offered without conferring with Gregor. The smile on the male's face assured Remy he was okay with Tessa's offer.

"That won't be necessary. We were going to surprise you, but I'll go ahead and tell you I have recently purchased a home not far from yours. New Orleans will always be our home, but there are few mated Goyles in our area, and she wants the twins to have cousins to grow up with."

The badass female sniffed quietly. "That'll be perfect. We'll see you soon." Tessa strode to the plane and climbed the steps. Remy was missing an important piece to the puzzle. Outwardly, Tessa seemed pleased her cousin was moving closer, but her sadness said otherwise.

"You'll get pregnant when the time comes, Brother. Don't give up hope," Dominic whispered to Gregor. Now Tessa's mood made sense. Kaya had recently given birth to the Clan's Prince, and several other mates were pregnant. If Tessa and Gregor had been trying a while, it had to hurt to see others succeeding. Remy remembered how excited he and Isla had been when they found out Rain was on the way. He sent up a prayer to the gods that the couple got their wish. Dominic and Gregor embraced, slapping each other's back. Dominic then grasped Remy's hand. "I hope you find the answers you need." Dom inclined his head, then strolled to the SUV. He was going to return the vehicle to the local rental company in New Orleans.

When Remy and Gregor boarded the jet, Tessa was

cutting up with the pilot. It was good to see her sadness had dissipated, at least for the moment.

"Would you like to sit in the cockpit?" Santiago asked Remy.

"I would, thank you." Remy figured Tessa had explained what Craven had done to Rain. It would be better to sit as far away from the human as possible.

He had flown many times in his life, but Remy had never given much thought to the specifics of flying or being a pilot. Santiago went through the motions of getting the jet fired up and moving while telling Remy each aspect. It was educational as well as entertaining. When they were rolling down the runway gathering speed, Remy couldn't help but grin. Santiago kept Remy's thoughts off Craven for the most part by talking about his own life and what it was like working with Tamian. When they landed at a small, private airfield, Remy was relaxed. As he went to stand, Santiago grabbed his arm.

"Why don't you wait here with me while they get the doctor on his way to the Pen?"

Remy agreed and remained seated until Gregor gave them the all-clear. Remy joined Gregor outside the jet, and his boss held out a set of keys. "Go home to Rain. Tessa and I will come by later to get the car. I'll see to getting Craven locked up. He's not going anywhere."

"Thanks, Brother. I'll be back to work tomorrow. I want a recorded confession from the human I can send to Isla's parents. They won't take my word against their own son."

"Have you considered letting Rain tell them his uncle was the one responsible?"

"Yes, but they'll think I coerced him into lying. They never liked me. I wasn't rich enough."

"I thought your family owned vineyards and hotels?" Gregor released Remy's shoulder and shoved his hands in his pockets.

"We do, and we have plenty of money, but it's nowhere

near what Isla's family has."

"Crazy. Like I said, he's not going anywhere, so take all the time you need." Gregor strode over to join Tessa at the transport van. Remy was lucky having someone like Gregor for a boss and a friend. After losing Isla and Rain, Remy had become depressed and pushed everyone away. When Rain was returned to him, Remy called his parents, and they were planning on visiting soon. If only Isla would be returned just as miraculously, his life would be perfect again.

On the drive to Frey's, Remy called ahead to let them know he was on his way. He went ahead and filled Frey in on what had transpired so they wouldn't have to talk about it in front of Abbi or the children. Rain met him at the front door, wrapping his little arms around Remy's legs. Remy picked him up and entered the door Frey was holding for him.

"Are you hungry?" Abbi said by way of greeting. "It won't take long to plate some leftovers." Remy readily accepted. He was a decent cook, but he never turned down a great meal. Isla had been wonderful in the kitchen, watching videos and trying new dishes every night. Remy had learned from watching her. When she was alive, he'd never been far from his mate. The ache in his chest remembering his female had eased, but now that Rain was back in his life, Remy wanted their family back together more than ever. Rain needed his mum.

He hated to eat and run, but it was late, and Remy was ready to get Rain home. Frey and Abbi walked him to the door. "I can't thank you enough for watching Rain." Remy waited by the door as Rain and Amelia said their own goodbyes.

"It's our pleasure. He's really coming out of his shell," Abbi said.

"He's a great kid," Frey added just as Remy's phone pinged with an incoming text.

When he saw it was a message from Gregor with an attachment, he turned the volume down so the kids wouldn't hear it. The video was of Craven. Remy glanced over at Rain.

Frey kissed Abbi on the temple. "Remy and I are going to step outside for a moment."

"I'll keep the kids in here."

Once outside, Remy turned the volume up and replayed the video. Craven's confession was much more detailed than what he'd given Remy back in the forest. He named Nash Hogan as the man responsible for sending his sister's blood as well as the kidnapping of Rain. Remy's heart was torn in two as Craven described exactly what the human had done to Rain and how he'd placed him in the tunnel beneath the church with the expectation Drago would find the boy. Remy already knew this, but the tears still fell, and Frey placed his hands on Remy's shoulders, pulling Remy back against his solid chest. As soon as the video ended, Remy wiped his eyes and let out a harsh breath.

"If you find Nash Hogan, let me know. I'll send someone with you to take the bastard down."

When Frey took a step back, Remy turned to him. "Thank you. It probably won't matter, but I'm sending this video to Isla's father. He needs to know what his son is capable of." Remy opened an email and attached the video, not waiting another second to send it to Felix. If his calculation was correct, it was around three in the afternoon in the eastern portion of Australia, so it wouldn't take long for Felix to see evidence of what Nash had done even if he were in a meeting. Whether or not Felix believed Craven was another matter. Frey put his hand on the doorknob and waited until Remy nodded. He was ready to be home with Rain. Before they made it to the car, Remy's phone rang. When he saw who it was, he closed his eyes. He didn't want to have the conversation with Felix in front of Rain.

"Now's not a good time," Remy said when he answered.

"You send this... this fucking bomb, and it's not a good time? Make the godsdamned time!"

Remy placed the phone on his chest. "Rain, can you go back inside? Papa needs to take this phone call."

"Come on, Rain. I'll get you and Amelia some cookies," Abbi offered from the porch where she, Frey, and Amelia were standing.

"Can I have cookies, Papa?" Rain asked.

"Yes. Now go with Miss Abbi." Remy waited for Rain to disappear back inside before putting the phone to his ear again.

"Rain? Rain's alive? Remy, what the fuck is going on?" Felix asked.

"It's just like the man in the video said. We found Rain in a church tunnel, scared out of his mind. Whatever Nash told you happened is a lie. He told Rain they were going to get ice cream and instead handed him over to the Greek who had been using Isla's blood because she's from an Original bloodline. If you want the rest of the truth, I suggest you ask Nash."

"But I don't understand. The ashes... If Rain's alive, then..." Felix cleared his throat. Remy had never heard the man anything less than put together, but with proof of what his son was capable of, the male was distressed. "I need to go." The line disconnected, and Remy fell to his knees. Had Felix come to the same conclusion Remy had? Since Rain was alive, it was possible Isla was as well. No. He wouldn't allow himself to believe it. He had already mourned her once. To do so again would kill him, and he needed to be strong for his son.

CHAPTER THREE

RAIN WAS WORN out from playing with Amelia. Remy carried his son into the house they were renting and didn't bother waking him for a bath. He pulled down the covers and lay him on the bed. After taking Rain's sneakers off, Remy pulled the covers over the boy and sat down beside him. Staring at the product of his and Isla's love, Remy sucked in a breath, trying to keep the tears at bay. Wouldn't he know if Isla weren't still alive? He always thought with their bond he would have felt her cross over. Remy figured that was what happened when Nash called and said she was dead. What if it was natural grief and not the severing of their bond? The not knowing was killing him all over again. Remy kicked off his shoes and settled against his son's small body, relishing the feel of his heartbeat.

Whimpering woke Remy several hours later. Rain was shaking his head. Remy pulled the boy tighter against his chest. "Shh. Papa's here. You're safe, Rainier. I've got you." Remy continued muttering until Rain settled. The Gargoyle psychiatrist Rain was seeing had informed Remy it would take time for Rain to get over the trauma of being taken, but she assured him with lots of love and patience, it would happen. If there was one thing he could give his son, it was love. There was no one more precious to Remy. Even when Isla had been alive, Remy had loved their child in equal measure. They had planned on having a houseful of kids, but Isla had been taken from him before that could happen. Remy was glad to have Rain. One child was better than none.

He admired Frey and Abbi for adopting Amelia. Abbi was a strong female, taking in the child of her cheating husband. Now they were expecting their first child together, and Remy couldn't be happier for the couple. Children truly did make life better when they were created out of love.

When Remy woke the next morning, he was alone. Low voices came from the living room, and he smiled knowing Rain felt comfortable enough to turn on cartoons while letting his papa sleep. After running through the shower, Remy padded barefoot into the living room. Rain was curled up under a blanket on the sofa, giggling at the silliness of the animated characters.

"*Bonjour, mon fils.*"

"Morning, Papa." Rain raised his head. "Can we have crepes for breakfast?"

"Strawberry or hazelnut?" Remy already knew the answer, but he offered a choice anyway.

"Hazelnut. Duh." Rain giggled when Remy gasped at the boy.

"Duh? Is that anyway to speak to your papa?" It was refreshing every time Rain joked with him, and his laughter was the best sound in the world. "I think Amelia is a bad influence. *Non?*"

"No, Papa. She's funny." Rain's eyes were bright as he spoke of his best friend.

"That she is." Remy winked before heading to the kitchen to make their breakfast. After loading their plates with bacon and crepes, Remy took them into the living room and placed them on the coffee table. They sat on the floor and devoured their food while watching cartoons together.

"Are you going to work today?" Rain asked after drinking the last of his milk.

"I thought we'd spend the day together."

"But what about school?" Rain frowned.

"If you'd rather study than spend the day with me, I'll drive you over to Frey's."

137

His son's eyebrows dipped as he decided. It was cute watching Rain contemplate studying or playing hooky. "Well," Rain drawled, exaggerating the L, "I guess one day won't hurt."

Remy chuckled. "You're a smart boy, and Marigold will catch you up tomorrow, I'm sure. What would you like to do?"

"Do we have any grapes?"

"Grapes? No, but we can get some at the store. Are you still hungry?"

"No, I want to smash them."

"You remember doing that?" The Durands now had machines which did the job on certain types of their wines, but some varieties were still mashed with feet. Rain had joined his parents several times in "smashing."

"Yeah. That was fun." Rain hadn't had a lot of fun in his life lately, but the more time he spent with Amelia and Connor, the better his little life was becoming.

"I don't know of any local wineries, but I'll check around." Remy stood and went to his bedroom for his phone. He'd plugged it up to charge while in the shower. He had a missed call from Henry as well as a voicemail. Remy tapped the screen to listen.

"Remy, this is Henry. I found Nash Hogan. He's been living in Amsterdam for the last year under the name of Nash Visser. With his family's fortune, he was able to create a new identity. I'm sending you his address in an email. Please let me know if I can help further." Remy shook with a mixture of rage and excitement. He was going to make his mate's brother pay for what he did to Rain. But before he did that, he would find out exactly what happened to Isla.

Remembering the reason he had gone to retrieve his phone, Remy calmed himself, then went back downstairs. He sat down on the sofa, his leg resting against Rain's shoulder where he sat on the floor. The boy ached for his father's touch, and Remy never failed to give it to him often, even in simple ways. Rain needed stability, something Remy wasn't capable of giving his son at the moment. Remy was supposed to return to California in a few months, taking Rain away from his new friends. Remy wasn't as close to the Gargoyles out west. None of the ones he hung around with had small children. That didn't mean there weren't any.

Remy's home in California was just as bland and unwelcoming as the one he was currently renting. The houses were nice enough, but Remy had yet to add any personal touches to either. Rain's bedroom had been set up by some of the mates, and it was filled with all types of things a kid could want. All their family photos were packed away. When Remy moved from France, he didn't bother taking the reminders of Isla and Rain out of their boxes. The memories hurt bad enough without staring at their shining smiles day after day. In the months since his rescue, Rain had yet to mention his mum. The psychiatrist said he would when the time was right, and Remy didn't want to push, especially when he didn't have all the answers as to what happened to Isla.

As badly as he wanted to hop a plane to The Netherlands, Remy didn't want to leave Rain again so soon after having gone after Craven. That had only taken one day whereas going to confront Nash would take much longer. Remy could take Rain with him, but only if he had others to go with him and watch over the boy. He could ask Gregor and Tessa, but he didn't want to ask Deacon to fill in for him again. If Tamian's mate wasn't working with Jonas on a project, Remy would love to have the couple accompany him. Tamian was a strong Goyle, and Lucy was a Gryphon. That wasn't common knowledge, but Tamian had confided in Remy on the flight to New Mobile. It was fascinating learning about another type of shifter, especially ones who could transform into both their Lion and Eagle separately. When Tamian described the massive Gryphon he'd fought when he rescued Lucy, Remy was curious to see one for himself.

Rain's giggles brought Remy back to the task at hand. He opened his phone and searched for local wineries. He found several in Georgia, and only one of those offered grape stomping. He sent an email requesting a private party where he could take Rain and possibly Amelia and Connor to enjoy a day out. He then sent a text to Frey and Dante telling them what he had in mind, stating it could be considered a field trip.

The event planner returned his call almost immediately. When she explained they didn't offer grape stomping on such a small scale because of cost, Remy told the planner about his family-owned vineyards in France, so he was aware of what went into putting the day together. He offered to pay full price with twenty percent added on top of that if she would accommodate their small group. There were other activities which wouldn't cost near what Remy was willing to pay, but this was part of Rain's past. What good was having money if he couldn't use it to give Rain a happy memory?

While he was on hold, Dante returned his text stating he, Isabelle, and Connor would love to accompany them and to add Gregor and Tessa to the list. Frey also texted, saying Abbi, Amelia, and Marigold were eager to take the trip too. Frey would send Lorenzo in his place to watch over his family since Frey needed to stay in New Atlanta. When the planner came back on the line, Remy told her the final count would be eleven, and she had gotten approval from the owners to set up their outing. They set the date for the following Saturday, and Remy paid her in advance. When he disconnected, Remy sent a text to Frey and Dante with the date and time of their outing.

Rain turned around and scooted onto his knees, propping his bony elbows on Remy's thighs. "We get to smash grapes?"

"Yes, but we can't go until next Saturday. Now, we have a whole day to do something else. Would you like to go see a movie? Or we could go to the Aquarium."

"I've never been to an aquarium. Do they have lots of fish?" Rain's accent was a combination of French and Australian. The more he was around Amelia, the less they came through.

"Thousands. They even have sharks."

Rain's eyes were huge. "Sharks? We have to go, Papa!"

Remy laughed and ran his hand over Rain's hair. "You go brush your teeth and change out of your pajamas. I'll clean up our dishes quickly, and then we'll be on our way."

Rain pushed off the floor using Remy's legs as leverage and climbed onto his papa's lap. Rain squished Remy's cheeks together, making him look like a fish. It was a move Amelia did often to Frey, and the large Gargoyle lit up every single time. "You're the best daddy ever." Rain smacked a kiss on Remy's fish lips, then hopped down and took off up the stairs. Okay, maybe Amelia wasn't such a bad influence after all.

After their day at the aquarium, Remy and Rain returned to their normal days. Remy stayed away from Craven because the urge to kill the human was too strong. As he made his rounds, he observed Isabelle interact with Gabriel. From what Remy was told, the male had changed since being captured. Isabelle spent time with her brother, helping him remember who he had been before being kidnapped and used for his shifter blood. He was no longer Vincent Alexander, cold-blooded killer. Gabriel was aware of the bad things he'd done for the man who created the Unholy, and he quietly spent his days in the Pen as atonement. If Isabelle had her way, Gabriel would not be locked up, but more than once, Remy overheard their conversations. Gabriel stated he wouldn't leave before he'd done his time, even if his sister were to somehow convince Gregor to let him out.

141

Isabelle and Dante continued to administer the antiserum to the Unholy, and so far, the treatment was working. Tessa hadn't been lying when she told Craven he was no longer needed. Isabelle had Jonas Montague as a father, and the man was a genius. Isabelle had inherited her father's smarts and was able to formulate her own antiserum. Tessa had inherited the male's penchant for mischievousness, and Remy was always delighted when she spent her days at the Pen with Gregor. The redhead was feisty and funny, and she reminded Remy of Isla.

When she caught Remy deep in thought the Friday before their trip to the winery, Tessa asked him if he was okay.

"I'm good. Just thinking about going after Isla's brother."

"So you know where he is?"

"Yes. Henry found him in The Netherlands. He's been working under an alias."

Tessa clapped her hands together. "Then what are we waiting for? Let's go get the bastard."

"What kind of trouble are you getting into now, Red?" Gregor asked as he entered the office.

"The best kind – taking out the trash." Gregor arched a brow, and she continued. "Remy found his dickhead brother-in-law."

Gregor growled low in his throat. "What are you waiting for?" Gregor's tone matched his mate's.

"I'm supposed to be learning how to run the Pen, not traipsing across the world for revenge."

"It's a good thing I'm in charge of that project, isn't it?" Gregor pulled Tessa's back against his chest and looked at Remy over her shoulder. "Other than worrying about that, is there anything else holding you back?"

"Logistics. I hate leaving Rain again, but I can't take him with me and go after Nash. I won't put him through seeing the man who sold him to Drago."

Tessa huffed and slashed her hand in the air as though Remy were being obtuse. "I can go with you and watch Rain while you go after Nash. I've been a lot of places but never The Netherlands." Tessa turned her head and looked up at Gregor. "What do you say, Stone? Fancy a trip to tulip land? If you can't go with us, I can ask Tamian. Lucy's going to be busy with Jonas a while, and I know he's always up for garbage disposal."

"I'll go. Deacon already offered to step in when and if Remy found Nash."

"Then that's settled. I'll ask Tamian for his jet. Remy, just let me know when you want to go." Tessa had a fire in her eyes Remy admired. She and Gregor were proving to be not only good Clan mates but good friends as well. He was lucky to know them.

"Find out when it's best for Deacon. I hate taking him away from Sabrina."

"Will do, Brother."

Remy left the couple in the office while he made his rounds. He thought about calling Felix with his plan to go after Nash, but he didn't want the male to tip his son off. Remy had no idea whether or not Felix was aware of where Nash was or that the male was using an alias. There was little Remy wouldn't do for his own son, but kidnapping and possibly murder were two things he would have a hard time being okay with. He didn't see his sweet child ever getting to a point in his life where he was that evil. Remy didn't know Nash well. He only knew what Isla had told him about her brother, and none of it was good. According to her, he had always been spoiled and felt entitled. How the two siblings turned out so differently having been raised by the same parents was a mystery.

Saturday's weather was perfect for their trip to the winery. The autumn air was crisp, and Halloween decorations were springing up everywhere he looked. Abbi and Frey were planning a party for the kids after taking them around to the Clan houses to trick-or-treat.

Rain chatted animatedly to his two little friends about stomping grapes. Connor, who was usually quiet and stoic like his father, was excited at the prospect of getting dirty. Amelia was dressed in her ever-present tutu, only this one was purple so it matched the color of the juice. Remy kept one eye on the road and the other on the kids in the back of the SUV. Lorenzo sat next to him in the passenger seat. He was used to the kids' conversations, having watched over them often, and he still laughed at Amelia's antics.

"You're lucky, Brother," Lor whispered at one point. "I can't imagine what you went through when you thought you lost him and your mate, but you've been given a second chance. For that, I thank the gods."

Lorenzo was an honorable male, helping the Clan wherever he could. He was one of the Goyles who had yet to meet his mate. "Don't give up hope. There's still plenty of time for you to find your own mate."

"Hope is all I have. In the meantime, I will watch over the young ones as best I can. I am looking forward to the next generation taking over. Times are changing, and I want to assure our future leaders have the best possible chance at leading our Clan. If I cannot have my own children, I will gladly be a guardian for all the others."

"Are we there yet?" the three children asked in unison, giggling when they did. Lorenzo grinned, and Remy rolled his eyes, but he was thrilled Rain had two friends to bring out the kid in him.

North Georgia was worlds away from New Atlanta. Sure they had suburbs, and the area where most of the Gargoyles lived was somewhat rural with lots of acreage, but the farther away they got, the more scenic the landscape became. Autumn in the south was different than in California, and Remy found himself feeling a bit homesick for his French vineyard home. When he lost his little family of two, Remy couldn't remain, so he traveled to the States, hoping to function without memories beating him down every moment of every day. He had Rain back, but Remy didn't think he could return to their home without Isla.

He was doing his best to be everything Rain needed, and most days he felt he succeeded. There were some days, though, his doubts crept in. He would never have another mate. Never love another female, but didn't Rain deserve to have a mother figure guiding him as well? No! No. Remy would have to be enough. He couldn't even think about bringing someone else into Rain's life. Into his own life. He would have to be enough.

Everything about their outing was perfect. The weather. The location. The owner of the vineyard had introduced himself, and when Rain mentioned their vineyard in France, the human had taken time to speak with Remy about grapes and processes and bouquets and all the other things that went into a great bottle of wine. It was easy to get lost in the business aspect of having a vineyard. When the owner's wife joined him, Remy excused himself to join the others in the reason they'd taken the trip. He rolled up his pants and stood barefoot alongside Rain. His son wasn't much taller than the last time they'd shared a vat of plump, purple fruit. Rain had been held inside during his captivity, not getting the needed daily allotment of fresh air and sunshine. Remy tried not to dwell on the trauma his son had endured. Instead, he made the most of their time together.

After cleaning up, the adults sat around the table to enjoy the included lunch and wine tasting, while the kids alternated taking bites of food and playing in the cool sunshine. Amelia was always a ball of energy, and her constant need to move was enticing to Rain and Connor. All three children had been through more in their short lives than most adults, but with the Clan's love, they were thriving. The females in New Atlanta had taken Rain into the fold, especially Abbi. Maybe it was because she, too, had endured being held captive. Remy had heard Abbi's story.

145

The mates never hesitated to share what they had gone through. They each had come out the other side better for finding their intended Gargoyle. Remy only wished Isla had her own happy ending.

Tessa, who was talking about one of her cousins, stopped mid-sentence just as Amelia yelled, "Izzy!"

Isabelle and Dante rushed to where Connor was standing frozen. Remy had never experienced one of the young boy's visions. Amelia became another child altogether as she ran to her mom and sat quietly, watching her cousin. Abbi pulled Amelia onto her lap as they both waited. Rain hadn't moved from Connor's side. He stood silently as Dante and Isabelle knelt beside their son. When Connor came out of his trance, he placed his forehead against Dante's. The two spoke silently for several long seconds, then like nothing happened, Connor returned to his former animated self.

Isabelle led both boys to the table and encouraged them to eat. "It's getting late. Please finish your lunch." Connor did as he was told, and Rain walked over to where Remy was sitting. Mimicking Amelia, Rain climbed onto Remy's lap. He was quiet as he ate, and Remy wasn't sure whether or not to be worried. As far as he knew, Rain had never witnessed Connor's visions either. If he had, he hadn't mentioned it to Remy.

"This was an excellent idea, Remy. Thank you for inviting us," Dante said. The normally laid-back male had joined in the festivities, even laughing along with his son.

"Thanks for joining us. We'll have to do it again soon."

"Like now?" Amelia asked, her cheeks full of cold pasta.

"No, silly girl." Abbi handed Amelia a napkin. "We have to make an appointment so they can gather more grapes. We have already stomped all they had today."

"But there's all them grapes out there." Amelia pointed to the rows of vines.

"True, but those aren't ready. Unless you want to pick enough for everyone? It would take a few days, but I think you could do it."

"Days? I don't have days, Mommy. I have dance class and school. And I'd miss Daddy."

When Remy caught Connor staring at him, he tuned out Amelia's chatter. The boy had always been polite whenever Remy was around, but the way he was focused on Remy was unnerving. Dante clasped Remy's shoulder and whispered, "Later." It wasn't loud enough for the kids to hear, but all those with shifter hearing caught it.

On the drive home, the kids were less chatty. Even Amelia nodded off slumped against Connor. Remy had figured the boy would ride back with his parents, but he climbed into Remy's SUV with the other kids. Dante and Isabelle didn't look concerned, so Remy tried not to worry either.

CHAPTER FOUR

REMY PARKED IN Dante's driveway, eager to learn what had spooked Connor. The boy climbed out of the back row and wordlessly made his way inside. Isabelle walked with her son, while Dante remained outside. Tessa followed her cousin, but Gregor stood next to his brother. Lorenzo strode off to check the perimeter even though all Clan homes were being monitored by Henry back in the lab.

"As you've probably deduced, Connor had a vision. Usually when that happens, he has his art supplies handy and can draw a picture of what he saw. Since he didn't, he shared it with me. Connor saw a woman with a young girl. He has gone upstairs to put his vision to paper. Until you see it, I am not going to speculate as to who the females are."

"I need to get to Rain. If Connor shows him the drawing, I don't want Rain to get upset if it happens to be his mother."

"Isabelle won't let that happen. Abbi and Marigold are keeping Amelia and Rain occupied. But let's say the female is Isla. You should head to Amsterdam immediately."

Remy dipped his chin and stared at his feet, trying to get his breathing under control. His beast wasn't offering assistance. It was too focused on their mate being out in the world somewhere waiting on them.

Gregor stepped closer and clasped his hand on Remy's neck, squeezing gently. "Tamian has his jet on standby, and Tessa and I are packed and ready to go whenever you say the word."

The front door opened, and Remy raised his head. Isabelle held a piece of paper, and Remy sucked in a breath. He wanted to look at what Connor had drawn, but he didn't. Isabelle's face was impassive. Whatever Connor had drawn didn't mean anything to the female considering she had never met Isla. Then again, neither had Connor. But somehow, the child was able to see future events. He could envision those he'd never met, the same way he had connected with Dante in the beginning. Isabelle stopped in front of Remy and held the page out to him.

"Fuck." It was a perfect depiction of Isla and a little girl walking hand-in-hand between rows of grapes. Remy's knees threatened to buckle. "This—" Remy cleared his throat, which was thick with excitement and regret. "This is our vineyard back in France. One of Isla and Rain's favorite things to do together was take a walk if I had business to attend."

"This is from the past?" Dante asked.

Remy had only glanced at the drawing. Inhaling deeply, he took a longer look. Studying his mate, Remy noticed subtle differences in her appearance. Isla was thinner, and her hair was a bit shorter.

"No. It's…" Remy's hand shook, and Dante grabbed hold, steadying him. "Isla's hair was longer, and she wasn't this thin. And I don't recognize the girl. I… I can't…" Remy closed his eyes against the tears threatening to fall. "I can't let myself believe she could be alive." His voice was barely more than a whisper. "I can't lose her twice."

Dante took the paper and handed it back to Isabelle. "Brother, you have no reason to believe me. To believe in Connor's abilities, but he has never had a vision that wasn't accurate."

"What if this is the first time? What if he's seeing something from the past? No, Isla doesn't look like she did, but Connor's never met her. What if he has her characteristics wrong because of that? I can't let myself

149

believe she's out there, because if she is? Then I failed her like I failed my son. I'm the one who didn't want to go visit her family. I'm the one who sent them to Australia without me to watch over them."

Dante placed both hands on Remy's shoulders. "Don't do that, Brother. You had no reason to believe her own brother would betray her. Isla took Rain thinking they'd be safe. You don't blame her, do you?"

"No! No, of course not."

"Then don't blame yourself. You both were under the impression Nash Hogan was a somewhat honorable male. This is on him. No one else. Now, instead of standing here wondering, get your ass on that jet and go find out the truth."

Tessa, who had been waiting on the porch, strode down the steps. "I can ask Tamian and Lucy to go with us. Both have the ability to get the truth out of others."

Remy shook his head. "No. Lucy's work is important." Tamian's mate was working with Jonas on a serum that would allow human mates of the Gryphons to live longer lives. Their species didn't have fated mates the way Gargoyles did.

"Do you still want to take Rain with us?" Gregor asked.

Remy scrubbed his hands down his face. "I don't want to be away from him, but what if..." He swallowed hard. "What if we do find out Isla is alive? There's no telling what the bastard did to her or with her. I mean, he sold Rain, for fuck's sake. What if he sold Isla to someone?" Remy turned to Dante. "What would you do if you were me?"

"I'd leave him here. Your son loves spending time with Amelia and Connor. He is thriving with Marigold." Dante fisted his heart. "I vow on all that's holy he will be safe with us."

Remy nodded once. "Okay. I won't take him. We don't know what we're going to find or how much trouble Nash is going to cause. He'll be better here." He turned to Gregor

150

and Tessa. "Since Rain isn't going, you don't need to come with me."

Lorenzo had returned from checking the area. "I'll go with you. You don't know who Nash has with him."

"Thank you, Brother. I'd be honored to have you at my side."

Remy went inside and had a chat with Rain, explaining he had another trip to take. He didn't tell his son where he was going or who he was confronting. Rain's experience with Nash had been traumatic, and Remy didn't feel the boy needed to think any more about his uncle than he already did.

Remy left Rain knowing he would be as safe as could be with Dante and Frey watching out for him. Gregor and Tessa had offered to go as well, but Remy declined. He didn't want to put Deacon out any more than he already had. Lorenzo picked Remy up on his way to the airport. When they arrived, Tamian was waiting with Santiago.

"Tamian?"

"I'm going with you. Tessa called and told me what was going on."

"But what about Lucy?"

"My mate is holed up in Jonas's basement laboratory. If there's any trouble, she's more than capable of handling it. She is a Gryphon, and she's a badass." Tamian's smile while speaking of his mate was brilliant.

"Okay then. I appreciate your assistance."

Lorenzo joined Santiago inside the cockpit, and Remy and Tamian took their seats across from one another. "Why was Santiago practically vibrating?" Remy asked. The pilot had seemed almost giddy.

"Because of a female. I have a chalet in Mont Blanc, and a pretty female named Mirabella oversees it when I'm not there. We can use it as our home base since it's only an hour's flight from Amsterdam."

"Are they mates?" Remy couldn't imagine not living where his mate did, only visiting every so often.

"Not in the true sense of the word, but neither of them has found their fated mates, so they enjoy each other's company whenever possible."

"What happens if either of them do find their intended?"

Tamian spread his hands. "Then they part ways as friends. Mirabella never leaves the area, so her odds of finding her true mate are slim. Santiago travels with me, but he is content in his life. At least he says he is."

Santiago called out from the cockpit that they were ready to take off. He didn't bother with the intercom since everyone on the flight was a Gargoyle. They were taxiing down the runway when he called out once more. "For the record, I am content. Mirabella is a fine female."

Tamian grinned, shaking his head. Remy asked about the chalet, and Tamian recounted how his father, Xavier, had it built for Elizabeth. Xavier was the Italian King, and Tamian was going to take over the throne soon. He and Lucy were using New York as their home base since her family was there. Tamian's parents also lived in the state, so it made sense.

"I have two of my Italian Clan on standby should we run into more trouble than the four of us can handle. I don't think we'll need them, but they are already waiting for us in Amsterdam. I gave them the address Henry found on Nash, and they're doing nothing but watching the house from a distance. Making sure the male doesn't leave the city. If he does, they'll follow but not engage."

Remy was surprised Tamian had already put males in motion. This wasn't his fight, but he was once again in charge in ways Remy hadn't thought about. Then again, Remy wasn't a leader. He had been a businessman for hundreds of years, and he learned the family business from his parents. He could tackle spreadsheets and budgets, but leading men into battle? No, that wasn't Remy. "You'll make an excellent King, especially having a mate like Lucy. Does your Italian Clan know she's a Gryphon?"

"No. Gryphons have kept the secret of their species for the same reasons Gargoyles have. A long time ago, a Gryphon found out about Gargoyles without admitting the truth of himself. He passed the knowledge to his son who in turn passed it on to his son, but they didn't spread the truth of our existence to anyone outside their family. Knowing there are two types of shifters leads me to believe there are more out there. Who knows?"

They had been in the air a couple hours when the jet rocked with what felt stronger than turbulence. Remy grabbed the edge of the leather sofa he was seated on, and Tamian gripped the arm rests of his captain's chair.

"Santiago?"

"Shit, this isn't another sabotage is it?" If the plane went down, the four of them would live, but landing would probably hurt like a mother.

After a few more seconds, the plane settled down. "It was turbulence. I've only felt it that strongly a couple times before."

"You're sure?" Tamian asked.

"Yes, Brother. I wouldn't lie to you. All systems are at one hundred percent."

Remy released his breath as Tamian closed his eyes. Henry spent most of his time tracking the mysterious hacker who'd helped Drago. Being able to take a jet out of the sky took scary levels of skill.

The rest of the flight was uneventful. It was ten in the morning local time when they landed. Once Santiago had the jet secure in a private hangar, they drove an hour north and met with one of Tamian's Italian Clan mates. Tamian introduced Leonardo, then the male gave his report. "Nash is currently at his office. He usually stays there until five on the dot, then drives straight home. He has no guards, and he lives alone other than a housekeeper, cook, and butler. The property is a small farm, and there is a working drawbridge leading to it. So far, we haven't seen the bridge up. The house is quite old, but the security system is new. The only time the alarm is set is when Nash turns in for the night. His employees live in a smaller house on the property, but they leave before he sets the alarm and aren't allowed in the house until he is already up and getting ready. If anyone else knows the code, we aren't aware of them. There are also security cameras located around the farm. They are located in such ways that all points of entry are covered, even the roof."

"How much time between when the employees leave and he goes to bed?"

"Anywhere from two to four hours."

"Thank you, Leo." Tamian scratched his chin. "We need to hit the house right after his employees have left. That will give us all night to get the information we need from the male. Leo, do you know if the employees are human?"

"They appear to be, yes. I didn't feel any shifter vibes from them."

"What about the cameras? He'll see us coming," Lorenzo asked.

"He will see two of us coming. We will split up. Two will approach from the front and two from the back. If he refuses to allow us inside, we'll force our way in. That leaves the other two as backup."

"Wouldn't it be easier to go inside and wait until he gets home?" Remy asked.

"Yes, but I don't want the humans involved. If they're like our family employees, they're aware of Gargoyles, but on the off-chance they aren't? They don't need to get a crash course in all things shifters, nor do they need to see their boss being tortured if it comes to—"

Leonardo's phone rang. "Pierre?"

154

"Hogan's on the move, and it looks like he's in a hurry. He rushed out of his office without his briefcase. I'm following to make sure he isn't headed to the airport."

"Keep us posted." Leo disconnected. "Something spooked him. Is it possible he knows you all are here?"

"With the amount of money he has at his disposal, anything is possible." Tamian rubbed the back of his neck. "Leo, you head to his house. See if there's anything off with his employees like they're scrambling to pack his things." Leonardo fisted his heart, bowed his head, then took off in his rental. Tamian pulled out his phone, tapped the screen a few times, then held it out in front of him.

"Tamian, how was your flight?" Henry asked.

"We hit a rough patch of turbulence, but otherwise it was uneventful. One of my men called. Hogan rushed out of his office like his ass was on fire."

"Where do—" An alarm cut off Henry's words. It wasn't loud, but it did its job. Remy stared at the phone as Henry cursed everything under the sun. "When I find this hacker bastard, I'm going to cut his balls off. I would venture to guess Nash is running because he's been tipped off. I'm sorry, Tamian. I wiped the system after I found Hogan, but whoever it is out there fucking with our Clan must have gotten through before it was wiped."

"Don't apologize. We have eyes on him. We just need to alter our plans. Go do what you need to."

Henry disconnected while cursing some more. Remy ran his hands through his hair. He was too close to catching Nash. He couldn't lose this opportunity to confront the male. "What now?"

Tamian's phone rang, and Remy prayed it was good news. "Pierre?"

"Hogan is headed south on the A9. That doesn't lead to his home or the airport. It looks like he's running."

"Stay on him, but don't let him see you. We're headed your direction. Keep me posted of every turn he makes. I'll let you know when we've caught up."

"Will do."

Tamian twirled a finger in the air. "Let's go." Back in their rented SUV, Lorenzo waited for Tamian to pull up the navigation system in the vehicle. Once they knew which direction to head, Lorenzo sped off, and Tamian made a call to Leo. "Pierre called. Hogan's headed south. Stay at the house once you get there and watch the employees. If they leave, get inside, and see if you can find anything. You'll probably trip several alarms, so make it quick. I don't want the police showing up while you're there."

Lorenzo deftly navigated the foreign roads without going too far over the speed limit. Texts from Pierre came in plenty of time for Lor to take the exits following the other two vehicles. The farther south they drove, the closer they got to France. Remy's house was twelve hours away by car. When Tamian mentioned using his chalet as a base, Remy hadn't mentioned his home. When he left for the States, he never planned on returning to the estate. His family oversaw Remy's vineyard. It had been too profitable to let sit dormant. He wasn't sure if he could visit it now even though Rain had been returned to him. Remy didn't think he was strong enough to handle walking the grounds without Isla by his side. Mont Blanc was nearly the same distance from their current location, so Remy didn't feel bad about not mentioning his home.

For the next few hours, they followed Nash south. Pierre had to stop off for fuel, so Lorenzo took the lead position. Then it was their turn to stop off. Having Gargoyle sight allowed them to hang back far enough Nash wouldn't realize he was being followed. After driving through Belgium, Nash finally pulled off the interstate for fuel. While Nash was paying, Lorenzo walked up and started a conversation with him, and Remy slipped into the backseat.

Sneaking out of his vehicle and into another with a sword was tricky, but he managed. They had decided to confront Nash and direct him to Tamian's chalet, since they had no idea where the male was headed.

Nash climbed back in after filling up his tank, and Tamian slid into the passenger seat at the same time. "What the... Who the fuck are you?"

"Who I am is no concern of yours. All you need to know is you're done hiding."

"You have no idea who I am." Nash's voice was low. Remy figured the other Goyle's beast was close to the surface. His own was ready to come out and meet Nash's head on.

"You're Nash Hogan, and you're going to do exactly as I say." Tamian extended his claws, and Nash's eyes widened.

"If you know who I am, then you also know I have my own claws."

"Yes, but I don't have a sword coated with wolfsbane pointed at me." Remy sat up and placed the tip of his weapon against Nash's neck. "Now, here's what's going to happen. You're going to drive. And if you attempt to do anything stupid, Remy will cut you. The wolfsbane will paralyze you. Yes, we may wreck, but seeing as we're all Gargoyles, we'll live. Also, there are two other vehicles full of Goyles following. You are outnumbered."

"What do you want?" Nash looked at Remy through the rearview mirror.

"I want you to drive. We're going to take a little trip, and if you are honest between here and our destination, I may let you live. Go ahead. Pull back onto the road and head west."

Tamian had tapped the address into the navigation system, and the electronic voice told him to turn left. Nash did as told, but he was cursing under his breath.

Once they were on the interstate, Tamian called Pierre and told him to head their direction. Then he began the interrogation. He had convinced Remy to let him do the talking, and Remy agreed. All Remy had to do was control his anger and keep the sword on the male's neck.

Tamian was still turned facing Nash when he began asking questions. "What did you do with Isla?"

"She died in a car crash. My parents scattered her ashes."

"Try again, and this time with the truth."

Remy tightened his grip on the hilt and pressed the tip harder into Nash's neck.

"That is the truth."

"Just like Rain was with her in the crash? We all know you sold your nephew to Drago Costas. You also sold him your sister's blood. What did you do with Isla?" Tamian's voice deepened yet came out barely above a whisper.

"I-I didn't do anything with her. I kept her hidden so some doctor could extract her blood, then she uh, she just disappeared." The car drifted closer to the shoulder of the roadway, but Nash corrected it, bringing it back between the lines.

"Let's assume you're telling the truth, which you are not. Why would you do that? Why would you offer your own sister up for experimentation, then sell your nephew for science? It's not like you needed the money."

"I believed in the cause. The doctors were using her blood to develop an antiserum to be used on the Unholy."

"Then why didn't you offer your own blood if you believed it was such a good cause? Why did it have to be Isla's? Your sister had a family. A good life with Remy and Rain. How could you in good conscience sell a small child as a science experiment?"

Remy called on his beast for patience. For calm. He was ready to take Nash's head.

"Isla mated outside the Original line. Rain wasn't ever going to be allowed to grow up and become part of the business."

"This shit again?" Tamian shook his head. "The fates decide who our mates are. Who are we to say they're wrong?"

"Those of us who believe the old ways. It's why I'm still unmated. The female the fates chose for me was impure like Remy. Until I find a female from an Original line, I will remain single."

"You denied your true mate? How is that even possible?" Remy asked.

"Because I'm strong. I know the value of keeping the bloodlines pure. My mother was not my father's true mate either, but he didn't let that stop him from doing the right thing for the Hogan bloodline. "

"Is your father aware of what you did with Isla and Rain?"

"No. At least he wasn't until you called him and he heard Rain's voice. Father had demanded I get rid of them. It's why I faked their deaths and sent him ashes I stole."

CHAPTER FIVE

ISLA PLACED BOTH hands on her stomach, praying she wasn't pregnant. She had long ago run out of tears. Losing Rain, being separated from Remy, not knowing what each day would bring, had all taken its toll on her mind and body. The first few months after finding out Rain had been killed were a blur. Isla had passed out at her brother's words, then she'd woken up to find herself strapped to a chair while a man named Craven withdrew her blood. More than once, Isla wished she were back in that dank room. Other than being bound so she couldn't lash out, the doctor had treated her well. Fed her. Gave her books to read. Allowed her outside as much as she wanted. The bonds were even left off when she agreed to having her daily needle sessions. Why fight the inevitable if it offered her a few luxuries?

She had just gotten used to her new normal until one day, Craven decided he was done with her. The doctor told her he was taking her to meet up with Remy. He lied. The couple he left her with were Gargoyles who bought her. Isla knew this because of her shifter hearing. After learning the high price Elias and Anna Weber paid all because they wanted a child with Original blood, she endured a different type of captivity. She was shoved into an attic set up like a mini apartment. It would have been nice except for the reinforced bars on the windows and the metal cuff on her wrist. Isla wasn't allowed out of the attic often, and she was never able to leave the house. If she tried, the band on her arm shocked her until she was rendered unconscious. She knew this from experience.

The past few months had been almost as bad as when she found out her son was no longer of this earth. The only good thing about her ordeal with the Webers was the fact that she wasn't being raped by Elias. A doctor was attempting to artificially inseminate her. With as many years as it took for her to get pregnant with Rain, Isla doubted these attempts would happen quickly. At least she prayed they didn't. She didn't want another male's child. She wanted her child back. Wanted her life back. And once they got what they wanted? What then?

"YOUR FATHER WANTED Isla dead?" Remy didn't believe it. The electronic voice of the navigational system interrupted their conversation, directing Nash to take the next exit onto a different interstate. When Nash didn't put on his indicator, Remy pressed the sword against his throat. "Take the exit," Remy demanded. Nash glanced briefly into the mirror, but he wasn't looking at Nash. Remy didn't turn to look behind them. He already knew Lorenzo and Pierre were there. Nash flipped on the turn signal and hit the exit.

"Instead of having your sister and nephew killed, you thought they'd be better off used as lab experiments?" Tamian asked once they were rolling down the next section of interstate.

"Craven assured me they would only be used for their blood."

Tamian narrowed his eyes at Nash. "None of that matters now. Where were you rushing off to in such a hurry?"

"I wasn't—" Remy pushed the blade he'd allowed to go lax, and Nash swallowed hard. "My father called. Said he had proof Rain was alive. He demanded I come home."

"So you were driving to Australia via Europe?" Tamian laughed. "Here's what I think. Isla was the oldest and next in line to run the family business. Sure, she left home to build a life with Remy, but she was still in your way. With her alive, she would inherit half of everything should your father cross over. If something happened to her, that half would go to her son. With them both out of the picture, you set yourself up to be the sole heir. "How am I doing so far?"

"No. That's not—"

"Now, your father knows you lied about Rain, so it makes sense you lied about your sister as well. A male like Felix Hogan who's made his mark on the world with no help from anyone surely knows how to dole out punishment to his wayward son."

"He said if I didn't bring Isla to him, he would not only remove me from the family, but he'd personally take my head. I tried to do the right thing. I thought Craven would let Isla and Rain both go once he had enough blood to create his antiserum." Nash licked his lips. "I honestly thought they'd find their way back to Remy. Gods, I was wrong."

"Nash, what happened to Isla?" Remy was vibrating with anger. His beast was ready to tear the male's limbs from his body and send them to Felix wrapped in a bow.

Nash hesitated. He eyed Remy in the rearview mirror as his hands tightened on the steering wheel. The sound of leather creaking was as loud as Nash's deep breaths. "After Craven was through with Isla, he sold her to a German couple."

"You motherfucker!" Remy sliced through Nash's neck. It wasn't enough to take the male's head, but the coating on the blade would slow his reflexes. "Fuck! Pull over. Pull the fuck over!"

"N-no. You'll kill me. I c-can take you to Isla. I know where she is."

Tamian pointed a sharp claw. "Pull the godsdamned car over before you can't. He wasn't kidding about the blade being treated. You're going to feel the effects in a matter of minutes."

Nash pulled over to the shoulder and sat, unmoving. Tamian got out of the passenger side and walked around the car. When there was a break in traffic, he opened the door and pushed the other male, urging him to crawl over the console. "Move your ass," Tamian commanded. Once they were seated, Tamian pulled out his phone. "Aldredge, it's Tamian. I need a favor. Go ask Craven who he sold Isla Durand to. Yes, sold her. Yep." Tamian glared at Nash who was staring back, his mouth hanging open.

"You have Craven?"

Tamian scowled. "Yes."

"Hang up. Fuck. Hang the phone up. Craven didn't sell Isla." Nash slumped against the door, his head lilting to the side. "I did."

Remy's fangs and claws came out. If he weren't in a confined space, his wings would have been spread behind him. He reached between the seats to grab Nash, but Tamian caught his wrist.

"Remy! If he sold her, he knows where she is." Tamian waited until Remy retracted his claws to release him. "Where is she?" Tamian's voice was low, and Remy felt the power behind it. He held his breath, waiting on Nash to answer.

"She's in Germany. Just across the border."

"You're going to need to be a little more specific." Tamian punched in the address Nash rattled off, then called the males in the two vehicles waiting behind them. Once they had the information, Tamian pulled back onto the roadway. The city where the German couple lived was in the opposite direction from where they had been traveling.

"You said Felix demanded you bring Isla to him, yet you were driving away from Germany. Why?" Remy no longer had the sword pointed at Nash. It wasn't necessary. He held a syringe filled with a stronger dose of wolfsbane Tamian had given him earlier.

"I'm not going to let our Father kill her. Despite what you think, I love my sister. I didn't agree with her mating with you, but that isn't a death sentence. Not in my book."

"But selling her into slavery is a better alternative?"

"It wasn't like that." Nash's words were slurring. The wolfsbane was taking effect. "They wanted a... child with... Original blood, and Isla—" Remy shoved the needle into Nash's neck.

"What the fuck?" Nash tried to raise his arm, but his muscles were no longer cooperating.

"And Isla what? You pimped my mate out like some brood mare?" Remy slapped Nash's head, but the poison had done its job. Too well. "Oh, gods. The child. That's who was in the picture Connor drew."

"Maybe or maybe not. The drawing depicted Isla and a girl at your vineyard. You said Isla's appearance was different, so there's a possibility that is your child with your mate in the future. The good news is there *is* a future with Isla in it. We're going to get your mate back."

"But what if it isn't my child? Nash said this couple wanted a baby."

"If that's the case, she somehow ends up with Isla, at least for visits. Will you be able to handle that?"

"What? Yes. I..." Remy didn't want to think about his mate being with another male. What if she'd been raped? He didn't know who this couple was, but they must be Gargoyles to know about Originals. Gods, what had his Isla endured these past two years? "I just want my mate back. I want her safe in my arms, and I want her to be reunited with Rainier. If these Goyles bought her for the purpose of carrying their child, they're not going to let the child go with her."

"And you'll deal with that together. The main thing is to get her back home where she belongs. Help her heal from whatever she's endured the same way you're helping your son."

Remy's mind was a tornado. It swirled between horrid thoughts of the worst his mate could have endured and the thrill of seeing her again. Knowing she was alive. Anticipating reuniting her with Rain. Those were the things he tried to focus on. Tamian was right – whatever she'd been through, Remy would help her recover no matter what it took. Then he was going to deal with her father.

When they were half an hour away from their destination, Tamian pulled off the highway. Remy didn't question the male until he parked behind a large church. "Why are we here?"

"To transfer Nash to one of the other vehicles. When we get Isla away from the couple, she doesn't need to see her brother slumped over and paralyzed."

"Or maybe she does. If she knows he's responsible for selling her, she might want to take his head herself."

"Maybe we wait and see about her mental stability? You showing up is going to be emotional enough, don't you think?"

"Yes, you're right." Remy got out and helped Tamian move Nash to the back of Lorenzo's SUV.

Lorenzo closed the hatch once they had the male situated and covered. "I had Henry look up the couple while we were driving. Elias and Anna Weber are the current owners of the address Nash gave you. According to the satellite image, the property is considered a farm, and it's on approximately seven acres. There are other houses around but not so close we should have trouble. How do you want to handle this?"

"Remy and I will use the driveway. If someone happens to stop us before we make it to the house, I'll say we're tourists and got turned around. If we don't meet with resistance, we'll take the front door. Leo, I want you to stay with Nash. The wolfsbane should keep him paralyzed for a while, but I don't want to take any chances of him coming around and causing trouble. Lor, you, Pierre, and Santiago will surround the house in case they try to leave either out the back or through a window. With Elias being Gargoyle, he could take to the sky in an attempt to escape. You will park on the road and come in from the sides and back. Remy and I will leave our swords in the car, but the three of you should be armed just in case. Be ready to rush to our aid if you hear me call for you. I doubt Weber will give us any trouble since he shouldn't be expecting us."

With a plan in place, they drove the rest of the way. The closer they got, the antsier Remy and his beast became. His Gargoyle wanted to be turned loose, but Remy kept it right at the surface. Once the others were in place, Tamian was able to drive up to the house without anyone coming to see who the strange vehicle belonged to. It was eerily quiet as they made their way to the front door. No voices were talking inside the house. Remy reached out with his senses searching for his mate. It didn't take long for her heartbeat to reach his ears. There were two other beings inside, but they weren't his Isla. He'd slept next to her enough times to know how her blood pulsed through her body. Remy fisted his hands to keep his claws from extending. Tamian rang the doorbell. It took almost a minute before footsteps sounded from inside. By the heaviness, Remy could tell it was a male. Since there were only three people in the house, he was ready for Elias to open the door.

"Can I help you?" The male who opened the door, wearing silk pajamas and house slippers, appeared to be in his late thirties, but his countenance was much older.

166

Remy pushed his way inside. "Where is she? Isla!" A strong hand gripped Remy's shoulder, but Remy jerked out of the male's hold. "Where is my mate?"

"I think you must have the wrong house. There's no one here but my wife and me."

"I know you're lying. I can feel her heartbeat. Isla!"

Elias's eyes flickered toward the stairs. Before he could take a step, Tamian clamped down on the male's bicep.

"We have your home surrounded. If you don't want to lose your head, you will let Isla go."

"Elias, what's going on?" a woman asked. Remy assumed she was Anna.

"Nothing to worry about. Go back to bed."

"No, don't," Tamian commanded. "Where is Isla?"

Anna's fear was tangible as she looked to Elias. "Who? There's no one here but my husband and me." Her voice shook, and her hands grasped her robe tighter around her chest.

"You're lying. I know my mate is somewhere in this house. I can feel her heart beating!"

Anna turned and rushed up the stairs. Remy chased after her. Elias yelled for Remy to stop, but he didn't. He trusted Tamian to keep the male from catching him. Remy caught up with Anna at the top of the stairs. She attempted to slip into a bedroom, but Remy was quicker.

"Isla!" Remy yelled. He didn't need to since his mate was a Gargoyle, but he wanted to make sure she heard him.

"Remy?" A faint voice sounded from above.

"Where the fuck is my mate?" Remy turned to Anna, his claws and fangs out.

"Anna! Don't you fucking touch her!" Elias yelled from downstairs.

The front door opened, then Remy heard Lorenzo's voice telling the male to stand down if he wanted to keep his head. Remy's beast was the flutter of a butterfly's wing away from bursting through. Anna must have sensed his anger because she pointed to a door behind him. He didn't trust the woman, so he gestured to the hallway. "After you."

Anna, wide-eyed, skirted around Remy, keeping her eyes on him as she moved to the door she'd indicated. A door which was thick steel and locked from the outside.

"You have five seconds to get that godsdamned door open before I send you downstairs where three sharp swords await."

"I-I have t-to get th-the keys," Anna stuttered.

"Then get them." Remy's patience was gone. "Isla? I'm here, my love. Hold on."

"Remy? Is that really you?"

"Yes, it's me. Are you okay?" Remy kept an eye on Anna as she retrieved a set of keys from the dresser in her bedroom.

"I'm okay." Isla's voice wobbled.

Anna's hands shook as she tried to put the key in the first lock. Since Remy didn't know which key went to which lock, he waited, trying not to growl at the female. As soon as the last lock was undone, Remy pushed the female out of the way, none too gently, and pulled the heavy door open. The most beautiful sight Remy had ever seen was rushing down the steps. When Isla saw Remy, she grabbed hold of the rail, catching herself. "Remy?"

"Isla!" Remy opened his arms and caught his mate as she launched herself at him.

"Oh, gods! I can't believe it's really you." Isla's words were muffled against Remy's throat. "Rain's..." Isla sobbed so hard her body shook.

"Rain's safe. He's with some friends, but our son is safe."

Isla jerked back, tears streaming down her pale face. "What? No. Nash said—"

"Nash lied. To both of us. Look." Remy pulled his phone out of his pocket and opened it to his photos. "See?

He's back in the States with my new Clan. He's going to be so happy to see you."

"He's really alive?" Isla hiccupped, her pale blue eyes shining through the tears.

"He is. And as soon as we deal with your captors, I'll take you to him." Remy picked his mate up and started down the steps.

"No! I can't leave." Isla slapped Remy's arm.

"What? You want to stay here?" Was this some Stockholm Syndrome bullshit?

"Of course not. Look." Isla held up her arm. There was a silver band around her wrist. "If I go outside, this shocks me."

Remy growled low in his chest. "Just outside or outside this room?"

"Outside the house."

Remy strode down the steps. Anna was nowhere to be seen, but her voice was coming from downstairs mixed with Elias's and Tamian's. When Remy and Isla reached the front room where the couple was surrounded by Tamian and the others, Isla ducked her head against Remy's neck.

Remy continued until he was just outside the circle. "Where is the key to remove this cuff?"

"We don't have it. The man who brought her here took it with him," Elias said, tipping his chin up. Lorenzo pressed the tip of his blade to Anna's throat. "Stop! I swear to you, we don't have the key."

Tamian placed a hand on Lorenzo's wrist. "He's telling the truth." The male walked over to where Remy was holding Isla. "May I?" he asked Remy permission to touch his mate.

"Yes. Please."

Tamian gently took Isla's hand in his and studied the cuff. "Does this shock you?" he asked Isla.

"Yes, but only if I go outside."

169

Tamian took a picture of the band. "I'm sending the picture to my uncle. He might recognize it." Remy assumed Tamian was referring to Jonas Montague. The male was a doctor, but he was also a scientist who created amazing gadgets like prosthetics and voice modulators for his family to use when they worked as watchers.

"Wait. He said the man who brought Isla here." Remy turned to Elias. "What's the male's name?"

"I'm not telling you shi—" Lorenzo once again pointed his sword at Anna who cried out when the tip punctured her skin.

"Nash! His name is Nash Hogan."

Tamian tapped his phone and placed it against his ear. "Leo, check Nash's pockets for a small key. It should be octagonal in shape."

"Nash did this?" Isla asked.

Remy cradled his mate tighter to his chest. "I'm afraid so, but it gets worse."

Tamian focused on Isla as he spoke to Leonardo. "Excellent. Please drive to the house." When he disconnected, he smiled at Remy. "There's an odd-shaped key on a chain around Nash's neck."

Remy walked Isla away from the others. "Before we go outside, there's something we need to talk about. Nash admitted to selling you to the Webers. He said he did it because your father wanted you and Rain dead."

170

CHAPTER SIX

"WHAT?" ISLA TREMBLED, her eyes filling once again with tears. "Dead? But why?"

"Because of me. Because I don't have Original blood, and you mated outside your 'station.' He said Felix didn't want his heir to be anything other than pure blooded. Nash said both he and Felix refused their true mates for the same reason. I don't know whether or not to believe him. Nash said he faked your deaths and sent someone else's ashes to your father. He delivered you to Craven. You and Rain both."

"But you said Rain was safe!"

"He is, Sweetheart. I promise he is. Now. I don't know all the details or timing. I don't know why Craven turned you back over to Nash when he did. We didn't get that far into our interrogation of Nash before we found out where you were. I had to get to you first. Answers were secondary."

"But my father..." Isla shook her head. "And my mother? Does she know all this? No, she can't. She wouldn't..."

"Do you think she knows she isn't his true mate?"

"She has to. At least I would think so."

"Remy, here's the key." Tamian held it out, and Remy took the small object hanging from a chain. He placed Isla on her feet, then unlocked the cuff from her wrist. He handed the metal and key back to Tamian before rubbing his mate's wrist gently.

"How do you want to handle this?" Tamian asked, gesturing to the couple still held at bay with swords pointed at them.

Remy turned to Isla. "Let's go outside. You don't need to see this."

"No. I'm not going anywhere. Remy, they took my freedom. They tried to use me as an incubator. I'm not strong enough to take Elias's head, so would you do it for me?"

Remy wasn't surprised at his mate's strength or her need for retribution. "What about Anna?"

Isla narrowed her eyes at the other female. An evil grin spread across her exquisite face. "I know the perfect punishment." She grabbed the metal cuff from Tamian and strode to where Anna was standing. Anna was shaking her head, muttering "no", but Isla grabbed the female's arm and snapped the cuff on her wrist. "That ought to do it." Isla returned to Tamian and held out her hand. "Key please." Tamian handed the metal to Isla who looped the chain over her head, the key settling against her chest. "Carry on."

"Are you sure about this?" Remy studied Isla's face for any hesitation.

"Positive. Then we're going to handle my brother." Her voice was steely determination, and that was all Remy needed. He kissed her forehead before turning and holding out his hand. Lorenzo passed his sword to Remy, and the others took a few steps back.

Elias had been quiet up until that point, but as soon as Remy put both hands on the hilt, the male began begging. "No, please. Don't do this. I'll give you anything. Money. My home. We didn't hurt your ma—" Remy swung, and Elias's words were cut off, replaced with the thud of his head landing at Anna's feet. Anna screamed, falling to her knees. The female reached for Elias's head but pulled back at the last minute.

"I'll kill you!" she yelled at Isla, not Remy. Anna lunged to her feet, intent clear. Lorenzo caught the female before she got two steps in. "Let me go! You can't just murder someone for no good reason!"

"No good reason?" Isla crossed the room, getting right in the other female's face. "You bought me like you would a piece of furniture. You locked me away for months. Used me in an attempt at getting a child with Original blood because Elias found you lacking. How does that make you feel, Anna? To know your own mate needed another female to give him the perfect offspring? You two deserved each other, and now you can see how it felt to be trapped inside." Isla turned to Remy. "Can we go now?"

"We sure can." Remy held out his hand, and Isla took it. Their group left Anna screaming at them. When they reached the door, Isla turned to the other female, waved, and closed the door.

Remy turned Isla so she was facing him. "Are you okay? Do you need a doctor? Are you…?" He couldn't bring himself to finish the question.

Isla's bottom lip quivered. "I don't think I'm pregnant if that's what you were going to ask, but it has been a couple weeks since the last time the doctor tried to, you know." Isla took a step back. "Remy, what if… What if I am?"

"If you are, then Rain will be an older brother. You said it's only been two weeks, so if the gods decided you were to have this child, it was for a reason. If you are pregnant, then this will be as much my child as Rain is. Do you understand me?"

Isla nodded as tears streamed down her face. "Gods, I love you. I love you, Remy Durand."

"I thought your last name was Doucet," Lorenzo said.

"I changed it when I moved to California. I didn't want anyone questioning if I was one of the Durands who own the vineyards in France."

"Makes sense."

"Remy, what do you want to do about Nash?" Tamian gestured to the SUV where Isla's brother was still lying.

"He's here?" Isla asked.

"Yes. I may have paralyzed him a bit. I injected him with wolfsbane, and, well, he pissed me off."

"You're not the only one." Isla fisted her hands. "He claims our father wanted Rain and me dead, so instead of carrying out his wishes, he sold us to be used. How was that any better? If he cared so much, why didn't he send me back to you where you could protect me?" Shaking her head, she muttered, "Stupid, fucking Hogan males." Isla began pacing, and Remy let her. His mate had a decision to make. If it were up to him, he would take Nash's head and send it to Felix in a box. The other males stood silently, watching and waiting. Isla stopped in front of Remy after the twenty-seventh time back and forth.

"I need to talk to my mother. What time is it?"

"It's going on midnight here, so it should be close to noon there, right?"

Isla counted silently on her fingers. "Ten, but close enough. Fath— Felix should be at the office."

"When Rain told me Nash was responsible for handing him over to Craven, we assumed Nash was acting of his own accord. I called Felix to ask him if he knew where Nash was, and he heard Rain's voice. He was genuinely surprised to find out our son was alive. When we caught up to Nash earlier, he admitted he was running from your father, so Felix may or may not be at the office. He might be looking for Nash. If you call your mother, be prepared, Sweetheart. She thinks you're dead. Maybe I should call first. Test the waters, if you will."

"Yes, that's a good idea. I don't know what I'll do if she agreed with Felix's ideals."

"There's only one way to find out." Remy pulled his phone out of his back pocket, found the contact number he needed, and pressed the call button.

"Remy, is that you?" Imogen answered.

"Yes, it's me."

"What the hell is going on? Felix has lost his mind, saying Rain is alive. He swears he heard the boy's voice when you called, but Nash sent his and Isla's ashes. I'm worried about my mate."

"Imogen, Rain is alive."

"But how? And why would Nash lie to me like that? Isla and Rain were my whole world. Don't get me wrong. I love my son, but he's just like his father, and both of them can be a little much sometimes. Isla was my calm amidst the storm."

Isla clamped her hand over her mouth, pale eyes shining.

"Nash mentioned something about Original blood and keeping the Hogan line pure."

"Remy, I'm so sorry. I should have been strong enough to shield Isla." Imogen's voice was strangled. "It's a long story, but Felix isn't my true mate. I've always known this, but I was young when he and I were thrown together. Both our parents had the same idea about the Original bloodline." Imogen sobbed into the phone, and Isla dropped to the ground. Remy fell to his knees beside her. He scooped her into his arms, the phone forgotten.

"Remy? Are you there?"

Tamian handed the phone to him. "Yes, I'm here. Imogen, I have some great news and some terrible news."

"Give me the great. I could use it."

"Isla is alive."

"Remy, don't lie to me. I don't think my heart could take it if I believe my baby's not dead and then find out she really is."

"Mum?"

"Isla? Is that really you?"

"Yes. It's me. Remy rescued me. Just now. I haven't seen Rain, but we're both alive."

"Oh, thank the gods! My baby!" Imogen sobbed some more, and Isla cried along with her mother.

When Imogen got herself under control, she asked, "What was the terrible news? Or do I want to know?"

"Mum, Nash is the one responsible for Rain and me disappearing. He said Felix ordered him to kill us. Instead, Nash sold both of us to a doctor for our blood."

"I'll kill him. I'll kill them both. Damnit. Felix is coming down the driveway. If you see Nash, tell him not to bother ever coming home. He's dead to me. Isla, I love you, but I have to go."

"Mum? Mum!" The phone was silent. "Shit. I need to get to Australia. Remy, I have to go."

"We'll go, if that's what you want. First, we have to take care of Nash."

"You heard her. He's dead to my mother, and he's dead to me. Might as well make it real in the truest sense. The bastard sold my Rainier. He didn't need the money, so that tells me he didn't really care what happened to us."

Tamian held out a hand to help Remy stand. "Let's go. We can either charter a jet from here or drive back to Amsterdam and take mine. Up to you."

Remy lifted Isla's chin. "I know you want to get to your mom, but it's well over twenty hours. Is a few more going to make a difference?"

"I honestly don't know. I don't think Felix will hurt her, but then again, I never thought him capable of wishing me or Rain dead either. I guess a few extra hours will be okay. There's no need to spend extra money if you already own a plane."

"Do you want to confront Nash before we leave?" Remy asked.

"No." Isla didn't elaborate as to why she didn't want to see her brother. There really was no need.

Tamian didn't question her either. "Santiago, you're with me. Lorenzo, please drive for Remy and Isla. Leo, you and Pierre handle Nash. Toss him into the house with Elias, then you can head home. Thank you both for the assist."

Leonardo and Pierre fisted their hearts and bowed their heads. "It was an honor," they replied to their future King.

Tamian and Santiago made their way to one of the vehicles. Remy led Isla to the other and helped her into the back, while Lor slid into the driver's seat. Remy pulled her onto his lap, needing her as close as possible. It was several miles to the interstate, so he would hold her until then.

Isla laid her head on Remy's shoulder. "Tell me about Rain. Do you have any more pictures? It's been over two years. I bet he's grown so much. At least I hope he has. Tell me, what did Craven put him through? Do you know?"

"Right after I got him back, he wouldn't talk about his time with Craven. He's been in therapy for a couple months, and he's opened up a little. At first, he was terrified to even leave the house, and he had nightmares several times a week. He's much better now. He has a couple little friends, and he's really thriving. We have been staying in New Atlanta. When I thought I'd lost you both, I left France and moved to California. I didn't want anything to do with grapes. It brought back too many memories, so when I was offered a job overseeing the new prison being built, I took it. The ones building it own the one in New Atlanta, so I flew there to learn all I could. The Stone Clan is like one big family. They have helped Rain and me these last few months. I can't wait for you to meet them."

Remy showed Isla all the photos of Rain he'd taken on his phone. Isla touched the screen with her fingertips, gushing over each picture of their son. "I can't wait to hold him." Isla kept Remy's phone opened to a picture of Remy and their son smashing grapes as she rested against his chest. It didn't take long for her to fall asleep, and Remy pressed his cheek to her hair, inhaling deeply. He sent up another prayer of gratitude to the gods for bringing her back to him. He also prayed she wasn't pregnant, but if she happened to be, he would love the child as his own because it was a part of her. She said it had only been a couple weeks since the doctor had last visited, so that wasn't enough time for a heart to form. He planned to keep his ears open, just in case.

When they reached the interstate, Remy had settled Isla on the seat with her head in his lap, and she'd slept the entirety of the drive without stirring. Remy had stared at his mate the whole time, much how he hadn't been able to let Rain out of his sight the first few days after he'd been found. It was early morning when they arrived back in Amsterdam. There was food on the jet, so he hadn't bothered asking Lorenzo to stop. Lorenzo parked next to Santiago in a secure lot close to where the jet was waiting. While they boarded the plane, Santiago went about his pre-flight routine, double-checking to make sure it was ready for their long trip.

Remy and Isla sat together on one of the sofas with Tamian across from them. Lor was in the cockpit. Once they were in the air, Tamian played host, getting them something to eat and drink. Isla wanted to hear all about Rain as well as what Remy had been up to over the last few months.

"Now that we're back together, are we going to return to France?" Isla asked.

"If that's what you want, but first, I'd like to take you back to New Atlanta for a while. I did make a commitment to the Clan for the new prison being built in California, but since my situation has changed for the better, they'll more than likely be willing to find someone else to take over."

"Honestly, I just want to be with you and Rain, wherever that is. You said Rain is doing well with his new friends, so maybe we shouldn't take him away from them so soon."

"I have a few more months with Gregor and Aldredge before the new prison is finished. I think you'll like it out in

California. We can buy a house on the beach or one up in the hills."

"What about friends for Rain?"

Remy ran his thumb over the back of Isla's hand. "I'm sure there are others who have children, but since I thought I lost you both, meeting those in the Clan who had families wasn't on my radar. I was only focused on work. I can call Sinclair and ask. He's Rafael's brother and oversees the Clan out west."

"Did I make the wrong call?"

Remy gripped Isla's hand tighter. "About what?"

"Going to confront Felix instead of heading to see Rain. I can't wait to see him. I know we should have headed to the States immediately, but I can't let this mess with my family go. I have to look Felix in the eye and let him know he didn't get away with wanting me and Rain dead just because you aren't from an Original line."

"I don't think so. The Clan in the States went to war with the Greeks for the same reason. Rafael's uncle disowned his own sister because she mated with an Italian. He also had Jonas Montague ostracized for mating with a human. That lasted over two hundred years until the Stone Clan went to Greece and put an end to his tyranny. But know this, my love - you aren't alone. I want Felix to pay, and I will be there by your side when you confront him."

"All of us will be there," Tamian said from across the aisle. "Felix is an older Gargoyle, which means he's strong. Not that Remy can't hold his own, but there's strength in numbers. I won't allow him to talk his way out of what he attempted."

"Thank you, Tamian. For your hospitality as well as helping Remy find me. It's a comfort to know he has Clan who cares for him."

Isla turned her face up, smiling. Remy pressed a soft kiss to her lips. He couldn't wait until they were alone. He needed his mate desperately, but he wasn't about to take her

179

to Tamian's bedroom where the other males would hear them making love. He and his mate tended to get a little wild between the sheets. Or they had before. Remy would let Isla set the pace whenever they came together. She had assured him she hadn't been harmed while in seclusion, but he worried about her mental state. He also worried about the possibility of her being pregnant. He hadn't lied when he said he would raise the child as his own, but Isla would be the one carrying another male's baby no matter how it had come about.

Isla fell asleep against Remy's shoulder, and Tamian insisted he take her to the bedroom to rest. Remy relented, praying his beast would contain itself and do what was best for Isla, not encourage Remy to ravage her. It had been years since they had been alone. He placed her on the bed, then curled up behind her. The bedroom was small but just as opulent as the rest of the jet. The pillows didn't carry anyone else's scent on them, so either no one had used the bed recently, or Tamian made sure the bedding was changed out.

Remy and his family had money but nowhere near as much as Isla's. Her family had been in the wheat business for centuries having bought up all the property they could get their hands on. Over the years, the Hogans had branched out into other ventures, but the grain was their main source of income. Remy had no idea what Nash had been doing in The Netherlands other than hiding. With Felix alive, Isla's legacy was in jeopardy. Not that his mate was worried about inheriting the business. She had never cared about the money.

Remy's vineyard would eventually go to Rain. If his son decided he didn't want anything to do with the grape business, he could pass it on to someone else in the Durand family, but it would never be sold to outsiders. Remy wondered what contingencies Felix had in place, if any. The whole debacle gave Remy a headache, and since Gargoyles didn't get human afflictions, that was saying a lot.

Closing his eyes, Remy inhaled deeply. He had missed her unique scent. Remy did his best to think about happier things, like reuniting Isla and Rain. Isla meeting the other mates. Showing her both New Atlanta as well as California. He wanted his little family to walk the beaches of the Pacific. Sit and enjoy the sunsets over the water. As much as he enjoyed the Clan in Georgia, Remy was looking forward to getting back to the West Coast. He was also ready to take vacations back home in France. His nephew, Renauld, was looking over Remy's vineyard in his absence. When Rain was older, Remy and Isla would take their son back and teach him everything there was to know about their family business. If he decided he'd rather do something else, Remy was okay with that. Maybe their second child would be interested. Because there would be more children for Remy and Isla. They had always talked about having siblings for Rain, whether they had them naturally or adopted. For Gargoyles, that option was more painful because any human child wouldn't live hundreds of years, unless Lucy and Jonas were successful in their endeavors.

Isla slept the duration of the flight, showing how tired she had been. Remy left her for about an hour so he could talk with Tamian, but he left the door open so he could keep an eye on her. Remy only woke her when it was time to land. The long sleep did his mate wonders, because as soon as her feet hit the ground in Australia, the fierce female he had first met came back to life. She was in familiar territory, and Isla took over their mission.

"She reminds me of my Lucy," Tamian muttered with a gleam in his eye. The half-blood merely inclined his head when Isla began barking orders.

It was over three hours' drive from the airport to where Felix and Imogen made their home. It was a gaudy monstrosity, and Remy hated it. The former abbey was a castle complete with dining hall and chapel. The building was less than three hundred years old, but it felt as though all the souls who ever walked the grounds still inhabited the place. Frankly, it gave Remy the creeps. It was another reason why he hadn't wanted to visit with Isla and Rain over the holidays. He'd never make that mistake again. If ever Isla wanted to visit her family, Remy would be plastered to her side for the duration.

CHAPTER SEVEN

ISLA WANTED TO call her mom since it had been a full day since she spoke to her, but she also didn't want to give Felix a heads up he was going to have company. Isla didn't want the male to call in reinforcements.

The castle her parents called home was located in a quaint neighborhood. Isla always wondered how Felix and her mum got away with living there hundreds of years with no one asking why they weren't aging. Per Isla's wishes, Lorenzo drove right up to the house. The four males exited the rental and flanked Isla as she strode up to the front door. When she tried the knob, it was unlocked, and they silently made their way inside.

Isla wanted desperately to call out to her mum, but they had a plan. One she had decided on, so she had to keep her mouth closed and her ears opened. Her mum's laughter rang out from farther in the house. Isla froze. If her mum was laughing, either Felix wasn't home, or Imogen had lied about knowing of his plans. The males surrounded her, and Isla stood on tiptoe to see why. Her mum had entered the hallway, accompanied by a male Isla didn't know.

"Isla!" Her mum broke into a run toward Isla. Remy and the others remained where they were, guarding her.

"It's okay, Remy. Stand down." Remy allowed Isla to move forward just as her mother reached her and strangled her in a tight embrace. The stranger remained where he was, hands in his pockets. The smile on his face as he watched Imogen and Isla embrace was kind.

"Mum." Isla hugged her mother just as tightly while keeping an eye on the male.

"Oh, my baby! What are you doing here? Not that I'm not happy to see you, but shouldn't you be with Rain?"

"Mum, you hung up on me. I was worried about you. Where's Felix, and who is this?"

Imogen released Isla and slid her arm around Isla's waist while grinning at Remy and the other males. "Hello, Remy. It's so good to see you, Son. It appears you brought a small army, but there really was no need. I have my own bodyguard." Imogen held out her free hand, and the stranger strolled to her as though Isla wasn't about to have a heart attack.

"Mum, where is Felix?"

"I'm getting to that. Isla, I'd like to introduce you to Benjamin Ward. Ben is my true mate."

"Say what?" Isla eyed the handsome male as he fisted his heart and bowed his head.

"On my honor." When Ben straightened, he turned to Remy with his hand out. "Remy, it's a pleasure. Imogen has told me so much about you and your vineyard. I hope she and I will be allowed to see it soon."

"Mum, what the hell is going on? And where the hell is Felix? I have something I want to say to him before he—"

"Ben took care of him yesterday."

"What?" Isla's head was spinning. "What do you mean took care of him?"

Ben rocked back on his heals, smiling. "He's currently fish food in the Coral Sea. I pretended to be a businessman who made him an offer he couldn't refuse. If there's one thing Felix Hogan was, it was greedy. I took him out for a business lunch on my yacht. He was there to swindle me out of millions. I was there to take his head. I won."

Isla was trying to comprehend all she was hearing. "But I just talked to you yesterday. How did you manage this in less than a day?"

184

"Do you want the truth?" Imogen asked.

"Yes. I'm sick of lies and manipulation."

"Ben has been planning on taking Felix out of the picture for a while. He and I met when we were young. His family worked for mine, and I'm sad to admit, my parents' thoughts on the whole Original bloodlines remaining pure were the same as Felix's. Ben and I knew we were mates, but my parents sent me away to live with my aunt in Western Australia. Ben's family was released from their duties, and they moved south. Once enough time passed my parents thought I'd forget my foolish notions, as they called wanting my true mate, they brought me home and introduced me to Felix."

Ben stepped up to Imogen and wrapped an arm around her waist. "I spent my life watching over your mum. I also kept tabs on Felix and all his dealings. Our family wasn't poor, just not from an Original bloodline. I mirrored Felix's business dealings, remaining a few steps behind on purpose. When I was able, I approached your mum. I let her know I was there for her in case she ever needed me."

Imogen caressed Ben's face. "Ben and I have loved each other from afar for quite a while now, but when you called and told me what Felix plotted, I was done being the good and faithful mate. So I called Ben and told him it was time."

"And I was just waiting for her call. Have been for years. I had plenty of time to come up with different scenarios on getting rid of Felix Hogan. If that makes me a bad Gargoyle, then so be it. I've waited eight centuries to be with my fated mate, and I won't apologize for getting Felix out of the picture. Especially now I know what he tried to do to you and Rain. If you tell me where Nash is, I'll take care of him as well."

"He's been handled." Isla shook her head and laughed. "Damn, Mum. This is all... I don't know what this is."

"It's the start of the rest of my life. Ben has offered to manage the business unless you want to come back and run it. If not, he'll take care of everything so it will be waiting for Rain or any other children you have."

"My life is with Remy and Rain in America for now. Ben, if you would manage the company, I'd appreciate it."

"No problem. I have an excellent team ready to step in. Your mum has already asked that you and Rain be listed as the new owners. The paperwork has been completed. I happen to have a wonderful computer specialist on my payroll."

Isla knew he meant a hacker, but she didn't care. "And you've managed this in the last twenty-four hours? What if Nash were still alive?"

"Like I said, I've been planning this for quite a while. If Nash *were* alive, he wouldn't be for long considering what he did to you and your son. I know I'm not your father, and we've never met before today, but I feel as though I know you already. Your mum has told me all about you and your family. I hope we get the opportunity to get better acquainted in the future."

Isla studied her mother's face. She wore a countenance of adoration, happiness, and contentment. It was something Isla had never seen before. Then again, being with your true mate was the only thing that mattered to a Gargoyle. That and the family you had with them.

"While we're putting your name on documents, do you want to own this place?" Imogen waved her arm around.

"You don't want it?" Isla didn't want to hurt her mum's feelings, but the castle was the worst place Isla could imagine living. Felix had purchased it after Isla and Remy were mated. When her mum wrinkled her nose, Isla snickered. "Uh, no thank you."

Imogene winked at Isla. "Me neither. This is the gaudiest piece of property I've ever seen, and I've seen some doozies over the years. Okay, I'll sell it and put the money in Rainier's trust fund. Now, how about you introduce me to the males who accompanied you?"

Remy made the introductions since Isla had been mostly out of it from the moment they all stormed into her life. Afterward, she and her mum enjoyed some alone time while the males took a tour of the castle. They talked about Rain and what he and Isla both had been through. Imogen gushed about Ben and how she finally had the male she was meant to be with. Isla's heart hurt for her mother having been denied a life with Ben for over eight centuries. They still had at least two hundred years to be together, if not more, so better late than not at all.

After visiting for a couple hours, Isla said goodbye to her mother and Ben, who promised to visit the States soon so they could love on Rain. Isla was looking forward to it. Between the drive back to the airport and the flight to America, it was almost another twenty-four hours before Isla was reunited with her son. She had wanted to call, but Remy advised against it. Their boy would be a bundle of happy nerves, and Remy didn't want Abbi and Frey to have to deal with a million questions about how much longer.

Remy did call Frey once they landed to give them a heads up. When they pulled down the long driveway nestled in the woods, Isla grabbed Remy's hand, squeezing until her knuckles were white.

"Relax. You have nothing to be nervous about."

Isla wasn't so sure. Her son had been through a traumatic ordeal, and he was so young. Isla knew it was Nash's fault, but she still blamed herself. It was what parents did when their child was hurt. Tamian had gone to see his mate, but Lorenzo was still single, so he offered to drive them. Lorenzo explained how he watched over the kids while Abbi and Frey were at the gym. Isla didn't miss the wistful longing in his voice as the male talked about Rain, Amelia, and Connor. After hearing stories during the long flight, Isla felt as though she already knew the children.

Isla shouldn't have been surprised to see several adults and three children standing on the front porch when the car stopped. From everything Remy told her about his new Clan, they were wonderful, caring beings. Rain was already running down the steps before Remy got the door opened.

"Papa! Is it really Mum?"

"See for yourself." Remy stepped back, and Rain's precious face filled the opening.

"Mum!" Rain climbed into the SUV as fast as his little legs allowed and dove into Isla's arms. They spent several minutes clutching each other, both crying happy tears. Remy urged them to get out of the vehicle, and Rain held both his parents' hands as they walked to where everyone was still waiting.

"Look! It's my Mum!" Rain shouted.

Amelia ran down the steps, her hair bouncing around her shoulders. Dark, mischievous eyes smiled as the little girl spun in circles. "This is a happy day!" She grabbed Rain's hands and spun him with her. Both kids were stumbling from the spinning dizziness, but they were laughing, and that was the best sound in the world to Isla. Well, maybe not *the* best, because Remy's sexy voice in her ear when they were alone was at the top of the list.

Introductions were made, and Abbi offered to feed everyone. Isla's stomach wasn't happy, but she chalked that up to all the traveling and lack of routine over the last couple days. She wasn't used to eating when she wanted. Her meals had been structured. The Webers only fed her nutritious items which were supposed to be optimum for pregnant women or those hoping to be pregnant. Isla had too much chocolate mixed with red wine on the flight back, two things she hadn't been allowed in too many months. Now, she was paying for it.

Isla could see why Remy wanted to remain in the States. The Stone Clan welcomed Isla and treated her as one of their own immediately. Abbi and Isabelle told her abbreviated versions of how they met their mates. Abbi said that once Isla got settled, she would be introduced to the others and hear their encounters. It was an initiation of sorts, but one that bonded the mates.

Remy had already filled her in on the bombings, so she didn't expect the females – and Trevor – to be in a hurry to have a get together. They were getting their homes and lives back in order. Plus, she had a son and mate of her own to get reacquainted with. Still, it felt good to be part of such a large, welcoming family.

REMY STOOD IN the doorway leading from the kitchen into the living room. Isla and Rain were huddled together on the sofa. Rain was chatting away about Amelia and Connor while Isla smiled at their son, taking in every word. She brushed his hair off his forehead, ran her knuckles down his cheek, pressed kisses to the top of his head. She constantly touched him in some way, much the same way Remy had done when he first got Rain back. When it was time for Rain to go to bed, Isla looked to Remy for direction. His heart broke for his mate. In her absence, Remy continued with their normal ritual of getting Rain settled for the night. Bath first, then story time.

"All right. Bath time, then a couple chapters," Remy said more for Isla's benefit than Rain's.

"Mum, will you read to me? Papa tries, but you make all the voices."

Isla laughed, her eyes bright with tears. "What are we reading?"

"Percy Jackson! His papa is a god." Rain jumped up and ran down the hallway into the bathroom. Remy didn't trust the boy to bathe properly when he was this excited.

"You go help with his bath, and I'll lock up the house." Remy pulled Isla to her feet. "Nothing's changed, Sweetheart. I've kept the same routines, and I know he'd rather have you take care of him now that you're home." Isla tipped her face up, and Remy gave her the kiss she was silently asking for. "There are other routines that need to continue, if you get my drift."

Isla slid her hands around to Remy's backside and squeezed his ass. "I get your drift. I've missed you, Mate."

"As I've missed you." Remy kissed her again before stepping back. "Go," he urged because if they stood there any longer, he would take her on the floor. That was not how he wanted their reunion to be. He planned on making love to his mate all night. In bed. Remy locked up the house, then he grabbed a beer from the refrigerator and leaned against the island. He took his time sipping instead of chugging to give Isla and Rain much-needed time alone. They had been apart for years, but as he listened in, he smiled at their laughter.

Remy enjoyed three bottles of his favorite ale before joining his little family. Rain was in his pajamas sitting against his pillows with Isla seated beside him holding the latest Percy Jackson book. The stories were for older kids, but Remy read the series before introducing them to his son. He also asked the psychiatrist, who told Remy to use his judgement as Rain's father. In the end, Remy decided they were the right amount of good versus evil, and if there were aspects Rain didn't comprehend, Remy took the time to explain whatever Rain had questions about.

Isla opened the paperback to the beginning. Instead of getting Rain an e-reader, Remy purchased the physical books so Rain would have them to read on his own when he was older. His bookshelf wasn't full, but it was getting there. Isla cleared her throat, but Rain placed his hand on the book.

"Mum?"

"What is it?" Isla placed the book on her lap, giving Rain her full attention.

"Where were you?" Rain picked at a small thread on his

blanket, not looking at his mother.

Isla glanced up at Remy, and he nodded. They hadn't discussed what to tell Rain, but Remy felt the truth was the best course of action.

"For most of my time away, I was with Dr. Craven."

"Did he leave you in a tunnel too?" Rain whispered.

"No. He sent me to live with a couple named Elias and Anna."

"Did they hurt you?" Rain's eyes were filled with unshed tears.

Isla wrapped her arm around their son's shoulder and pulled him to her. "No, Baby. They didn't hurt me. They didn't let me go outside the house, but other than that, they took care of me."

"If they were nice, why didn't they let you come back to me and Papa?" Rain had reverted back to calling Remy *Papa* more often than not.

"I didn't say they were nice; I just said they didn't hurt me. There's a difference. They wanted something from me, and until I gave it to them, I couldn't leave."

Rain raised his eyes to Isla's. "What did they want?"

Remy held his breath. Maybe the truth wasn't such a good idea, but Isla made the right call when she said, "My bloodline. You know how Percy Jackson has a god for a father?" Rain nodded. "I'm kind of the same way, except instead of my papa being a god, he and my mum both come from a long line of shifters who date back to the original Gargoyles put on Earth. That makes my blood, and now yours, special. In a sense, you're like Percy."

"Really?"

"Yes. There are always going to be those – human and shifter alike – who want more than they have. I'm so sorry your Uncle Nash lied to you. I'm sorry I wasn't there to protect you."

"But you were there. In here." Rain tapped his heart. "And so was Papa. I felt you with me. It's why I wasn't scared." Rain looked up at Remy, then back to Isla. "Well, I was scared a little. Especially when they locked me in that tunnel. Mum, please don't make me visit Uncle Nash. He calls me names."

"I promise you will never have to see Nash again. Neither will I. Now, how about we see what Percy is up to?"

"Okay." Rain held out his hand, and Remy crossed the room to sit with his mate and son. As Isla read the opening chapter of book two, Remy tried to follow along, but his mind was full of the future and how to best take care of these two amazing creatures. He thanked the gods several times for bringing them back to him. Neither had been physically harmed, but they weren't without scars. Remy was going to do everything in his power to ensure they healed mentally. Rain was doing better since he'd been seeing the therapist, and Remy would get Isla an appointment as well.

Four chapters later, Rain was asleep. Isla pulled the covers up around his shoulders and kissed his forehead. Remy rose and stood by the door, but he didn't rush her. He knew what Isla was feeling. At least he thought he did. Being separated for years had been torture, and the first night he had Rain back, Remy had watched his son sleep all night. He wouldn't take that away from Isla if she wished to remain by Rain's side. Surprisingly, his beast wasn't pushing him. It wanted what was best for their mate too.

After half an hour, Isla kissed Rain again, then rose and walked into Remy's waiting arms. She leaned her head back, eyes filled with that glint they got when she wanted him. Isla ran her fingers through Remy's hair, then tugged his head down for a kiss. There was no mistaking what his mate wanted by the way her tongue tangled with his. His mate could be a fierce lover, and that was who Remy was getting. He welcomed her. Grabbing the back of her thighs, Remy picked his mate up, and Isla wrapped her legs around his hips, settling her jeans-covered core against his erection.

"I need you, Mate," she husked against his mouth.

Remy's cock lengthened, ready to reclaim his female. "And you'll have me."

Chapter Eight

REMY CARRIED ISLA to their bedroom, locking the door behind them. Rain was aware of his parents' nighttime activities. Not sex specifically, but they had explained to him years ago that as a couple, they needed their own play time. The first time Remy had shouted his release, Rain came running, scared his Papa was hurt. That had been the last time they left the door unlocked. Remy had a feeling he would soon be just as loud. It had been too long. With his hands full of his mate's ass and his mouth filled with her tongue, Remy needed to fill something else.

Releasing his claws, Remy carefully shredded the clothes Isla was wearing. He had wanted to get her out of the items all day because they had been given to her by Elias. Remy didn't want anything touching his mate purchased by another male. Especially one who thought it was okay to buy another being and use them for their own gain. Isla made quick work of Remy's clothes, and when they were both naked, she dropped to her knees, wrapping her smaller hand around his hard length.

"I've missed this." Isla's eyes flared with need before she sheathed his cock in her wet heat.

"Fuck!" Remy had missed that too. His mate loved giving head, but it had been years since they'd last been intimate, so when she tried taking all of him, she gagged. "Easy, Love."

Isla pulled off, wiping her mouth. "I'm out of practice."

Remy pulled her to her feet and carried her to the bed. "There's plenty of time for that later. I need you, Isla. I need

194

to be in you."

As soon as her back hit the bed, Isla spread her legs and pulled Remy down on top of her. "I need you too. I want you to mark me again when you come. I need that connection."

Remy would do anything his mate asked of him, and if she wanted the mate bite, who was he to deny her? His beast rumbled in his chest at the thought. Remy didn't make her wait. He slid his cock into her already slick passage. She squeezed her inner muscles, making them tighter around his length. As he moved in and out, they stared into each other's eyes, becoming reacquainted in body and soul. His thrusts weren't hurried. Remy wanted their first time to last, but it had been years, and his body had other ideas. Remy tried to hold off on coming, but Isla urged him to move faster. Harder. Again, he couldn't deny his mate. He pushed up on one hand so he could reach between them and rub her clit. Isla never had trouble getting off when they had sex, but he wanted to give her that extra push. As soon as he touched her nub, her fangs dropped, encouraging Remy's to do the same.

With his orgasm close, Remy rubbed harder, stroked faster. "Remy." Isla gasping his name was his cue. He pounded her core, sending her over the edge. When her inner walls clamped down, she curled her body up and sank her fangs into his neck. Remy shouted the house down as his own climax hit like a freight train, and he latched onto Isla's neck. They retracted their teeth at the same time, licking the wounds closed. Isla flopped back, grinning. "Now that's a proper welcome home."

"Je t'aime, ma belle femme."

"I love you more." Isla brushed Remy's hair off his forehead and threaded her fingers through his locks. "I wanted to die when I thought you and Rain were gone. When I was first with Craven, I had no desire to live. Then one day, I was sitting outside in the sunshine, and a wave of

195

peacefulness washed over me. At first, I thought it was the gods letting me know it was okay to cross over, but as soon as I had that idea, a gust of wind swirled hard enough to lift my hair. All the while I was outside, the air had been still. When the blast came out of nowhere, I got to thinking. If you, my true mate, were no longer of this world, I would have known the second you crossed over. The bond would have snapped in two. I never felt anything like that. So, I held onto hope that one day, you and I would be reunited."

"I'm glad you held onto that hope." Remy rolled to his back and pulled his mate close. Isla rested her head on his chest just over his heart. "I'll admit I didn't handle things quite as well. I fell into a deep depression, locking myself away. Eventually, I left France and headed west. I needed to get away from everything that reminded me of you and Rainier. I ended up in California. The depression lessened, but my heart was still shredded. I was looking for an outlet for my frustrations, and when I found a gym run by local Gargoyles, I found more than I bargained for. I told them my story, and the manager hooked me up with Sinclair Stone. He offered me the job overseeing the new penitentiary, and I accepted. In doing so, I became part of the Clan. I was no longer alone. I had a purpose. Sin sent me here to learn everything about running a prison, but between finding Rain and going after both Craven and Nash, I haven't been as invested as I should be. I'm not sure I'm the best candidate for the job. They need someone they can count on."

Isla rose up to look at him, slapping his hard abs as she did. "Remy Durand, you are the most capable male I know. You are smart. You have a head for business. You're the take-charge type. Rain and I are back where we belong. We're safe. If this is something you want to do, then do it. I've never been to California, but I'm sure it's a beautiful place. And you know me; I have no problem making friends. If the Gargoyles there have mates, Rain and I will be fine while you're working. You already said you made the commitment."

"If you're sure." Remy only wanted his mate's happiness. She and Rain had been through so much, and he would do anything to ensure both had everything they wanted, even if that meant moving back to France.

"I am. All I want is to be with you and Rainier. I have lost time to make up for, and I'd like to do that by focusing on our child. I can do that from anywhere. He's in a good routine here with his friends and tutor. I'd like to observe his interactions so I can mimic them in California. And I would like to meet with his psychiatrist."

"Do you have nightmares?"

"Sometimes. I don't think they'll be as bad or as frequent now that I'm back with you though."

"Whatever you need, My Love."

"You. I need you." Isla crawled on top of Remy and kissed him deeply. He gave her what she needed several times that night.

ISLA WAS IN love with the other mates. She met most of them during the Halloween party Frey and Abbi hosted. Over the course of the next two months, Isla had the opportunity to talk with them one-on-one. While Remy went to work, Isla accompanied Rain to the Hartleys' home, and when Abbi didn't have dance class to teach, she invited the other mates to visit. Isla had been reluctant to share her story, but the more she heard of what the others had gone through, the easier it became. She cried with them as they shed tears for her, and those bonds became stronger each day.

After meeting Connor, Remy shared the drawing the young boy had drawn. Isla couldn't stop staring at the little girl in the picture. She had asked Abbi to get her a pregnancy test, and when it showed up as negative, Isla secretly rejoiced. All the poking and prodding, the invasive injections hadn't worked. The Webers paid a small fortune to have Isla in their home, and she considered it a victory on her part the artificial insemination never took. Looking at the girl in the drawing, Isla felt in her heart the child was hers and Remy's. Or would be some day. It had taken years for Rain to come into their lives, so Isla knew this child would happen when the fates deemed it so. Isla could wait. She had her precious Rainier to focus on now.

Since they were moving to California so Remy could honor his agreement to run the Pen there, Isla searched online for houses. Money was no issue, so she took her time in finding the perfect home for their little family. Knowing one day a daughter would be added, Isla chose houses with plenty of room. She had narrowed it down to two she really liked, and when Rain and Amelia broke for lunch, she sat her son on her knee and showed him the pictures.

"I like this one, Mum. It has a swimming pool." Rain chewed his bottom lip and turned his eyes to her. "Will you teach me how to swim?"

Before she could answer, Amelia twirled around the kitchen in a red and green tutu. She had them in every color, plus several for each holiday. Since Christmas was a few days away, red and green were the colors of the day. "I want to swim too! I can do water ballet!" Amelia's dark hair had fallen from the bun it started out in, and when she stopped spinning, she grabbed onto Isla's arm. "Will you fix my hair please?"

Isla grinned at the girl. Amelia was a breath of fresh air, and Isla was thankful Rain had such a good friend. Isla set Rain on his feet, then she fixed Amelia's hair into a braid because the bun, while cute, just wasn't practical for someone as active as Amelia. "Yes, Rain. I'll teach you to swim. Maybe when we're settled, Amelia can come visit."

"Yes! It'll be an adventure. I've never been to California." Amelia's butt wiggled, making it hard for Isla to get the braid finished, but she managed. If Connor's vision was right, Isla needed the practice.

Remy had reached out to Sinclair and gotten names of Clan members in California who had younger offspring. Not that they were opposed to Rain befriending human children, but it was nice to have friends they could be themselves around. The new prison had been completed, and they would be moving within the next month. Isla was going to miss the mates in New Atlanta, but she was looking forward to the next part of their lives. She was ready to have a home she could decorate with all their things Remy had in storage. Isla had been relieved her mate hadn't gotten rid of everything when he thought she'd died.

Marigold fixed lunch for everyone, and after the kids had eaten, they went back to studying. While sitting there scrolling through the photos of the house Rain liked, Isla's shifter nudged her. It had been so long since the Gargoyle had interacted with Isla. When she was held captive, that part of her retreated as though it were pissed off. She had tried coaxing it out of hiding, but it wouldn't budge. So to feel it stirring brought tears to her eyes.

I've missed you.

I was always here.

It didn't feel like it.

I was making things worse by fighting with you.

No. We were just in an impossible situation.

I'll never abandon you again. Especially now.

Why now?

Because I have to look out for our girl.

What girl? Wait! Are you saying…?

Yes. Rain is going to be a brother.

How far along? Can you tell?

Far enough there's a heartbeat.

Isla bowed her head and thanked the gods for giving her such a blessing. She also thanked them for keeping her from getting pregnant while being held at the Webers'. Then she jumped up from her chair, whooping and twirling much like Amelia did. Remy. She needed to call Remy. They were going to have a baby! She trusted her shifter to tell her the truth. It had alerted her when she was only days' pregnant with Rain, so Isla didn't bother with a pregnancy test. Instead of calling, Isla decided to meet him at work. She had visited the Pen a couple of times taking her mate lunch, and his only rule was she call first so he could meet her at the car. It wasn't that he didn't trust the other males around her, but he explained the prison was no place for a female to wander around unescorted.

Isla texted her mate. *I'm coming to see you.*

Remy's response came less than a minute later. *I'll be waiting.*

Isla slipped into the room where Marigold was going over a math lesson and told them she was headed out to see Remy. After kissing both kids on the temple, Isla practically skipped down the hallway and out the door. They had bought a second vehicle so Isla wouldn't be stuck at home with no transportation. It was a smaller SUV with the highest safety rating available, and Isla loved it. The drive to the Pen took roughly half an hour, and during that time, Isla didn't stop smiling. They hadn't been expecting a baby, but the hope was always there just below the surface. Isla would have a houseful if it were up to her.

True to his word, Remy was waiting outside when she pulled into the employee parking lot. She bounded out of the car and ran to her mate. If Remy weren't a Gargoyle, he might not have caught her as she lunged herself at him. He laughed at her exuberance.

"Not that I'm unhappy you're here, but what has you so excited?"

Isla wiggled out of Remy's embrace and pushed on his shoulder. Normally when she did that, she was asking for something completely different.

"Uh, as much as I would love to get frisky with you, I'm not sure here is the right place," Remy teased.

"At least bend over," she urged.

"Isla. What's going on? Bend over for what?"

Isla tapped her flat stomach. "Listen," she said, grinning.

"No."

"Yes!"

Remy squatted and placed his ear to her sweater. With his shifter hearing, he didn't need to get that close, but it was the intimacy she craved. Now that her shifter had informed Isla she was pregnant, Isla was able to detect the second, faster beat coming from her body.

Remy nuzzled Isla's belly. "Hi there. I'm your papa, and I can't wait to meet you." Remy looked up at Isla with so much love in his eyes it nearly brought her to her knees. She cupped his face and bent over to kiss him.

"We're having a baby," she whispered against his mouth.

"Merry Christmas to us," he responded. While they didn't believe in the human God, they did celebrate the holiday. They had taken Rain to pick out a tree and let him and Amelia decorate it however they wanted. Lights adorned the exterior of the house. Cheap baubles as well as expensive keepsakes lined the mantel and just about every other surface inside. They had gone overboard hoping to make up for the last two years their son had missed the holiday.

Remy surged to his feet, lifting Isla off the ground, and twirling her around. "We're having a baby!"

Aldredge ran out the back door, clapping and hooting with Remy. "Congratulations, Brother."

"Thank you. This is..." Remy shook his head.

"This is everything," Isla finished for her mate.

"Take the rest of the day off. Go celebrate," Aldredge offered.

"Thank you. I think I will." Remy, still holding Isla, carried her to her car and put her in the passenger seat. Once he was seated next to her, he leaned over the console, and she met him halfway. "I guess we already know it's a girl," he said after showing her with his mouth how happy he was.

"We do. My beast confirmed it. Let's go tell Rain he's going to be a big brother." Isla threaded her fingers with Remy's once he got the car started and on the road. Isla leaned her head against the seat and turned her face so she could stare at her mate. For over two years, she lived through hell. Not because of how she was treated, but because she'd been separated from her mate. Isla loved Rain with her whole being, but Remy was the other half of her soul. Now she was once again complete, and she didn't think she could be happier.

"I have a better idea." Remy lifted their joined hands and kissed Isla's knuckles. "He has a few more hours with Marigold. Let's go home and celebrate, just the two of us."

"You have the best ideas." Their sex life wasn't lacking by any means, but having a child meant they had to keep their lovemaking in the bedroom. Isla missed the days of spontaneous sex whenever and wherever.

By the time they arrived at Frey's to pick up their son, Remy had reminded Isla how creative he could be. She was more than sated, and she couldn't stop smiling. Abbi asked them to stay for supper, but they politely turned her down. Isla took her friend aside and confided what was going on. They wanted to tell Rain about the baby and celebrate with just the three of them. Abbi hugged Isla tightly, her own baby kicking against Isla's stomach. Abbi was due in just a few weeks, and baby Jonathan was making his presence known.

Abbi pushed on her son's foot. "I swear, he's going to be a fighter like his father."

"Or," Frey interjected from the kitchen doorway, "he

202

could be a dancer like his sister." His eyes were focused on Abbi's belly. Isla knew that look. It was the same one Remy used to get when Isla's tummy had been swollen with Rain.

Isla squeezed Abbi's arm, then went in search of Remy and Rain. Amelia was chattering about water ballet. Remy raised his eyebrows, and Isla grinned, shaking her head. When the little girl came up for air, Isla jumped in. "Amelia, we'll see you tomorrow, okay?"

"Okay. Bye, Rain!" Amelia went in for a hug, and Rain embraced her back. Isla thought they were cute together. She could imagine the two of them becoming mates when they were older, and Isla would be quite okay with that. She loved Abbi, and Frey was an honorable male. Having them as family would definitely be a plus.

Since they were celebrating, Remy asked Rain what he wanted for supper. The boy chose pizza, and Isla was happy with his choice. She had been cooking almost every night since she returned, only going out on the weekends. Remy suggested calling the order in, then eating at home since they had something private to talk about. Isla called the local mom-and-pop place that had the best pizza she'd ever tasted. She agreed that eating at home was the right idea. Isla was nervous about telling Rain she was pregnant. If this had been before he had been taken, she wouldn't think twice about his reaction. Considering he had just gotten his mum back, Isla didn't want him to think—

"Stop," Remy said. He grabbed her hand and kissed her fingertips. "I can hear you thinking. It's going to be fine," he promised. She gave her mate a smile, trusting he was right.

"YOUR MUM TELLS me you picked out our new house." Remy handed Rain a plate with his favorite pizza.

"It has a pool. Mum is going to teach me how to swim."

They had decided to excitedly talk about moving to California with all the state had to offer, like beaches and sunshine. They casually mentioned the other kids who Rain would have the chance to become friends with too. Isla thought if they let Rain get used to the idea instead of merely declaring they were moving he would better handle the situation. They had been correct.

"Now that is exciting. I need to call Sixx and have him put in the offer for us so someone doesn't snatch it out from under us." After Isla chose several homes in the area close to where the Pen was located, Sixx had vetted the properties then performed walkthroughs of each, and he did so with his camera showing Remy each property as he toured them. "The one you like has plenty of bedrooms. One for your mum and me. One for you. One for your little brother or sister." Remy held his breath.

Rain nodded as he chewed. "That would be so cool. Amelia is getting a baby brother, but I'm getting a sister."

"How do you know that?" Remy asked.

"Connor said so. He saw her in a vision."

Remy was so happy at Rain's acceptance of a sibling he didn't chastise the boy for speaking around a mouthful of food. Isla's eyes were filled with happy tears when she leaned over and hugged their son.

"What?" Rain asked his mum. "What was that for?"

"Can I not hug you because I love you?"

"I guess. When do I get my sister?" he asked, then took another bite of cheesy pepperoni goodness.

"In early September. We have plenty of time to get settled into our new home before she arrives." Isla brushed her hand across Rain's hair. "Would you like to help set up her room?"

"Yes. She's going to need lots of stuffies. Babies need soft things, don't you think?" Rain took a drink of his soda, then let out a burp. "Sorry, but that's bubbly. Oh, can I name her? I think she should be Rain too. Is September in the summer?"

"At the end of it, yes." Remy was pleased Rain was taking the news so well. "But do we really need two Rains? Won't that get confusing?"

"No, Papa. I'm named after you, and that's not confusing."

"You're right; it's because we don't call you Remington." Isla had chosen Remington Rainier after Remy and his father. He wasn't sure she would agree to their daughter being named Rainier as well.

"And we won't call my sister Rain. We can call her Summer." Rain shrugged like it was a done deal. When Remy raised his eyebrows at Isla, she nodded.

"Summer Rain. It is catchy. What do you think, Mum?" Remy asked, reaching for Isla's hand.

Isla blinked back the tears, but they were happy ones. He could feel her joy through their bond. "I think it's a lovely name. I also think you're going to be the best big brother ever."

"Can her bedroom be next to mine? If I'm going to look after her, I need to be close."

Remy's heart was full to bursting. "It sure can. Let's finish eating so I can call Sixx. Then we can discuss what color you want your room painted."

The house they'd chosen had just been completely remodeled, and the rooms all had fresh coats of paint in colors Isla adored. Still, they had agreed Rain could decorate his room however he liked. They wanted their son to be excited about moving, not dread it.

"Mum, when do we get to see Summer? Amelia has pictures and videos of Jonathan in Abbi's tummy."

"Well, she's not very big. Right now, she's about the size of a pepperoni slice. She's going to need to grow a little before they can show us a picture."

"Cool. Can I go with you when you see her? I need to be there."

Isla smiled down at their son. "If that's what you want."

"It is. Summer needs me to protect her. That's what big brothers do." Rain was so matter of fact, and Remy wondered what was going through his son's mind. Did he not think Remy would protect the baby? Oh gods! He blamed Remy for what Nash did.

"Well not all big brothers. Uncle Nash didn't protect Mum. Or me. He was a bad big brother, right, Mum?"

"You're right. Nash wasn't a good big brother at all."

"Then I'm going to show him how it's done. Summer will never have to worry about me lying to her." Rain climbed down from his chair and bent his head over Isla's stomach. "You hear that, Summy? I'm your big brother, Rain, and I'm going to take care of you. I'm going to protect you, just like Papa protects me and Mum." Rain kissed Isla's sweater, then placed a kiss on Isla's cheek. "Love you, Mum."

"Love you too, Rainier."

Rain then went to Remy. When he stopped in front of Remy, the boy fisted his heart and bowed his head. "On my honor, Papa."

Remy choked back a sob, grabbed his son, and hugged him tightly. "You're the best son in the world, and I love you more than life itself."

"Love you too, Papa. Now can I go read?"

Remy released Rain. "Of course." Rain took off running up the stairs, and Remy watched until Rain was out of sight. When he turned back around, he got a lap full of his mate. Isla snaked her arm around Remy's neck and rested her head on his. No words were needed. Their son had said it all.

Epilogue

Toulouse, France
2056

ISLA FIXED SUMMER'S hair in a tight Dutch braid. Her daughter was on the go from the time she woke until she went to bed, chasing after her big brother. Summer sat still for Isla until the band was secured around the ends, then she stood and held out her hand. If they had been at their home in New Atlanta, the girl would have been off like a shot, but they were at their French vineyard for a couple weeks while the kids were out of school. Summer wasn't familiar with the sprawling estate, thus the hand holding.

Isla escorted her daughter through the rows of grapevines as they made their way to where Remy and Rain were helping set up vats of grapes waiting to be stomped. There were several small vineyards in Georgia where she and Remy took the kids to get their "smashing" fix when they couldn't get to France. California had been a wonderful place to live, but when the offer came for Remy to switch places with Aldredge, he took it. They had made friends on the West Coast, but the Clan in New Atlanta had become family.

Rain and Amelia were tighter than ever. Frey and Remy were keeping their eye on Rain. He was fourteen, and they expected him to transition any day now. When that happened, they would have to keep him away from Amelia until he learned to control his beast. Amelia was well aware of all things shifter, and she promised to run if Rain began phasing around her. As much as Amelia loved Rain, Summer equally loved Jonathan. The two families spent most of their free time together.

As soon as Isla and Summer broke through the rows of vines, Summer took off running. She tackled an unsuspecting Jonathan, and the two kids rolled around on the ground, trying to get the upper hand. Summer was a year younger than Jon, but she was a full-blooded Gargoyle. She was already strong, and with Frey teaching her along with the other kids in one of his many classes, Summer was grappling with the best of them.

"Shift your legs, Jon," Frey instructed. His son did as told, and soon he had the advantage.

Abbi came to stand by Isla. "You would think they'd get enough of this at the gym."

"Grab his wrist, Summer." Frey didn't play favorites when it came to teaching. He used every opportunity to coach them to be the best they could be. Things were changing in the world around them, and when the kids got older, they would be the ones leading the Clan. Frey wanted to give them every opportunity to be prepared, even if it meant impromptu wrestling at the French vineyard.

Jon was large for his age, but that wasn't surprising considering who his papa was. He was stronger than Summer, but she gave him a run for his money. Seeing the kids were pretty evenly matched, meaning they wouldn't stop until someone made them, Remy announced, "The vats are ready."

Summer rolled off Jon and held out her hand. "Let's go smash some grapes." Jonathan took it, and after popping to his feet, the two kids rushed over to a free vat. They pulled off their shoes and jumped in. These particular grapes would not be used in the winemaking. They had been set up purely for entertainment.

Remy led Isla off to the side instead of to their own vat.

"What's wrong?" she asked. Instead of speaking, Remy

pulled out his phone. After tapping the screen a few times, he held it out to her. Isla had seen the drawing Connor presented Remy all those years ago, but she had forgotten about it. Until now. Isla glanced down at her clothes, then looked over at Summer. They were dressed exactly as Connor had imagined them.

Remy looked behind Isla. "Seeing the two of you walking between the vines was like déjà vu. I don't understand his gift, but I will never doubt Connor's abilities again."

As she and Remy stepped into their own vat and took part in stomping the grapes, Isla thought about Connor and the recent drawings he had created. If all the teen had seen in his visions did come to fruition, life as they knew it was going to get interesting.

If anyone was up to the task of protecting the world, it was all the kids of the Stone Society.

GABRIEL

CHAPTER ONE

ISABELLE STUDIED THE picture of Rebekah. If Connor was drawing Gabriel's mate, it meant something. To her, it meant there was the possibility of finding the female and reuniting her with Gabriel. It didn't mean a happily ever after though. Not with her brother sitting in the Pen. Gabriel was paying for his crimes, plus his mental health was still shaky. With all that had happened recently, with the threat against their clan still out there, Isabelle didn't want to bother Henry. Julian was taking some well-deserved time off, so Isabelle had called the one other person she knew who had some computer experience.

Tessa, dressed in her usual jeans and biker boots, tapped away at a laptop. She was sitting at Isabelle's kitchen table, her long, red hair in a braid down her back. "Take a look at this." Tessa pointed to the screen.

Isabelle looked over her cousin's shoulder. "That's the same garden Connor drew."

"It is. At first, I thought it would be in Asia, but turns out it's in New Portland, Oregon. There's a Japanese garden there." Tessa had started searching for Rebekah using the female's name, and when that didn't garner any hits, she focused on the landscape.

"But what if she was just visiting?" Isabelle straightened and wrapped her arms around her waist.

"What if she isn't? Belle, you know Connor's drawings are always spot-on. They mean something, and in this case,

211

it probably means that's where you'll find Rebekah."

"What if she doesn't want to be found?"

"And what if she does?" Tessa stood and grabbed Isabelle's biceps. "What has you so worried?"

"She's human. They didn't complete the bond, so she's aged while Gabriel hasn't. I'm going to need to explain everything to her. What if she doesn't believe me? What if she does? She probably moved on with her life. She could be married with kids."

"She very well could be, or she could be pining for the love of her life. Belle, Connor saw Rebekah for a reason. Don't you owe it to Gabriel to find out what that reason is? Maybe she's not meant to reunite with Gabriel. Maybe she's in trouble."

"You're right. But damnit, New Portland's a big city. How am I going to find her?"

"I'll help. Gregor and I will go with you. Between the three of us, we'll cover more ground."

"Four of us." Dante strode into the kitchen and cupped Isabelle's face. "I'm coming with you."

"But what about the morgue? Trevor and Jasper are out of the country."

"I'll call in a favor. Speaking of, Tessa, since Tamian and Lucy are here, why don't you call and see if we can borrow his jet?"

"On it." Tessa grabbed her phone off the table and went outside to call her brother.

"Dante —"

"No, Beautiful. I'm not letting you do this alone. Simon Lowell is an old colleague of mine and happens to be in New Atlanta. He and I went to lunch yesterday. Simon is a medical examiner who currently lives on the West Coast. He's also a Goyle, and his time is up in his current location. He is looking to relocate, and I think New Atlanta would be perfect for him."

"Does that mean you're really stepping down?" Dante

had mentioned retiring more than once. At least from his position in New Atlanta. He had been in the city for many years, as had all his family.

"I think it's time. With this latest threat to our family, we need to consider our next steps. But let's worry about that later. For now, let's go see if we can't find Rebekah."

Isabelle leaned her forehead against her mate's chest. She didn't know what she'd do without her strong Gargoyle.

Tessa was all smiles when she returned inside. "Tamian is calling Santiago. The jet will be ready whenever we are. I've already called Stone, so I'm going home to pack. Are you bringing Connor with us, or do you want me to drop him off with Abbi on my way home?"

"As much as I don't want him out of my sight right now, I think he'd be better off staying here." Things had calmed down somewhat since several of their homes had been bombed. Drago Costas was dead, but whoever had helped the male was still out there somewhere.

Dante kissed Isabelle's temple. "You go start packing, and I'll call Frey. Tessa, if you don't mind dropping him off, I'd appreciate it."

"Nothing but a thing," the redhead said, sitting back down at the laptop. "I'll make hotel reservations while I wait."

"FANCY MEETING YOU here."

Four words were all it took to disturb the peacefulness Rebekah relished standing on the Moon Bridge of her beloved Japanese Gardens. She had found this place soon after she moved to New Portland, and it became a much-needed haven. When she fled New Atlanta all those years ago, doing her best to escape the memories, the man, she put as much distance between them as possible. Had she not fallen in love, not completely given her heart away, the miles might have helped. It didn't. The pain dimmed with the years, but the memories wouldn't leave her mind, no matter how much Rebekah wished it so.

"Christopher." Rebekah glanced over her shoulder at the man standing a few feet away. A few years older than her, Christopher Hadley was handsome. The two had met on that same bridge several months ago, and despite her many protests, he was relentless in asking her out. During a moment of weakness, she agreed to coffee. One date turned into a weekly thing, and that was all Rebekah was interested in. More than she was interested in if she were being honest. She had no room in her life for a man. Not again.

"I can never get enough of this view." Christopher's words might have indicated the stunning gardens over her shoulder, but his eyes were focused on her. In her younger days, Rebekah might have been called pretty, but age and other things had taken their toll. Her face was lined. Her former slim body now held a few extra pounds. She hadn't necessarily let herself go, but she was no longer diligent in daily self-care.

Rebekah turned her head away from the man, hoping he would get the hint she wished to be alone. When his feet carried him closer, she closed her eyes briefly and sighed. It wasn't in her nature to be rude, so she remained quiet instead of telling him to go away.

"I was hoping you'd join me for dinner. I know we have our standing coffee dates, but I have a business meeting, and the others are bringing their wives. I'd prefer to not attend alone, and there is no one else I'd rather have on my arm than you." Christopher touched her shoulder. "Just this once, as a favor. Please."

Rebekah considered it. Their coffee dates weren't uncomfortable. Christopher was intelligent and a good conversationalist. He was a widower with two grown children who had long ago moved away. She could do worse for company. "When and where?"

"Friday evening at The Bowery. Dinner begins at six, so if I pick you up at five-thirty, will that give us enough time?" As far as she knew, Christopher didn't know where Rebekah lived. She had given her maiden name when she introduced herself. She had never mentioned the large estate her late husband left to her when he passed away, nor had she shared who her husband had been. Knowing Jacob's name would make it easy enough to figure out where she lived.

"I'd prefer to meet you there. And Christopher? Just this once."

The man's shoulders settled as he nodded his acquiescence. "I can accept that. I'll let you get back to your solitude. Until Friday." Christopher tipped an imaginary hat before walking away.

Rebekah pulled her coat tighter before shoving her gloved hands into the slanted pockets at her thighs. She tried to regain the peacefulness she'd felt before Christopher showed up, but the moment was gone. Instead of taking up space someone else could enjoy, Rebekah made her way to the exit. She knew every inch of the Gardens and was familiar with those who worked and volunteered there. Most days, she found someone to speak to, if only to say hello. Not today. No, she got in her car and headed to the estate she called home.

When she had first come to live on the property, Rebekah wasn't sure about being secluded, but after a while, the grounds, the fence surrounding the property, and the massive structure she shared with Jacob all became another sanctuary for her. The older man had been a colleague who befriended Rebekah. Theirs had been a relationship borne of loneliness on both their parts. His wife had passed away, and Rebekah filled the void for him, while his kindness did the same for her. After a couple years, Jacob convinced

215

Rebekah to marry him. He had no children from his first marriage, and he wanted to provide for her. For fifteen years, the two of them lived together as friends. He never pushed her for a physical relationship, knowing her heart belonged to someone else. When Jacob passed away, he left Rebekah with an estate worth millions, but once again, her heart was shattered. She lost her best friend the day she laid Jacob to rest.

Rebekah had lost her heart the first time over thirty years ago, and no man had been able to retrieve it in all that time. She'd tried. Heaven knows she had tried to forget Gabriel, but her one and only love was always there, right at the surface. Rebekah had been brokenhearted when Gabriel turned her away. She had stuck around for a while, keeping in contact with his mother, but eventually Gabriel disappeared.

He had been different the last time she'd seen him. Quiet. Withdrawn. Whatever happened to change his appearance also changed Gabriel on the inside. Gone was the effervescent man she fell in love with. In his place was someone she didn't recognize. Rebekah remained for a couple years, hoping and praying Gabriel would reach out to her. He never did, so she moved out west, hoping to put Gabriel behind her with the distance between them.

It didn't work.

Trying to move on with her life, Rebekah threw herself into her profession and studies. She became a psychologist in the hopes that if she ever found Gabriel again, she could at least understand whatever he'd gone through. She wanted to help him, but if she never saw him again, at least she could help others. She had met Jacob at the clinic where she worked. He had first been her boss and mentor, then her friend and husband. His daily presence was a comfort until she lost him too. Now she was content with her tabby, Esmeralda.

Speaking of the feline, Esmeralda greeted her at the

door, winding through Rebekah's legs as she tried to navigate through to the kitchen without falling.

"Esme, one of these days, you're going to make me fall, and then who's going to feed you? Hmm?"

Esmeralda responded with a long "mrawr."

Rebekah set her purse on the counter, then bent to pick up the menace. Rubbing at the M on Esme's forehead, Rebekah carried her pet into the living room and sat down on the sofa. Esme nudged Rebekah's hand for more loving. Toeing off her shoes, Rebekah relaxed, letting the cat's purring do its job of soothing Rebekah's soul. She closed her eyes as she stroked Esme, thinking about Christopher's request for dinner with colleagues. The last time she had dined out in a group had been with Jacob before the heart attack took him suddenly. Rebekah used to love going to restaurants, meeting up with friends. If Christopher's coworkers were anything like him, Friday wouldn't be a hardship. It was the wives she was leery of. Still, she could hold her own for one evening.

Friday rolled around, and Rebekah was nervous. She dabbed concealer under her eyes, doing her best to cover the purple skin. It wasn't like she was trying too hard to impress Christopher. Her makeup was subtle. Always had been. When satisfied with her face, she brushed her dark hair now interspersed with gray. She rummaged through her closet to find the perfect outfit. The Bowery was an upscale place, so she opted for one of her more stylish dresses, then added simple pearl earrings instead of her preferred diamonds. She didn't want to come across as the wealthy woman she was. Not that she thought Christopher was after her for her money. Then again, she didn't know him well enough to say that for sure. She wasn't one to flaunt her wealth. Yes, she lived on the estate she'd shared with Jacob, but Rebekah had always been a simple woman. She spent her money on things that made her happy. Books. Artwork. Giving to charities.

When Jacob passed, Rebekah had been lost, and she retired from her position as head psychologist at the local hospital. She spent the next two years traveling. Revisiting the places Jacob had taken her on vacation. Tuscany had been their favorite. Rebekah stayed two months in a villa in the central Italian countryside. Those two months helped heal her heart enough she was able to return home. The estate was too large for one person, but it became her haven. Her refuge. Instead of losing herself in the large home with Esme, she found new hobbies, and she volunteered.

With one last glance in the mirror, Rebekah grabbed her purse and keys. The drive to the restaurant took less than twenty minutes. Christopher was waiting by the front door. His smile was genuine when he saw her, but Rebekah didn't feel anything for the man other than kind affection. She'd lost her heart twice, and there was nothing left for her to give someone else other than friendship.

"Hello, Gorgeous." Christopher leaned down and kissed her cheek. He placed his hand on her back as he held the door for Rebekah, and once inside, he led her to a large table where three couples were seated. The men stood when the two of them approached. Christopher said, "This is Rebekah Collins." When she was seated, the men returned to their seats, and each one introduced themselves and their wives.

"It's a pleasure to meet you." Rebekah sipped the water already waiting for her.

"So, Rebekah. What is it you do for a living?" Constance Alder asked from her right.

"I'm a psychologist, though I retired a couple years back."

"I thought you looked familiar. You're Rebekah Nieman."

Rebekah tried not to cringe at the use of her married name, but she wasn't going to lie. "Yes. How did you know?"

"I'm a nurse in the OR at the hospital. Several patients were referred to you when they were brought in for overdoses."

Rebekah should have known someone would recognize her name if not her face. She smiled at Constance, and the two of them chatted about other employees they both knew. When their food arrived, Rebekah turned back in her seat to find Christopher staring at her. She raised her eyebrows, and he shook his head. Rebekah would eventually have to address the fact that she'd not shared her married name with him. Dinner was enjoyable for the most part. Rebekah had missed being out with friends. And although she'd just met the three couples, she found herself intrigued by each of the women. The men had been talking about an investment they were partnering on, and Rebekah found it interesting, until Dan Sykes turned his attention to her.

"We could use a fifth partner."

Rebekah took a sip of wine, giving herself time to tamp down her frustration. "I appreciate the offer, but it's not something I'd be interested in."

"Please think about it. It's a solid investment. We've worked out the logistics, and the building will be perfect for what we have in mind."

"I'm sure you've done your due diligence, but like I said, it's not something I want to invest in."

"Rebekah—"

"If you'll excuse me." Rebekah stood and grabbed her purse. "It was a pleasure meeting you all, but I think I'm going to head on home."

Constance gave her a sad smile and handed Rebekah a folded piece of paper. "It was a pleasure to see you. If you ever want to get coffee, please give me a call."

"Thank you. I might take you up on that." Rebekah turned to her date. "Thank you for a lovely evening," she lied.

"I'll walk you out." Christopher gestured for Rebekah

to proceed in front of him. When they reached the sidewalk, he grabbed her hand. "Why did you lie to me about who you really are?"

Rebekah pulled away. "I didn't lie. I simply chose not to offer my married name because of what just happened in there. Whenever someone finds out who I am, they think they can hold out their hand, and I'll drop a donation or get involved in their investments."

"I apologize for Dan, and I promise I didn't know your real identity. Please don't let this tarnish our relationship."

"We don't have a relationship. We had a tentative friendship, but I think it's best if we part ways now. Take care of yourself, Christopher." Rebekah turned to walk to her car, but Christopher grabbed her arm.

"Don't walk away from me." His grip wasn't as harsh as his words.

"Take your hands off her," a female voice demanded.

Rebekah turned to see a stunning redhead standing there, her face a mask of fury. He dropped his hand. "I was just—"

"Leaving. You were just leaving." The woman took a step toward Christopher who raised his hands.

"Fine. Rebekah, I'll call you." Christopher strode back into the restaurant.

"Are you okay?"

Rebekah nodded. "Yes, thank you."

"No problem." The redhead didn't hang around. She strode in the opposite direction, meeting up with a handsome man who held his hand out. The woman looked back at Rebekah one more time before clasping her partner's hand and walking away.

Rebekah made her way to her car and headed home, thinking about the woman who'd come to her rescue.

CHAPTER TWO

"AT LEAST WE know they aren't together." Tessa adjusted the vent on the dash as Gregor followed Rebekah away from the restaurant. They had been sitting in the Bowery enjoying dinner when Rebekah walked in with her date. Tessa had wanted to introduce herself, but before she got the chance, Rebekah had made her exit. When Tessa saw Christopher grab Rebekah's arm, it was all she could do to keep her Gargoyle at bay.

"Truth, Red. But we also know Rebekah was married."

"She's not now, so she won't have any reason not to come back to New Atlanta."

They had listened in on the conversation happening a few tables over. After her identity had come to light, it didn't take long for Tessa and Gregor to figure out Rebekah had money. It also didn't take long for one of the men to ask her to join their endeavor. It was then Rebekah had made a hasty retreat from the restaurant. Tessa and Gregor had decided to dine separately from Dante and Isabelle, giving them better odds of seeing Rebekah while out. Tessa paced the hotel suite waiting for Isabelle and Dante to return. She had called her cousin while following Rebekah home and told Isabelle they had seen the female.

The door opened, and Isabelle grabbed Tessa's arm. "Tell me everything."

Tessa recapped what happened, then explained where Rebekah lived. "It's a large estate surrounded by a fence and iron gate. I did a little research when we got back. Her husband passed away a couple years ago."

"That's good. Not that he's dead. That's not what I meant. It's good that she's free to come back with us if she wants. I'm not sure about showing up at her house though."

Tessa sat down next to Gregor on one of the sofas in the common area of their suite. "I still think The Gardens is our best bet. Connor drew it for a reason. It must mean something to her."

"So we just show up there every day waiting for her?"

Dante put his arms around Isabelle from behind. "There are worse places to wait. The photos on the website are stunning. I say we look for her there. If for some reason she doesn't show up after a few days, then we'll try her home."

"Okay. We'll give it two days, and if she doesn't show up, then we'll go to her home. Now that we know she's here, I'm ready to get this over with and get back to Connor."

Tessa leaned against Gregor, and he wrapped his arm around her shoulder. "I've already bought tickets for tomorrow. We'll be there when the doors open."

Isabelle and Dante said goodnight, then retreated to their bedroom. Tessa turned to her mate. "You ready for bed, Stone?"

"With you? Always." Gregor stood and lifted Tessa from the sofa as if she weighed nothing. Tessa kissed Gregor's neck as he carried her to their room. For months, she had worried about not being able to give him babies. They talked about it, and Gregor assured her they would adopt if they needed to, but Tessa wanted to have *their* kids.

Gregor placed her in the middle of the bed, and Tessa propped up on her elbows. "I want to go away."

"What? Red—"

"I want *us* to go away. Once we talk to Rebekah and get back home, I want the two of us to go somewhere like Acapulco. Somewhere warm where it's just the two of us. Deacon has the Pen under control, and I'd just like to get away from New Atlanta for a while."

"Whatever you want." Gregor unbuttoned his shirt, and Tessa licked her lips when his defined chest came into view. It was a sight she never tired of.

"I want you." Tessa slid from the bed, and they undressed each other, taking their time. Lately, Tessa had been so focused on getting pregnant she hadn't allowed herself to enjoy the act. Tonight, she vowed to lavish her mate with all the attention he deserved.

REBEKAH TOOK A sip of her coffee and grimaced. It had gone cold as she sat and stared out the back door. Sleep had been a long time coming the night before as she went over what happened at the restaurant. It didn't surprise her that Dan Sykes had asked her to partner in their investment. What she had trouble with was whether or not Christopher had known who she was beforehand. Regardless, she didn't want to see him anymore. That didn't bother her. A weekly coffee date was all they had. And while those meetings were mostly pleasant, she wouldn't miss them. Maybe it was time to do some more traveling. Other than her cat and The Gardens, there really was nothing keeping Rebekah in New Portland.

Speaking of The Gardens, Saturday was her day to volunteer, so she rose from the table and dumped her cold coffee in the sink. Rebekah prayed Christopher wouldn't show up and sabotage her day. She needed the peacefulness to wipe away the previous night. After giving Esmeralda lots of loving, Rebekah showered and dressed. The drive to The Gardens wasn't long enough for Rebekah to do a lot of thinking. She didn't want to think, so she turned on what she called her guilty pleasure playlist. It was full of pop songs that were upbeat, and Rebekah sang along with each one.

Her job as a volunteer varied each week. Sometimes she helped in the gift shop, but more often than not, she was stationed at the concierge desk for the first three hours it was open. Afterward, she was free to roam. Since she hadn't seen Christopher come through, she was fairly certain he was going to leave her alone, at least for today. So once she was relieved, Rebekah stopped off at the café for some tea, then made her way around the pathway by the Flat Garden, passed underneath the Wisteria Arbor, then turned right toward the Moon Bridge. A couple was standing at the railing. Rebekah turned toward the opposite railing, but the woman stepped toward her.

"Rebekah? It's me. Isabelle Montague."

Rebekah gasped. "Izzy?" Talk about a blast from the past. Rebekah hadn't seen Gabriel's sister since she was a toddler. "Is it really you?"

Isabelle nodded. "Yes. It's me. I'm so glad I found you."

"Found me?" Rebekah took a step back. Why would she be looking for Rebekah unless she wanted something? The woman was dressed in nice clothes, and the man with her was dressed even more sharply.

"Yes. I have so much to tell you, and afterward, I was hoping you'd come back to New Atlanta for a visit."

"But why? Wait, is this about Gabriel? Did you find him? Did he come home? Is he okay?" Rebekah's heart was trying to beat out of her chest.

Isabelle smiled. "It's a long story. One best not told out in the open. Is there somewhere we can go to talk?"

Rebekah looked at the man who was standing stoically behind Isabelle.

"I apologize. Rebekah, this is my husband, Dante Di Pietro. He's New Atlanta's Chief Medical Examiner." Dante stepped forward and held out his hand.

Rebekah switched her tea from her right hand to her left so she could shake. "It's a pleasure, Dr. Di Pietro."

"Please, call me Dante."

"If you'd like, you're welcome to come to our hotel suite," Isabelle said just as another couple walked toward the bridge. It was the same redhead from the night before.

"Hello again," the woman said, stepping right next to Isabelle.

"Hello. Uh, do you two know each other?" Rebekah was getting worried about this being a trap. But why would Isabelle want to trap her?

"Yes, I'm Tessa, Isabelle's cousin. This is my husband, Gregor Stone."

"Stone? As in the Stones who rebuilt New Atlanta?"

Gregor inclined his head. "Yes, ma'am."

Rebekah turned back to Tessa. "Did you know who I was last night? What's going on here?"

"I did know, but it was pure luck we ran into you at the restaurant."

Isabelle leaned back against her husband's chest, and he slid a hand around her stomach protectively. "Like I was saying, I have so much to tell you, and yes, it's about Gabriel. He's back in New Atlanta."

"Then why didn't he come with you? Is he okay?" Rebekah wanted to leave right then and go to him. Or did she? He disappeared without a word to her. Broke her heart. She didn't know if she could go through that again.

"He's been through a lot. It's one of the things I wanted to speak to you about, but not here."

"Then let's go to my home. We'll have plenty of privacy there."

"We'll follow you," Isabelle said, gesturing toward the pathway.

Rebekah probably should have gone to their hotel instead of allowing them into her sanctuary, but she had a feeling she would need the comfort of being in her own space. She would listen to what they had to say, and then she'd decide where to go from there.

Thirty minutes later, Rebekah pulled into the driveway

with their rental car following. Instead of pulling into the garage, she parked out front. After unlocking the door, Rebekah turned off the alarm. Esmeralda took one look at the newcomers, hissed, then took off running down the hallway. That was strange. She was usually a social cat.

"Please make yourselves at home. Can I get you something to drink?"

"No, thank you," all four said in unison. Isabelle and Dante sat next to each other on the sofa, while Tessa and Gregor took the love seat. Rebekah sat on the edge of the chair opposite Isabelle.

Isabelle laced her fingers with Dante's. "Instead of making small talk, I'm going to come right out and tell you everything. What I'm going to say is going to be hard to believe, so please keep an open mind." When Rebekah promised she would, Isabelle continued. "The first thing you need to know is like the four of us, Gabriel is special. Have you ever read a fantasy book about shapeshifters?"

"You mean like werewolves?"

"Yes. Where people can change into something other than human."

"It's been a while, but yes, I have."

Isabelle looked at Dante, and he nodded. "We are all shifters. Gargoyles, to be exact. Dante and Gregor are full-bloods, meaning both their parents were Gargoyles as well. Tessa and I are half-bloods because our mothers are human. We can show you so you know I'm not lying." Isabelle held out her free hand, and claws extended from her fingertips. Fangs extended over her bottom lip. "The females of our kind only have claws and fangs. The males have wings and special skin which is practically impenetrable. We all have extended lifespans. Full-blooded Gargoyles transition for the first time when they reach puberty. Gabriel, like me, is a half-blood, and we don't transition until we meet our mate. I didn't know about any of this until I saw one of my brothers going through his transition."

Rebekah held up her hand to stop Isabelle. "I need a drink." She rose from her chair and headed to the stocked bar at the back of the room. She wasn't a big drinker, but this crazy story called for hard liquor. She poured two fingers of whiskey, downed it in one go, then poured another shot which she took back to her chair. Instead of sitting, she remained standing as she studied the four people. No, they weren't human if she believed Isabelle's story.

"I know this sounds crazy, and believe me, I understand. I wasn't aware of shifters. Had no idea I was one. I also didn't know I had fifteen siblings either. But back to Gabriel. When you and he were together, it caused his transition. Since our parents didn't tell us about being Gargoyles, Gabriel wasn't aware of what being around you would do to him. He was out one day when his first shift came upon him. It just so happened that when he began changing into his Gargoyle, he wasn't alone. Are you aware of the Unholy?"

"Of course. He's not one of them, is he?"

"No, but the men who saw Gabriel transitioning were scientists who worked for a man named Gordon Flanagan. They took Gabriel to Flanagan, they studied him, extracted his blood, and used it in an attempt at creating super soldiers. What they ended up with were the Unholy. When they had what they needed from Gabriel, they dumped his body, thinking he would die. Only he didn't. He made his way home, and that's the Gabriel you saw the last time you came over. After what was done to him, he wasn't the same."

"I hung around, just in case he wanted to see me, but eventually I moved out here. I gave up."

"I understand. We all did. Gabriel disappeared until last year. When he showed back up, he was someone different. It's not a happy story."

"Tell me anyway." Rebekah's head was spinning, but

she needed to know all about her first love.

"What Flanagan did to Gabriel, it messed with his mind. Gabriel went to work for Flanagan. Changed his name. He basically became Flanagan's flunky because he didn't feel like he belonged anywhere else. Not with you. Not with his family. Anyway, he killed people. A lot of people, and then he kidnapped the chief of police who happens to be our King's mate. Dante's and Gregor's brother, Rafael, is the leader of the Gargoyles here in the States. Kaya is his mate, and when Gabriel, a.k.a. Vincent Alexander, took her, it was like this epic showdown. They managed to rescue Kaya and put Gabriel behind bars. I work as the penitentiary's doctor, and when he and I were in the same room, I recognized him. It's been a rough year and a half, and he's shown only slight improvement."

"Why are you telling me this? Why trust me with your secrets? I assume the truth of Gargoyles is a secret since I would have heard if there were shifters out in the world."

"It is a secret. My son, Connor, is special. He has an amazing gift of seeing the future, but he communicates what he sees in drawings. Everything he's created in pictures has come to pass. He drew your picture standing on the Moon Bridge. It was how we knew to look for you in New Portland. Here, let me show you." Isabelle pulled her phone out of her purse, and after a few seconds, handed it over.

"That's..." Amazing. Incredible. Eerie. The picture on the phone was so realistic it could have been a photograph. "How old is your son?"

"He just turned seven. Before Dante and I got together, Connor was kidnapped. Somehow, he and Dante, whom he had never met, had a bond. Dante could speak to Connor in his mind, and Connor was able to draw pictures of the area where he was being kept. Dante could see what Connor showed him, and that led us to him. In Greece."

"This is all too much. I'm a psychologist, for God's sake. I study the mind, and I've never come across anything of

228

this nature in all the years I practiced." Rebekah handed the phone back. "So why did you come here?"

"I'm hoping since you're Gabriel's mate, you can help him. Help heal his mind and heart. He won't be getting out of prison anytime soon because his sins are too great, but as his sister, I want him to stop hurting. And Rebekah, he's hurting badly."

"But if he's in prison, how am I supposed to do that through a plexiglass window?"

"Gregor's the warden there, and he can get you in to see Gabriel. Not through a barrier but in his actual room. I know it's asking a lot, but I really think you can help him."

"What do you mean I'm his mate? We were only dating when he disappeared. We didn't..." Rebekah wrapped her fingers around her neck, embarrassed. "We weren't intimate," she lied for some reason.

Tessa laughed and slapped Gregor's thigh. "You don't have to be. I ran into this one" — she nudged Gregor's shoulder with her own — "in a convenience store. I had dropped some cash, and when I bent over to grab it, I bumped into the male standing behind me. That was all it took. I transitioned for the first time after that brief encounter."

Rebekah chugged the rest of her whiskey. Was she willing to leave her life in New Portland and travel back to New Atlanta to see Gabriel who was a murderer? "What if he tries to hurt me?"

Dante was the one who answered. "He wouldn't. He would rather die than harm you. You were married?"

"Yes."

"I assume you loved your husband. Would you have harmed him?"

"Ours wasn't a typical marriage. He was a colleague. He lost his wife, and the two of us became good friends afterward. We were married, yes, but it was purely platonic. Two people easing the pain and loneliness in the other. But no, I would never have harmed him in any way."

"Was your pain from losing Gabriel or something else?" Dante asked.

"I never got over Gabriel. He was my everything, and it broke something inside of me when he disappeared. I became a psychologist in the hopes I could figure out what might have happened... Oh my God. I became a psychologist to help Gabriel should I ever see him again." Rebekah laughed, but it wasn't joyful. "This is what I've been waiting for my whole adult life. When can we leave?"

Dante stood. "I'll call and get the jet ready."

Isabelle rose to her feet. "Is there someone who can watch after your cat? Animals don't like Gargoyles. They sense the beast inside us. Not that we'd ever hurt them, but they don't know that. If not, we'll get Tessa's brother to talk to her. Tamian's like an animal whisperer."

"I'd rather not leave her behind since I don't know how long I'll be gone."

"Okay. Do you have a carrier to put her in? She'll be upset until we can get her on the plane. We can put her in the bedroom and close the door."

"Yes, I do. I need to go pack. Please, help yourselves to anything in the kitchen or to something to drink."

Tessa pushed against Gregor's leg and got to her feet. "Do you need to call someone to watch over this place? If not, I'll toss the perishable food so your home doesn't stink once you return."

"No, there's no one. I would appreciate you taking care of that for me."

"Not a problem." The redhead sashayed out of the room with her husband following.

It took longer to coax Esmeralda out of hiding than it did to pack and ready the house to be closed up for a while. Rebekah packed as many clothes as she could in her three bags. Her hands shook, and her heart thumped heavily in her chest. She was going to see Gabriel. Rebekah was worried as much as she was excited.

Three hours later, they were in the sky. Rebekah peppered them with questions about their lives as Gargoyles, and in return, she told them about her life in Oregon. When Tessa relayed about the latest attacks on their families, Rebekah cried for the ones she'd never met. Her heart broke when she found out the Queen, Kaya, had nearly been killed in the explosion that tore apart hers and Rafael's home. The closer they got to New Atlanta, the more Rebekah wanted to be part of their lives. Not only did she want to help Gabriel but all those who were hurting. Yes, she was getting ahead of herself, but if she had her way, Rebekah might never leave Georgia once they landed.

CHAPTER THREE

GABRIEL LOST COUNT of the handstand pushups he had done. His mind hadn't allowed him to focus on the book he was reading, and the only other thing for him to do was exercise. Being stuck in the small room sucked, but it was his life now. After a year, he'd learned to deal with the lack of freedom. Footsteps sounded in the hallway, and Gabriel paused and lowered his head so he could see the door. Figuring it was the guard bringing his breakfast, he was pleasantly surprised to find Isabelle's smiling face filling the small window of his door, so he dropped to his feet and waited for his sister to come in. Their parents visited every once in a while, but it was Izzy who visited almost daily. She had been absent the last couple of days, and Gabriel was glad to see her.

"Izzy, where have you been? Is everything okay?" Isabelle kept him apprised of everything going on in the world outside the prison's walls. She showed him pictures on her phone, mostly of Connor and his two friends, Amelia and Rain. She did her best to keep things lighthearted, but when she told him what Drago Costas had done, he wanted to dig up the male's body and kill him all over again.

"Everything's good. As a matter of fact, I have a surprise for you." Isabelle was practically pulsing with excitement.

"You brought me a carton of smokes? I get to go outside for the rest of the day?"

"Even better. There's someone here who wants to see you."

Gabriel reached out with his senses, expecting it to be their parents or maybe Connor. Instead, he found... "No."

"No? Gabriel —"

"No, Izzy. I don't want her to see me like this."

"Gabriel?" The sweetest voice he had ever heard said his name from the doorway. Rebekah, his mate, was just as beautiful as he remembered. Unlike him who looked like a fucking monster.

That's because you are one.

Gabriel's inner voice never failed to remind him of every bad thing he'd ever done.

Rebekah stepped farther into the room, her happiness outweighing her hesitance. It amazed Gabriel how in tune he was with other's emotions. He practiced this ability with each guard who entered his room. Being able to read his mate... That was both a blessing and a curse. Gabriel wanted her happiness. Wanted Rebekah to be glad to see him. He was frozen in place as he took in the sight of his mate after all this time. Her hair was graying, and she had lines around her eyes, but she was still the most magnificent creature he'd ever seen.

"Rebekah," he managed to whisper. Unlike him, Rebekah wasn't frozen. She ran across the room and threw herself at him. He didn't hesitate to catch her. He would always catch her. "Rebekah," he muttered against her hair and hugged her tighter. His mate's body began to shake, and the sobs escaping her throat pained his cold heart. If anyone could thaw the organ, it was her. The sound of the door closing caught Gabriel's attention. For the first time in what felt like forever, he was alone with his mate.

"Let me look at you." Gabriel set her on her feet and brushed the tears from her cheeks with his thumbs. "Just as beautiful as the last time I saw you."

"Y-you remember that day?" Rebekah's voice was small and pained. He had done that.

He went to take a step back, but Rebekah grabbed onto

his forearms. "No. Don't. Please." She slid her hands down until they were clutching his. Squeezing, she smiled up at him. "The past doesn't matter. I'm here now. I'm here, Gabriel, and I've missed you so much."

"I—" Gabriel stopped the lie from spilling from his mouth. Until he was reunited with Isabelle, he hadn't given much thought to the past other than the bad things he'd done. "I'm glad you're here. *Why* are you here? And how?"

Rebekah pulled him toward the bed and sat down. Gabriel sat next to her, turning so he was facing her. "Honestly? Connor drew a picture of me, and Isabelle saw it as a sign. She, Dante, Tessa, and Gregor flew out to New Portland to find me. Not a day has gone by in these last thirty-one years that I didn't think about you. I waited around after the last time I saw you hoping you'd change your mind, but I didn't know what you'd been through. Isabelle told me everything, Gabriel. I'm so sorry for what happened to you."

"Not as sorry as I am. But if you know everything, why did you come here? You have to know I'm never getting out of prison."

"Maybe not, but that doesn't matter. What does matter is I now know what happened. I know you're alive. You may not well, but you're well enough for me to want to talk to you. Get to know you again. Gabe, I never stopped loving you."

"So you didn't move on with your life and find a man?" Fuck, Gabriel didn't want to know the answer. She was his mate. His heart and soul.

"I did get married, but he was only a friend. Our relationship was one borne of loneliness. I loved him as a friend only. I gave my heart to you, and it's still yours."

Gabriel couldn't stop himself from reaching for her. He placed his hand on her cheek, and Rebekah leaned into his touch, her eyes closing, and her mouth tilting up at the corners. Gods, she was still stunning.

"Where's your husband now?" Gabriel pulled his hand away.

"He passed away a couple years ago. In those two years, I traveled a bit. I volunteer at a place called The Japanese Gardens. I mostly read and spend time with my cat, Esmeralda."

"Sounds lonely. I'm sorry you lost your husband." Gabriel meant it. If Rebekah had remained in New Atlanta for him, she'd have missed out on having someone in her life. Gabriel was glad the relationship had been platonic, because she was his mate, even if he couldn't do anything about that. He was incarcerated, and they would never have a normal life together.

"He was a good man, and he left me with enough money to retire. I am free to move about as I wish, so now I'll be able to stay here and be with you."

Gabriel pushed to his feet and rounded on her. "Be with me?" He huffed. "Rebekah, look around you. This is my life. There is no being with me."

Rebekah stood and placed a hand on his chest. "It won't be conventional, but I'm not going anywhere. Gabe, I never thought I'd see you again. But now, here we are. No, we won't be together on the outside of these walls living a normal life, but I don't care. I still love you. Always have. Always will. Don't you get that? I'll take as much time as I can get with you, even if it's visiting an hour a day."

"That's no kind of life for you though." Gabriel placed his hand over hers and pressed it harder against his chest. The need to kiss her, to make her truly his mate, was getting stronger by the second. But he wouldn't do that to her.

"Shouldn't I get to choose? We've missed out on so much time already. Years, Gabe. Years I've walked this earth with a shattered heart. I feel as though I've been given a second chance. I know I'm older, and you might not feel the same—"

Gabriel cut her off with a kiss. He had never kissed

another woman. Never held anyone other than his mate. In the years after he disappeared from his family, Gabriel had never so much as looked at another female. Any time he jerked off, it was her face he pictured. He'd given his heart to her as well. Had been planning to propose before Flanagan got hold of him.

Rebekah slid her hands up his chest and secured them behind his neck, holding him in place. She kissed him back with all the fervor and love he remembered. His cock throbbed behind his cotton pants, and his beast urged him to take her. To toss her down on his shitty bed and complete the bond.

"Gabriel." Rebekah pressed her body to his, rolling her hips against his erection.

"No." Gabriel jerked away.

"I'm sorry. I thought..." Rebekah turned away, but Gabriel didn't miss the pain in her eyes.

Scrubbing a hand down his face, Gabriel sighed. "Rebekah, I won't do this to you. I'm a killer. I murdered both men and women with no remorse. I am not a good male."

"You don't regret killing? Now that you've had time to think about what you did, are you saying if you were let out today, you would go back to killing without a second thought?"

"Yes, I regret it, and no, I would never harm an innocent again. But that doesn't change the past." Gabriel ran his hands through his hair and pulled the short strands. "You can't tell me you would willingly choose me, a stone-cold killer, as a mate."

"From what Isabelle told me, you and I don't have a choice in the matter. The fates choose who the mates are, and they chose me for you, which means they chose you for me. If that's true, we are supposed to be together in whatever capacity your current situation allows."

"What else did Izzy tell you?"

236

"Everything. Well, as much as she and the others could cram in during the flight from Oregon."

"Did they tell you how the mate bond works?"

Rebekah hugged herself. "Yes."

"My life is forfeit. I won't be selfish and tie you to me that way. You deserve to live freely, not bound to someone unworthy."

Rebekah stood stiffly, her face a mask of fury. "What if that's exactly what I want you to do? Gabe, do you honestly believe if they thought so badly of you, they would seek me out and bring me here? Isabelle is your sister, so maybe she's biased. But the others? All of them think you are worthy of redemption. You have an extended lifespan. If we complete the bond, my life will be prolonged as well. You will eventually get out of here. It might not be for many years, but it will happen. Gregor said so. I've waited thirty-one years for you, and I'm willing to wait that many more. Longer if that's what it takes. I will visit you every day until you get out."

"And what will you do while you aren't visiting me an hour a day?"

"The first thing I'll do is find somewhere to live. Isabelle has already offered to help with that. If it weren't for Esmeralda, I would stay with her and Dante."

"Esmeralda?" Gabriel prayed Rebekah didn't have a child. She said her relationship with her husband had been platonic.

"My cat. She wasn't crazy about being around the others since they are Gargoyle. Tessa is going to ask Tamian to fix it so she's okay with those shifters who come around, but until then, I don't want to keep her crated. I will need to travel back to Oregon and pack up some things, then get the house ready to sell."

"Don't be so hasty. What if you realize after a few months or years you don't want to be here? Rebekah, don't go making all these changes without really thinking about

237

it."

"Do you not want me?"

"Of course I do. I want you more than I want to breathe."

"Then don't push me away again. Please." Rebekah's eyes filled with tears.

"What kind of life will that be for you? Coming to a prison every day? Waiting around years for me to *maybe* be released?"

"I'm not living now!" Rebekah fisted her hands as she yelled at him.

Gods, she was breaking his heart. Not the one in his chest. That one continued to beat steadily day after day. For the last thirty-four years, Gabriel believed he could no longer feel anything, but his mate was proving him wrong. And it hurt. Gods, did it hurt. He moved quickly, not giving her time to retreat. He picked his mate up and kissed her again. This time, he poured his own love into her mouth. Their tongues tangled, entwining as though they were making love. Memories flooded Gabriel's brain from their time together all those years ago.

When they broke apart to catch their breath, Rebekah threaded her fingers through his now-white hair. "Gabriel, please. Please don't ask me to leave you again."

Gabriel should turn her away for her own good, but he couldn't. Not with her begging. He had to trust she knew her own mind and heart, and if she wanted him, as limited as their time together would be, he would give it to her. "I have conditions."

"Anything."

"You become my true mate. I can't promise you a future without doing so. I can't know you are out there waiting on me while you continue to age. Not that I would love you any less, but I need to know there will be a day when I get out of here and we can be together the way we should have been all this time."

"Yes. Absolutely yes," Rebekah agreed without hesitation.

"Second, before we complete the bond, you spend some time here in New Atlanta getting to know the area and my family again. Visit me as often as you like so you can get to know who I am now. I'm not the same male I was when we were younger. I'm not the same male I was a year ago either, but I'm trying. Being in here" — Gabriel waved his arm around the room — "doesn't offer much chance at redemption. I read and exercise. I get to go outside for an hour each day. Isabelle visits when she can, but other than that, I don't have conversation."

Gabriel squeezed the back of his neck and sighed. "I'm still messed up in here." He tapped the side of his head. "I've *been* messed up for a long time, and I don't know that I will ever get better."

"I became a psychologist because of you," Rebekah said, surprising Gabriel. "I wanted to learn all I could about how the mind works so that I could help you if we ever reunited."

"You want to dig inside my head?" Gabriel took a step back. What if she didn't want a relationship with him, but instead, wanted to pick his brain for science?

"No, Gabe. I want to help you. If I can. There's no guarantee of that since I only studied cases which had been documented. I never came across anything like what happened to you. So maybe I can't help, but I can listen. I can be here for you, offering an ear or a kind word, both of which you seem to have little of."

"And what if you don't like what you find? What if the damage is irreparable? I won't claim you until you've spent enough time to know what you're getting into."

"You gave me your conditions, now I'll give you mine."

"And those would be?" Gabriel fisted his hands, then crossed his arms over his chest. He would call on his beast to help steady his breathing, but it was the shifter that was demanding he throw Rebekah onto the bed and claim her. Their mate was right there for the taking.

"Just one. Give me a chance. A chance to show you I'm willing to go all in with you. Willing to do whatever it takes to make this work. I already knew you were different. I knew that the last time we were together. I'm willing to put in the time if you're willing to show me the real you. I don't expect this to be easy, but the fates brought us back together. Our relationship won't be conventional, and it will wear on both of us." Rebekah closed the distance and gripped his forearms, tilting her face up to his. "But it will be worth it in the long run."

Rebekah moved one hand behind his head and urged Gabriel to kiss her. He wanted to. Gods, he wanted so much with this female. He pressed their lips together but kept it chaste this time. He was adamant about his conditions. But if he expected her to agree to his, he had to give in to hers. If Rebekah decided she was willing to wait, he would be willing to complete the bond.

"Are we in agreement?" she asked.

"Yes. I figure we have about an hour before they make you leave, so how about we begin getting to know one another? Tell me about this Japanese Garden."

LEAVING GABRIEL ALONE in his cell every day, even though it was more like a dorm room, was the hardest thing Rebekah had ever done in her life. The hours passed by too quickly, but she was thankful for them. As agreed, she and Gabriel spent their time talking. And kissing, though not as much as she wanted. Rebekah could feel the strain in Gabriel as he kept his distance. With it being winter, the weather was cold, but she knew how much Gabriel cherished his time outside, so when the temperature wasn't too low, she shared his time outdoors with him.

During the months after they were reunited, Rebekah spent time with Isabelle and Connor. The child was amazing. Not only was he brilliant in mind, he was also a talented artist. Rebekah did her best not to analyze the boy, but she had never met someone so young who was smarter than most of the adults surrounding him. Rebekah also met with Caroline for coffee once a week. It was strange being around Gabriel's mother knowing the woman was over two-hundred yet looked so much younger than Rebekah. Caroline confided in Rebekah about all her children and how guilty she felt at giving them up for adoption. Rebekah, using her psychology experience, helped the female with her guilt.

Gabriel was worried about Rebekah missing her house in Oregon after she talked about her life with Jacob and how she enjoyed the serenity of her home, but she assured him she was enjoying getting to know his family and the area. When she first arrived in New Atlanta, she stayed with Isabelle after Tamian performed his magic on Esmeralda, but during the third week, she asked Izzy and Dante for help in finding her a home of her own. She also asked for help in selling her place in New Portland, and they called on a Clan member named Sixx who lived on the West Coast. Sixx and his mate, Desirae, oversaw packing up Rebekah's home and having her things shipped to the new house she purchased not far from Isabelle.

Once she had her new place set up and all the boxes unpacked, Rebekah took lots of photos to show Gabriel. Isabelle had given her the drawing Connor made of his vision, and Rebekah had it framed. She hung it in the living room where everyone who visited could enjoy it. Rebekah had more company in the first week in her new home than she had in her entire life in Oregon. It seemed that Gabriel's family and Clan accepted Rebekah into their lives as a given. It was then she realized how lonely she truly had been.

"Thank you, Aldredge," Rebekah said to the assistant warden after he unlocked Gabriel's cell. In those first few days of visiting the Pen, Rebekah was self-conscious, but the guards who accompanied her to Gabriel's room were kind. If they thought she was crazy for wanting to be mated to a killer, they didn't let on. She got to know them little pieces at a time during the walk from the back door through the hallways. Gabriel wasn't kept in one of the cell blocks with the other inmates, and for that, she was thankful. She also spent time with the guards when they watched over her and Isabelle as they met with the Reborn. When Isabelle asked Rebekah to assist with their project of reforming the Unholy, Rebekah jumped at the chance. She felt good having a purpose. Gabriel had been vocal in his disapproval, but Dante had been the one to assure Gabriel Rebekah would be safe in her meetings.

After the door was closed behind them, Gabriel kissed Rebekah good morning. "I brought your favorite." Rebekah had begun taking breakfast to Gabriel so they could start their day together. Today's offering was something she picked up at the diner where Marley worked. Dane's mate was adorable.

"You're my favorite," Gabriel quipped, taking the bag from her.

Rebekah laughed at his cheesiness. Gabriel had opened up to Rebekah after much hesitancy on his part and stubbornness on hers. She assured him every time he refused to talk about his past that she wasn't going to judge him or think less of him for all the bad he had done. It took weeks, but he finally shared small parts of what he could remember during his time as Vincent Alexander. Rebekah knew they were going to be okay the day Gabriel broke down in tears and begged forgiveness for his transgressions.

His remorse wouldn't get him out of his jail sentence, but it went a long way in healing his pain.

They shared breakfast, and when they finished, Gabriel stood and took Rebekah's hands.

"Ready to go outside?" The weather was warmer, and the sunshine helped Gabriel's moods.

"Not today. I need to ask you something."

"What is it?" Rebekah squeezed his hands.

"You promised to take time and get to know me. I promised to keep an open mind. I was wondering how you feel now about being my mate."

"That wasn't a question, but if you're asking have I changed my mind, the answer is no. I want you now more than ever."

"But this life... Having to visit me here... You deserve so much more." Gabriel's eyes glistened, and Rebekah wished she could turn back time to make sure what happened to Gabriel never did.

"So do you. You didn't deserve to be captured and tortured or left for dead. What happened to you was a tragedy of the worst kind. And yes, you committed your own horrible acts, but now you're paying for those. But that doesn't mean you don't deserve good in your life to make up for what they took from you. I love you, Gabriel. I have always loved you. That never stopped. I spent over half my life without you. Without your love, and I'll be damned if I go through that again. Even if you don't complete the bond, I will still be right here, every single day, because you are my life. I want to be your mate for many years to come. Whether that's here visiting you or on the outside one day."

"Gods, I love you. I just had to be sure." Gabriel released her hands and walked over to the door where he closed the covering over the window. When he turned back around, gone was the hesitation. In its place was determination, and hummingbirds took flight in her stomach. After three months – no, after thirty-one years – she was going to be with her lover once again.

CHAPTER FOUR

GABRIEL HATED THE fact that they were in a modified cell in a prison instead of Rebekah's nice home with its lavish bedroom. His mate didn't deserve to be made love to somewhere so dire, but it was their only option. He walked over to the door and closed the covering on the small window. Gabriel had spoken to Izzy during her visits about Rebekah. He confided in her his deepest fears, and she reassured him often that Rebekah was happy. She was making a difference in the lives of the Reborn, and she was getting to know their family.

Dante had also visited with him. The first time was when Gabriel yelled the Pen down until he got a meeting with the male. Gabriel was beyond pissed when Rebekah mentioned working with the Reborn. Dante calmly explained the working environment and how neither Rebekah nor Isabelle were left unguarded for one second while in the prison. Dante praised Rebekah's work. He also talked about her time outside the Pen and how she was already deeply entrenched with Gabriel's family as well as some of the other mates. Dante assured him Rebekah was happy in New Atlanta, and he would be a fool not to mate with her. She wasn't going anywhere regardless of whether or not Gabriel completed the bond.

When Gabriel made up his mind to take the plunge, he asked Isabelle to come up with a way to cover the small window on his door. Even though most of the guards were shifters and would be able to hear them through the walls, they would at least have that small bit of privacy.

He had taken his time getting to know this version of Rebekah. Gone was the young woman he'd fallen in love with, and in her place was the older version who was stronger than anyone he knew. Knowing she wanted him no matter what he had done in his past made him love her more.

Gabriel had requested an early shower that morning, and during his walk with Aldredge had admitted he wanted today to be the day. Isabelle had spoken with the assistant warden, and they had built a frame around the window with a metal door that could be closed while Rebekah visited. When they installed the covering inside the room, Aldredge explained it was so Gabriel could close it himself whenever he and Rebekah wanted privacy.

Gabriel didn't rush the few steps between them. He crossed the room slowly, giving Rebekah time to change her mind. When he stood within arms' reach, Rebekah tugged at the hem of his T-shirt, sliding the garment up. Gabriel reached behind his neck and pulled the plain, white tee off. Rebekah ran her slender hands over his chest. Whatever Flanagan's minions had done to Gabriel in the past turned all his hair white. His mate didn't seem to mind. She threaded her fingers through the coarse strands as she scraped the skin below with her nails. Rebekah leaned closer and placed soft kisses over both rounded pectorals. When her hands drifted lower to the cotton pants he wore, he took a deep breath.

Rebekah's hands trembled. She had admitted to not having sex with anyone since they were together all those years ago, but her hesitation was unwarranted. He placed his hands over hers, moving them back to his chest.

"Do you remember our last time together?" Gabriel asked as he began unbuttoning her blouse.

"Like it was yesterday."

"Then you have no need to be nervous. Nothing has changed."

"Everything has changed." Rebekah closed her eyes when he pushed her shirt apart, putting her bra on display. "I'm not the young girl you last made love to."

"No, you aren't. You are the mature woman I love more than anything. Our bodies might look different, but our hearts are still the same. Our souls are still connected." Gabriel ran a fingertip across the top of Rebekah's bra. When she shivered, he did it again. "I'm not a good male, but I'm trying to be. In these past few months, I have felt more like my old self. Before you came here, I had a hard time remembering who I was before this happened." Gabriel gestured to his body. "But you've helped. So, no, we don't look the same on the outside, but I have a feeling once we are together intimately, what's on the outside won't matter."

REBEKAH HADN'T MEANT to make Gabriel feel bad about himself. He was still as handsome to her as he had been when they first met, even if his hair was white and his skin was pale. So maybe he felt the same about her more mature body. "You're right, and I'm sorry."

"No need for that. I want you now as much as I did then. Probably more, because now, I know you're my mate. I know what you're willing to sacrifice."

"I'm not sacrificing anything." Rebekah reached behind her and unclasped her bra and let it fall to the floor. A low rumble emanated from Gabriel's throat as his eyes filled with desire. "Touch me. Please." Gabriel did. He cradled both breasts in his hands, sending fire racing from her belly to her core. "Gabe, I need you."

Gabriel pushed his pants down his legs, stepping out of them. She admired his body while she finished stripping, and within seconds, she found herself on her back with

Gabriel stretched out above her. His erection teased her entrance, and she raised her hips. Gabriel didn't make her wait. He entered her body, and it was as if no time had passed. He was gentle with her. They had talked about this moment. He admitted to being afraid of hurting her. He hadn't been with anyone since the last time they were intimate, and Gabriel was afraid the beast would take over.

In that moment, she didn't want gentle. Didn't want him to hold back. This was more than lovemaking. He was claiming her, him and his shifter both. Rebekah ran her fingers through his hair, gripping the strands. "Don't hold back, Gabe. I want you to let go and claim me."

"Bek—"

"No, Gabe. You're not going to hurt me. I was made just for you. Please."

Gabriel took her mouth in a fierce, passionate kiss as his lower body moved faster. Gabriel amped the intensity, his powerful hips surging forward, his erection filling her, lighting her up from the inside.

"Yes, oh..." Rebekah slipped her arms under his, hands clutching the bunching muscles of his back.

"Bek, I'm... close... Oh, gods, I'm gonna..." Gabriel's fangs dropped, and Rebekah braced for the bite. The initial sting was quickly replaced with euphoria as he erupted inside her. He drank from her neck as he pumped his seed deep inside her core. Rebekah's own orgasm pulsed as she gasped to breathe through it. Isabelle had told her it would be otherworldly, and god, it was. It was as though their souls combined. Two became one. When Gabriel released his fangs, he licked her neck once, and her thighs trembled as another orgasm tore through her. Her muscles clamped down on Gabriel's still hard cock.

Gabriel rocked back and forth, stroking her inner walls through the tremors until he came again. Rebekah was once again the young woman who had made love to the handsome young man in her bedroom one night while her parents were away. She was also the mature woman who knew she would never love another as she did this male. They were united in body and soul, and no matter what the future held, they would endure it together as mates.

THE FIRST THREE years passed with Rebekah spending most of her weekdays at the Pen. After her mornings with Gabe, she counseled the Reborn, helping them make sense of what had happened to them. She also worked with any of the human inmates who wanted someone to talk to. Her life was full if not conventional. As the days wore on, so did her energy. Rebekah chalked it up to being on the go constantly until one day, Dante and Isabelle sat her down in the Pen's infirmary, and they both convinced her to see a doctor.

When she got the diagnosis, she just stared at the physician. Sabrina was mated to a Gargoyle. The woman had taken over as chief of staff when Jonas stepped down. Before that, she had led the oncology department, so Sabrina knew what she was talking about. "But I'm mated to Gabriel," Rebekah whispered. She couldn't have cancer. She was mated to a Gargoyle, and they were going to live happily for centuries to come.

Sabrina came around the desk and sat next to Rebekah, gripping her hands. "You are, and their venom can help with many things, but so far, cancer isn't one of them." Sabrina showed Rebekah the scans. Explained her options. Offered to get a second opinion. Rebekah didn't need one. She trusted Sabrina. Over the course of the next couple months, Sabrina was the one who cared for Rebekah, overseeing each treatment. Rebekah tried to hide the illness from Gabriel, but being Gargoyle, he could not only sense something was bothering her mentally, he could somehow smell the disease. Going through treatment was hard, but seeing Gabriel break down each weekend was harder.

The first time Gregor and Aldredge approached Gabriel with the offer of a weekend pass, Gabriel wouldn't talk to them about it. Said it wasn't right for him to have special privileges. It took a lot of begging and tears on Rebekah's part until he finally caved, sensing something was wrong. When Rebekah admitted to having the disease, he donned the prosthetic his father made specifically for Gabriel and spent time away from the Pen with her in their home. After that, Gabriel never hesitated to change into the disguise. When Rebekah went into remission, they celebrated at home in bed for five days. Sex was off the table since she was still weak, but Gabriel tended to her every need, healing her heart while the chemicals healed her body.

REBEKAH DID HER best to take care of herself. For six years, everything was fine. She worked with the inmates. Spent time with her family – she'd stopped thinking of them as Gabriel's family a long time ago – and watched over the kids on the weekends Gabriel wasn't home. Her life was filled with a comfortable routine, and she thrived. Every year she met with Sabrina for a checkup, and every year the tests came back clear. Until one day they didn't. Rebekah didn't want to tell Gabriel the truth. If it was like last time, she would dread the conversation. Together, they had gotten through the treatments. Her hair falling out, then growing back. The sickness and pain. It was going to be much harder this time. On them both.

When she arrived at the Pen to pick him up for his weekend out, she put on her bravest smile as Gabriel exited the back door.

"This is cheating," he said after kissing her hello.

"It is," Rebekah replied as she did every time they made the drive for his weekend away. "But I like having you home. I like it when you can let your wings out." Making love at the Pen had been fulfilling, but it wasn't nearly as fun as when they had sex at home where they could be as loud as they wanted, and Gabe could let his wings out without worrying about hitting the wall next to his bed. The first weekend he got a free pass, they had made use of almost every available surface in the house. Rebekah spent hours afterward soaking in the tub.

They stopped having sex at the Pen once he started going home, and their intimate times waned when she got sick. Their love, however, grew stronger, as did their relationships with his family who visited often, bringing their kids. It was the younger Clan that kept a smile on Rebekah's face when she couldn't be around her mate.

"Who do we have invading our home this weekend?" Gabriel asked as soon as they walked in the door, removing his prosthetic as he headed toward the kitchen. She cooked for her male when they were together, and he enjoyed a cup of coffee while she worked at the stove. It was their quiet time before the family invaded. Her male liked to complain about their weekends being compromised with nieces and nephews, but he was a big softy when it came to the kids. Having missed out on their own, they never turned down the opportunity for visits. On the weekends when Gabriel remained at the Pen, Rebekah offered to babysit so the parents could have alone time. Being with the younger Clan members so often abated any longing for her own children.

"Actually, we have the house to ourselves." Rebekah dreaded telling Gabriel the truth, but she needed to prepare him for the inevitable. She went about making pancakes, eggs, and bacon. When she set his plate in front of him, Gabriel dug in. She pushed her own food around the plate, not able to stomach more than a few bites.

"Bek, what's wrong?" Gabriel was in tune with her moods, and he had more than once questioned her health. She did her best to hide her paling skin with makeup and her lack of energy with a smile. He saw through it all, but she had always played it off. She could no longer do that.

"Let's go in the living room."

"You're scaring me." Gabriel moved out of his chair to kneel at her feet. He grabbed her hands and studied her face. "You're sick again, aren't you?"

"Please, let's go sit." Rebekah gently pushed on his shoulder, and Gabriel relented. Once they were seated on the sofa, she gripped his hands in hers, using their connection to strengthen her resolve. "I went to see Sabrina for my annual checkup. It's back, only this time, it's worse."

"How much worse?" Gabriel asked on a whisper.

"It's pretty much spread throughout my body."

Gabriel jumped from the sofa, pacing the living room. "What can we do? There has to be something."

"Gabe—"

"I'll call Jonas. He can figure something out. He's a fucking genius for the gods' sakes!" Gabriel shouted. Rebekah sank back into the cushions. She didn't want him to accidentally lash out at her, so she curled her legs underneath her bottom and let the tears fall.

Gabriel glanced at her, and when he saw her face, he dropped to his knees and wrapped his arms around her waist, burying his head in her stomach. Rarely in all their years together had Gabriel cried, but in that moment, he sobbed like a baby. They held each other, neither saying anything for a long time. When Gabe got his emotions under control, he picked Rebekah up and took her to their bedroom. He didn't undress her or ask for sex. He removed her shoes, then held her in his arms.

"I have a request." Rebekah lifted her head so she could gauge Gabriel's reaction.

"Anything," he vowed.

"Sabrina said I don't have much time. How much, she couldn't say for sure. A couple months at most. I can either spend my time taking treatments that will make me sicker and only prolong the inevitable, or I can spend my time with you. I would like what time is left to be spent here, together. I want you to stay here with me."

Gabriel's eyes filled with tears once again, and he nodded. Rebekah had already told Isabelle what was going on so she could inform the rest of the family. Rebekah had also cleared it with Aldredge for Gabe to remain with her. Rebekah had needed to get his approval before she requested that Gabriel stay with her. She wanted what little time they had left to be spent together in their home. She was already feeling drained driving back and forth, and soon, she wouldn't be able to make the trips.

The next three weeks passed with Rebekah doing her best to hide her fears. She wasn't afraid of dying but of leaving Gabriel behind. He had changed over the years, but she was his whole life, and she was afraid of what her death would do to his tortured soul. If it were her in his place, she wasn't sure she would want to go on without him, but she wasn't stuck in a prison cell with little contact with the outside world.

When her body began shutting down, Sabrina wanted Rebekah to go to the hospital. "What do you want me to do?" she asked Gabriel.

"I want you to live," he whispered.

Rebekah weakly raised her hand to his stubbled cheek. What little hair grew in was white, but it was enough to prickle her palm. "I mean about going to the hospital."

"I know what you mean." Gabriel closed his eyes, and tears seeped from the corners. Rebekah wiped them as best she could until she was no longer able to hold her hand up. When he looked at her, she knew in her heart he would follow her in death. It might not be immediately, but the defeat was clear. It was on the tip of her tongue to make him promise not to give up living, but she wouldn't do that to him. If he made the vow only to appease her, he would continue living a miserable existence for her own selfishness, or he would break the vow and be tormented further.

"I want you to be where you want to be. If you want to stay here in our home, I'm good with that." Jonas had already brought equipment to Rebekah. She had pain medicine running through an IV to keep her comfortable. "No matter where it happens, it's going to gut me. And it's not like I'll be coming back here after you're..."

"This is your home, Gabriel. Everything I have is yours."

"No. *You* are my home." Gabriel kissed her on the forehead, his cool lips lingering against her heated skin.

"I want to stay here. I don't want to go to the hospital where you have to disguise who you are. I want to look at the face of my mate until I no longer can."

Gabriel nodded against her head. He kept his face pressed against her hair as his shoulders shook with silent sobs.

"I love you, Gabriel Montague. Thank you for giving me the best years of my life," Rebekah whispered before closing her eyes.

Epilogue

December 2057

"Please just take me back to the Pen, Izzy." Gabriel was drained. He was broken-hearted and had little drive left inside. Gabriel still took his monthly weekend passes at Isabelle's insistence. Today they were gathered at Isabelle and Dante's house for Christmas. Gabriel didn't want to be around family. He didn't want to be anywhere. For almost a year he had sat in his cell, recalling every moment he had with his mate. Her scent had faded from the pillow he took from their home. Her voice no longer whispered to him in his head. If it weren't for the pictures he kept, he would have probably forgotten the gleam in her eyes and the way her cheeks pinkened when she blushed. Gabriel's imprisonment hadn't been punishment enough for his crimes. The fates saw fit to reunite him with his mate only to take her away again.

"No. We're already here. You can sit and stare at nothing in there just as easily as you can at the Pen. Besides, your niece misses you." Christina was Isabelle's youngest, and for whatever reason, she loved Gabriel.

Gabriel pushed open the car door and trudged inside. Kids were scattered all around either playing or running, and the adults had already started drinking. Not that those who had Gargoyle blood could get drunk. If they could, Gabriel would have grabbed a bottle of whiskey and hidden out in a corner. Instead, he headed for the recliner and parked his ass.

"Hey, Brother." Dante walked over to Gabriel, cradling a sleeping Christina.

"Hey." Gabriel held out his arms, and Dante handed the child over. He knew it was pointless to refuse. His family tried to use the kids as weapons. Before Rebekah passed, it had worked. Now, it just intensified the ache where his heart used to be. Dante didn't hang around to make sure Gabriel took care of his child. Isabelle brought a bottle and burp cloth, setting them on the end table next to the recliner.

"In case she gets fussy," Isabelle said.

Frey's kids were on the floor with Dane and Marley's toddler. Gabriel was happy for his youngest brother. Marley was a good mate. She was spunky but sweet. She and Rebekah had become fast friends, while it had taken Dane longer to open up. He still hadn't forgiven Gabriel for kidnapping Kaya and trying to kill her. Gabriel didn't blame his brother. Gabriel still hadn't forgiven himself.

Gabriel inhaled deeply, letting the new-baby smell wash over him. Tessa's twins were in trouble for something, but that wasn't anything new. They were always in trouble. When the adults managed to get all the kids gathered and settled, Tabitha asked Jonas to read from a journal she and Anthony had found in Isabelle's closet.

When Jonas flipped the journal open, he was quiet for a moment. "Wouldn't you rather hear about Santa Claus or some other nonsensical story?" he asked Tabitha.

"No, sir. I want to hear about you and Grandma."

Jonas glanced at Caroline who nodded. Settling back with Tabitha in his lap and Anthony sitting on the hearth holding his twin's hand, Jonas read his own words, telling about meeting his mate, Gabriella. Caroline was her middle name, and she adopted it once the two of them went on the run. He spoke of their kids and how they put them up for adoption. When it came to the part of what happened to Gabriel, Jonas paused and looked over at him.

"It's okay, Jonas. I'm not going to lose it if you continue with what happens next."

Jonas didn't continue reading, though. He suggested they open presents instead. Gabriel remained in the corner, watching the kids. He closed his eyes as chaos ensued, and his mind drifted to all the Christmases before when Rebekah was with him. The evening wore on with the children being sent upstairs to play with their new things, while the adults peppered Jonas with questions about cloning and Tamian being a full-blood.

"I had selfish reasons for what I did. I was trying to find the cure for cancer, but I also wanted to figure out if I could create a full-blooded Gargoyle using Tessa's DNA as well as my own. Don't get me wrong. I am not ashamed of my children, but I wanted to know if there was a way to engineer the cells so a child would be full-blooded. I succeeded with Tamian, and that fact needs to remain a secret. If word got out I managed to clone a full-blooded Gargoyle, I'm afraid he would be targeted the same way Gabriel was."

Before they could argue about Tamian's safety, someone knocked on the door. Isabelle surprised Jonas with a special gift. She had traveled to Cairo and convinced their oldest siblings to come visit. Lucian and Marcella had never wanted anything to do with Jonas and Caroline, but there they were, all the way from Egypt. Gabriel continued rocking Christina, half listening to the conversations. When he overheard whisperings that Marcella had cancer and Connor had finally come up with a cure, that was when Gabriel knew he needed to get out of there. He couldn't listen to how they would be able to treat his oldest sister when they had been a year too late for Rebekah.

Gabriel didn't blame Connor. No, he blamed the fates. And himself. If he had been stronger, been able to resist

257

going back to work for Gordon Flanagan, he wouldn't be in prison. Wouldn't be paying for his crimes. Rebekah wouldn't have paid with her life. And without her, there was no point in living. Getting out on weekend passes was only breaking his heart further, and watching his family with their kids living happy lives when he would never have that was the worst punishment of all.

His reason for living was gone. It was time he was too.

ISABELLE SOBBED AS Jonas placed the urn containing Gabriel's ashes next to Rebekah's. She blamed herself for pushing her brother to leave his cell every month and join their family. She thought their happiness would rub off on him, only it had the opposite effect. After Christmas Eve at her home, Gabriel shut down. He refused to leave his cell even to go outside and smoke. He sat in his room with Rebekah's urn cradled in his arms. He stopped eating. Stopped drinking. Isabelle continued visiting, talking about anything and everything, but the day she mentioned their sister Marcella had been cured, Gabriel lost his shit. It was the first time he yelled at her. The first time she honestly feared her brother.

Isabelle should have thought about how insensitive her words were. How it cut her brother that his mate had died from the same disease Connor found a cure for too late to save her. Gabriel kept the window blocked so Isabelle couldn't see in, and at her request, Aldredge removed the covering. Gabriel ignored Isabelle after he yelled at her to get out. He ignored everyone. She wanted Dante to do something, but her mate sat her down and told her she needed to be prepared – Gabriel was letting go.

It took a lot of soul searching on her part, but Isabelle finally got it. Even if Gabriel got out of prison someday, he would never find happiness. His mate was gone, and he had nothing to live for. The next time she visited him, she stood outside his door and told him she understood. Isabelle told Gabriel she loved him. That she would miss him greatly, but she would be okay. The next day, he crossed over.

Caroline stepped beside Jonas and straightened the already perfectly placed vessel. When she turned, she had her hands cradling her stomach the same way Isabelle did when she was...

"Mom?"

Caroline's smile was sad, but she was smiling nonetheless. "I have some news." She grabbed Jonas's hand, and he raised their joined fists to kiss her knuckles. "Jonas and I... We didn't plan it. I never thought..."

"We're pregnant," Jonas finished for her. "In six months, we're going to have another child. A girl according to Connor."

Caroline wiped a tear off her cheek. "If it would be okay with everyone, I would like to name her Gabriella. Not after me, but after your brother."

Tabitha was the first to say anything. She had claimed the name upon learning it was Caroline's first name, but now, Isabelle's niece ran up to Caroline and hugged her. "I think it's perfect, Grandma. In fact, I think you should name her Rebekah Gabriella."

Isabelle thought the same thing. It was the perfect way to honor the male, the brother and son, who had been through more than anyone should have to endure. It would also honor the female who brought light into an otherwise dark world. Both Gabriel and Rebekah would live on in their hearts, and this new baby would carry their names to honor their memories.

RAFAEL & KAYA

CHAPTER ONE

RAFAEL THANKED FREY for the update, then disconnected and went to check on Sebastian while Kaya was in the shower. His cousin was doing a wonderful job in Rafe's absence. It was one reason he was in no hurry to return. Another reason... that was more complicated.

When Rafael entered the room, his son gave him a toothless smile. Bas was standing in his crib, holding onto the edge and wiggling front to back. "Baba." Rafe insisted Bas was saying papa, but he could be trying to say momma since he babbled the word no matter who was around. Kaya interpreted it to mean bottle.

Rafe changed his son's diaper, then took him to the kitchen where Priscilla was cooking breakfast. She paused long enough to hand over a ready-made bottle so Bas could have his breakfast before the rest of them ate. Priscilla had been prickly as of late, as had Kaya. His mate wanted to go home, but Rafael wasn't ready. Before the explosion, Priscilla had always been loyal to Rafe, but having spent the last couple months in Italy, it seemed she had moved that loyalty to Kaya. She wasn't rude to Rafael, but she didn't go out of her way to appease him as she usually did. Rafe really missed his cookies.

After Bas finished his bottle, Rafe placed his son on his shoulder to burp him, patting his back while dancing around the kitchen. Bas loved when Rafael sang to him, so he obliged his son every morning. It was a routine they'd gotten into while Kaya was in the hospital and one Rafael continued once they were in Italy.

As soon as Kaya had been strong enough, Rafe hired a doctor to travel with them on the Clan's jet, and he brought his little family to the villa. He told himself it was to give Kaya her best chance at healing. He loved his Clan, but her room at the hospital had been a revolving door of mates. In truth, Rafael couldn't look them in the eye knowing he failed at keeping them safe. Houses had been destroyed and couples displaced.

While Rafael kept his family in Italy, the others were busy rebuilding their homes. They used the original drawings he had designed to put their houses back the way they had been before Drago fucking destroyed them. Gregor had been the one to inform Rafe they were taking care of the manor in his absence. His brother asked if he wanted anything changed, and Rafe told Gregor he didn't care. Rafe couldn't bring himself to take Kaya back to where she'd almost lost her life. He didn't want her living somewhere that could possibly trigger a reaction, causing more trauma. She assured him she was fine. When he reached out mentally, he didn't sense any stress when talking about the manor, but he didn't want to risk it.

Rafe avoided a lot of phone conversations with his family while Kaya talked to the other mates often. She and the others chatted over video conferences, sometimes one-on-one, and other times there would be four of five of them laughing together. Kaya wanted to return so they could see the new additions to the Clan. Sophia had given birth to Lydia, and Jasper and Trevor had returned from their honeymoon with Jasper's baby sister, a full-blooded female named Cailín. The Clan was putting their lives back together the way they should after a tragedy by helping one another. Rafael didn't feel as though he had any right to be part of the rebuilding, yet guilt was eating him alive that they were trying to get the manor ready for a homecoming he wasn't sure would ever happen.

Kaya didn't understand the guilt, nor did she blame

Rafe for what happened to her. She blamed Drago. If Rafael had taken the threat more seriously, if he had moved against Drago as soon as the male showed up in New Atlanta, things would have turned out differently. None of their homes would have been destroyed. The mates' plane wouldn't have been targeted. Kaya wouldn't need a cane to help her walk, and her face would be the same one she'd had since birth.

Not going home was putting a strain on all of them, but Rafael felt it was for the best. At least for the time being. Speaking of strains, Kaya ambled into the kitchen, and Rafael danced over to her. When Sebastian reached for his mother, Rafael pulled him back. She wasn't strong enough to hold their child and walk, but the look Kaya gave him said she felt differently.

After sitting at the table, Kaya held out her arms. "Give me," she insisted, and Rafe handed the baby over, but he sat down next to her in case she needed him.

KAYA LEANED HEAVILY against the bathroom counter and stared at her reflection. The woman looking back was different yet the same. The surgeons had done an amazing job putting her face back together, and scarring was minimal. It was just strange not to look exactly like she always had. Kaya wasn't vain, and she knew she was lucky. It could have been so much worse. She could have died in the explosion. Sebastian would more than likely have been killed if Priscilla hadn't chosen to take him to the garden. They were all alive, and their home could be rebuilt. It *was* being rebuilt. The Clan back home had bonded together to get the destroyed houses put back to rights, starting with Nik's since he and Sophia had a new baby girl.

After brushing her teeth and pulling her hair back in a

ponytail, Kaya grabbed her cane and made her way to the kitchen. She paused at the doorway to enjoy the sight of her mate dancing with their son while Priscilla cooked breakfast. Rafael was singing in Italian, and Bas was patting his papa's face, cooing along. At six months, Bas had Kaya's bright blue eyes and Rafe's darker hair. He was happy and healthy, both more important than his features. If she could only say the same about her mate, all would be right in her world. Rafe was healthy, but he wasn't happy. He put on a good front, but Kaya knew her male. Knew how he hid his worries from her. Knew he blamed himself for what happened.

"Look, Bas. There's your pretty momma." Rafael danced over to where she was standing. Sebastian reached out for her, but Rafe pulled him back. That was another thing that needed to change. Kaya could manage without her cane, and damnit, she could hold her son.

She shuffled over to the table and sat down, holding out her arms. "Give me," she ordered. Rafael placed Bas in her arms, then sat down next to her. Kaya loved her mate more than anything in the world except maybe Sebastian. She loved her child in equal measure, just differently. She appreciated how well Rafael had taken care of her during her rehabilitation. How he continued to be there for her every step of the way, but in doing so, he had abandoned his other responsibilities. Frey, according to Rafe, was doing a fine job of leading the Clan, but Kaya reminded him often it wasn't Frey's duty. Rafael was still the King.

Kaya missed their Clan. Missed being around the other mates. Their Italian villa was a glorious sanctuary, but the longer they remained, the more it felt like a prison. She was ready to go home even if it meant staying with Frey and Abbi for a while. Kaya could use a dose of Amelia's brand of happiness. Going home meant convincing Rafael she was well enough and he was good enough.

Priscilla placed Kaya's plate in front of her. "You're

looking spry this morning," Priscilla said with a wink.

Kaya hid her smile behind Sebastian's head. "Thank you. I feel spry. As a matter of fact, after we eat, I want to take a walk to the cliffs."

"Kaya," Rafael started to object.

"You heard the doctor. As long as I have my cane, I can walk as much as I want. He recommended getting more exercise, and I need the fresh air."

"I don't want you to overdo it." Rafe reached for Sebastian, but Kaya pushed his hand away.

"I've got him." Kaya settled the baby in her left arm, then began eating. Her arm had healed nicely, and she had gotten the cast removed a couple weeks ago. It was entertaining trying to get the food to her mouth with little grabby hands making for the fork, but Kaya managed. More than once Rafael reached out to help, and every time, Kaya glared at her mate.

Finally, Priscilla slapped Rafe's shoulder. "Your food is getting cold." Their beloved housekeeper had gotten bolder with her interference, and she was on Kaya's side. Both women were ready to go home. Priscilla loved their little family, but she missed the others more than Kaya did. She had been taking care of the Clan a long time, and they were her adopted sons and daughters. To her, Sebastian was her grandchild, but so were Connor and Amelia. Sophia had given birth to Lydia, and Priscilla was anxious to see the baby girl, as was Kaya.

Priscilla joined them at the table. That was something else that had changed. Before coming to Italy, the woman had always waited until they finished eating to feed herself. Kaya insisted she join them, and Priscilla, after very little fussing, did so. She waited until Rafe had a mouthful of food to drop her bomb.

"I have prepared several meals and put them in the freezer. Penelope will be coming back to stay with you for a while." Priscilla's sister and her family watched over the villa when it wasn't occupied.

Rafe swallowed his food and wiped his mouth. "Why is Penelope coming? We have you."

"I'm going home. Kaya is doing well, and I have a grandbaby to meet."

"But we need you here."

"And Sophia needs me there. Penelope can take care of feeding you in my absence."

"It's not about the food." Rafe slapped his hand on the table, startling Sebastian. His little face scrunched, and Kaya set her fork down so she could cradle him against her shoulder.

Patting Bas's back, Kaya glared at her mate. Again. "We'll be fine with Penelope. Have you already talked to Bryce?" she asked Priscilla. The Clan's pilot had remained with them at the villa instead of traveling back to the States.

"I'm flying commercial. I didn't want to leave you without the jet."

"Nonsense. It's not like Rafael's going to take me anywhere, so you might as well fly in comfort."

"Now wait a second. Last time I looked, I was King." Rafael pushed his chair back and stood.

Kaya didn't miss the opportunity to snap back. "And I'm still Queen. Although hiding out halfway across the world really isn't affording me the opportunity to be there for my Clan." The words had the intended effect. Rafe's face went from mutinous to hurt, but Kaya was tired of the pity party for one. He tossed his napkin onto his unfinished breakfast and strode from the room, slamming the back door on the way outside.

"That went well," Priscilla deadpanned before sipping her coffee.

"If I thought I could get away with it, I'd pack my bags and go with you. I've tried talking to him. Reasoning with him. I'm tired of being used as his scapegoat." Kaya kissed Sebastian's temple before placing him on her lap. "What are

266

we going to do with your papa?" she whispered to her son.

Priscilla's face softened. "I would say give him time, but..."

"As long as Frey is taking care of the Clan, he has no reason to go home. Is it horrible I wish something would happen so Rafe had to return? I love my mate, but I don't know how much longer I can take this."

RAFAEL DIDN'T GO far. He never strayed too far away from Kaya. Rarely did he invade her privacy, but he couldn't help but listen in as his mate and housekeeper talked about him. Kaya had asked more than once to return to the States, and he refused every time, claiming she wasn't ready. In truth, *he* wasn't ready. He had failed his family. Failed his Clan. He wasn't fit to be King, but Kaya didn't see it that way. Kaya was right that Frey was doing a wonderful job in his absence. More than once he considered turning the crown over to his cousin. Frey was a born leader. He had military experience. If only Roberto had been the eldest brother, Frey would have been the rightful heir to the throne.

Kaya was also right that he was using her as an excuse to stay away, but hearing her desperation was breaking his heart. When the back door opened a few minutes later, he didn't have to look to know it was her. Kaya was as much a part of him as his Goyle.

"Walk with me?" she requested. The hesitation in her voice was a kick to the nuts. Kaya should never have to doubt him, but lately, he had given her no reason not to.

"Of course." Rafael wanted to pick his mate up and carry her to the cliffs. It wasn't a short walk, but she needed this. Needed to not only get exercise as the doctor suggested, but to also feel capable. Kaya was a strong woman. Determined. It was one reason she was on her way to a full recovery so quickly. She had been moving about the villa without using her cane as often, but when she did, it was more for his benefit than hers. Or maybe she kept it handy so she could beat him over the head with it. He wouldn't blame her if she did.

When they arrived at the edge of their land, Kaya stood silently, gazing out over the water. She had remained quiet during the walk, but he sensed her thoughts were as tumultuous as the sea below. The wind coming off the vast expanse of dark water whipped at the tendrils of hair that had escaped her ponytail, but Kaya ignored it. When she finally spoke, she kept her eyes on the horizon.

"One day in the not-so-distant future, Sebastian will be King. Everything important he learns will come from you. Frey will teach him to fight. Julian or Henry will teach him about technology. I will do my best to teach him how to love. But the most important things about being a good leader will come from you." Kaya turned her face toward him. "Before we know it, he will learn to walk. He's going to fall down. Are you going to scoop him up and carry him or pick him up and encourage him to try again? He's going to face adversity. There will be those who try to take him down the same way Alistair and Drago did with you. Will you teach him to trust in the Clan, in our family, to stick together? Or will you tell him to run when things get tough?" Kaya searched his eyes before turning her gaze back to the sea.

"I don't know what it's like to lead a Clan," she continued. "But I do know about being in charge. As Chief of Police, I had to make hard decisions. I had to delegate responsibilities to my officers and detectives. I had to trust that those who were under my direction would do their best to keep our city safe. It didn't always work. Crime didn't cease. People still died. Was that my fault? Could I have done more to ensure the evil in the world suddenly became good? Stopped killing, stopped selling drugs, stopped robbing and causing chaos? I became a cop because of my father. I wanted to follow in his footsteps to try and make a difference. I'm not sure I succeeded, but at least I tried. That is the lesson I want our son to learn. To try his best. To lean on those around him to help. To know that when he fails – because he will – that he has a Clan surrounding him who won't blame him for failing, but will be there to pick him up, dust off his backside, and push him forward. I want Bas to know it's okay to not have all the answers all the time. I want him to be the best King for our future Clan. Are you going to teach him how? Or are we going to stay hidden away while his cousins learn those lessons from their parents?"

Rafael touched Kaya's chin and turned her face toward him. "Please forgive me. For trying to shelter you too long. For not listening when you asked to go home." Rafe leaned down and pressed their foreheads together. "I'm not sorry for bringing you here to recuperate, but I am sorry for making you stay after you requested we return. I have been feeling sorry for myself. I failed to keep the Clan safe, but more than that, I failed to keep *you* safe. I thought by bringing you here I could shelter you and Sebastian from further attacks. I thought I could outrun the guilt, or at least hide from it if I wasn't around to see the destruction. But while I've been here having a pity party, our family has been hard at work rebuilding our homes. I should have been there for them. I helped rebuild New Atlanta after the world fell, but when my family needed me most, I let them down. Not because we were attacked, but because I ran.

"You are absolutely right in everything you said, and that's why you are the perfect Queen. It is your place to keep me in line and tell me when I'm fucking up. It is my place to teach our son, and I'm not setting a good example by staying here while the world continues to spin. So again, please forgive me."

Kaya cupped his cheek with her free hand and kissed

him softly. "You're forgiven," she mouthed against his lips. "Let's go home."

Epilogue

New Atlanta 2053

FAMILY DAY WAS in full swing at the manor, and Rafael smiled at the chaos. Coming back from Italy had been the right decision. When they first returned, Rafael drove straight to Frey and Abbi's. After a couple weeks, Frey encouraged Rafe to take his family home, but Rafael used Kaya's trauma as an excuse for not doing so. The mates kept Kaya busy, visiting almost daily. Sophia brought Lydia over for play dates even though the baby couldn't do more than lie on a blanket next to Sebastian.

They had been back in the States for almost a month when Frey informed Rafael it was time to not only return home but to also return to being King. His cousin had done an amazing job leading their Clan in Rafael's absence, but the responsibility wasn't Frey's, so Frey took Rafael for a short road trip. When they pulled up at the manor, Rafael cursed his cousin until he noticed all the cars parked in front of the garage. The males of their family had gathered to not only show Rafael the reconstructed house, but to also have an intervention. Before they all lit into him like family and not Clan, Frey gave him a tour. Once they finished going over all the upgrades, the males ganged up on him. Frey told Rafe to get his head out of his ass and be the leader they had followed for two hundred years. Julian had a large part in convincing Rafael he wasn't to blame for the bombings when he asked Rafe if he blamed Julian for all the trouble with the unknown hacker.

271

He couldn't get over the changes to the manor. Instead of rebuilding it exactly as it had been, his brothers and cousins took it upon themselves to make quite a few changes. The dining room had been expanded to accommodate their whole family plus about fifty more, with a set of French doors leading to the patio. Priscilla's kitchen was also larger with state-of-the-art appliances any master chef would envy. A new, larger game room had been added to the back of the house. The living area which had been destroyed and where Kaya was injured had been transformed into two rooms. One was Rafael's office, and the other was a play room. The area where his office used to be was now the living area. In some ways it still felt like the old manor, but the new version was so much better. Rafe had been worried about Kaya's reaction to being home, but there had been enough modifications to make it different while still being theirs.

Now Connor was sitting at the patio table drawing. Amelia and Rain were being chased by Sebastian, Lydia, and Scotty. Deacon and Sabrina's oldest was getting stronger every day, evidenced by how fast he was running with the others. The younger kids were toddling around, watched over by a stoic Cailín. A couple babies were being passed between the mates, several who were pregnant again, Kaya among them. Rafael's chest filled with love and pride as he looked over his Clan. They had been through so much individually and collectively, yet here they were. Their Clan was thriving, and some day in the near future, these little ones would be leading the way.

Kaya wrapped her arm around Rafael's waist. "What are you smiling about?"

Rafael gestured to the kids. "All of them." He placed his hand on her round belly. "And her. They are the future, and I couldn't be prouder." Rafael hadn't become King until he was over five hundred, but he wouldn't wait that long to pass the crown to his son. As soon as Bas was old enough,

Rafael would begin teaching him everything he needed to lead their Clan. He wanted to spend time with his mate without the burden of ruling the Americas. He had competent males leading the Clan in Central and South America, the same way Sin watched over the Clan on the West Coast. Rafe wouldn't just hand over his duties and abandon Bas. He would be there for his son and all the other kids just like his brothers and cousins would be. The same way Sutton Lazlo was doing for his offspring and their kids. Sutton and Rory had been to visit more than once, and the couple had become close friends with the Clan. Seeing as how their granddaughter was also part of the Stone Society, it made sense the two families blended together.

Sebastian ran over to where Rafael and Kaya were standing long enough to kiss his momma's belly. It was something he did often. Bas also talked to his little sister, promising to be the best big brother ever. Whenever Connor was close enough to hear Sebastian make his claim, the older boy would get a far off look in his eye, then smile. Rafael didn't need Connor's visions to know his son was telling the truth. Bas had Kaya for a mother, and she was the best at teaching their son how to love while Rafael taught him everything else. Yes, Sebastian would be the best big brother, something Rafael strived to be with his own family.

"Love you, Momma. Love you, Papa," Bas said before rushing off to play again.

Rafael was loved, and that knowledge brought him back to being his old self after their time in Italy. It was what kept him going every day. Because when you were loved as he was, there was nothing that mattered more.

A NOTE FROM THE AUTHOR

When readers ask me to write about their favorite characters, I do my best to give them what they want. Sometimes, though, the storyline just isn't enough for a full book, and that's when I came up with the idea for Spectrum. If you enjoyed the book, I would appreciate you scrolling to the end and leaving a review. It doesn't have to be long, just honest and heartfelt.

This one was a little harder to write than most. As with the other books that deal with death, my heart was heavy. I cried. Then I cried some more. I went into writing Gabriel's story knowing he would never get out of prison, but I didn't know how heartbreaking it would be. I don't think the next book will be quite as heavy.

Speaking of the next one, it will be the last in the series. If you get my newsletter or are part of my Facebook reader group, you know it's not really the end. The next generation is set to take over, and I am looking forward to seeing what the "kids" do. At the end of Malakai, I intended the last book to be titled "Achilles," but the more I think about it, the last book will be about so much more than his and Hunter's story.

As of now, the next and final book will be titled "Stone Society." It will be a culmination of all the characters' trials, tears, and hard-fought happily ever afters. I don't have a release date, but I'm shooting for November 11.

ABOUT THE AUTHOR

Multi-genre author Faith Gibson began writing in high school, and through the years, penned many stories and poems. As her dreams continued getting crazier than the one before, she decided to keep a dream journal. Many of these nighttime escapades have led to a line, a chapter, or even a complete story.

"Love is love, and there's not enough love in the world." This belief she holds strongly, and it's the prevailing theme in her works, all of which come with a happy ending.

Faith believes her purpose in life is to entertain the masses, even if it's one person at a time. Living just outside of Nashville, Tennessee, with the love of her life and her pit bull pup, when she's not hard at work writing her next adventure, she can often be found playing trivia while enjoying craft beer, listening to live music, or off on an adventure of her own.

www.ingramcontent.com/pod-product-compliance
Lightning Source LLC
Chambersburg PA
CBHW070102030726
47506CB00002B/561